COUNTDOWN TO DOOMSDAY

"Terrorists have stolen one of our most sophisticated nuclear weapons," Groot told Wagner, "and we haven't the slightest idea as to where it might be. It was being convoyed from the depot at Wolfratshausen, in Bavaria, to the airbase near Fürstenfeldbruck. The convoy was hit in a rural area between Weilheim and Landsberg. All the convoy troops but one were killed on the spot, and when investigators arrived, the bomb was gone."

Wagner gave him a less-than-awed glance. "We've had nukes stolen before. So why all the excitement this time?"

"Because the bomb is programmed for Doomsday," Groot told him. "It's in what the designers have dubbed 'Stage Nemesis.' Which means that unless the grenadelike fuse is adjusted every two weeks, the bomb will trigger. Which further means that if the U.S. is wiped out in a first-strike war, the surviving bombs spotted in hidden depots will go off two weeks later."

"Hidden depots? Hidden where?"

"There are two of them in Moscow alone," Groot said.

"How much time have we got?"

"Eleven days to trigger time. But only eight for us. We've got to give the terrorists three days to get the bomb back to our control."

"God-amighty!" breathed Wagner.

FLORIDA
IS CLOSED
TODAY

Jack D. Hunter

LEISURE BOOKS ❧ NEW YORK CITY

A LEISURE BOOK

Published by

Nordon Publications, Inc.
Two Park Avenue
New York, N.Y. 10016

PROLOGUE

The convoy sped directly west, tires singing and motors keening in that high-pitched whine of military vehicles under full throttle. Colonel Skelly sat beside the driver of his command car, eyes half closed, body rocking gently from side to side with the machine's motion. To the sides, soft in fall's chalky hues, fields and hedgelines and pastureland and huddles of naked and sullen trees; above, cloudless and glaring, the blue vault; inside, an emptiness, a numb indifference. He rode, listening to the sounds and feeling the things around him and the nothing within him.

At Sindelsdorf the column turned northwest on the two-lane blacktop highway. Headquarters had selected the route because it avoided Munich and other major traffic congestions. This way they could cross the rolling Bavarian plain to Weilheim, from which they would jump to Rott and Landsberg-Buchloe, finishing up on Highway 2 to the base south of Augsburg. Back roads, to be sure, but with fewer complications than they would have found on the Autobahn. Full-scale NATO maneuvers made much of the turnpike systems, but the shell-game shifting of nukes assigned to U. S. military components was, more often than not, a matter of low-key routine. When the Hansels and Gretels saw blinking lights and warning signs and heard sirens and police bleaters they tended to get nervous, and write letters to editors, and hold rallies. But show them what seemed to be the workaday delivery of cucumbers, coal, and candy bars and they would—if they reacted at all—sneer in that way of theirs at the Yankee-Doodles playing soldier.

They despise us, Colonel Skelly thought behind his closed eyes. *They despised us in the old days because we were winners—rich in money and goods and the pizazz that goes with success in war and politics and self-assertiveness. Now they despise us because we are losers; pale imitations of our old selves, limp-wristed with glut and laziness and self-indulgence. Well, to hell with them.*

"May I smoke, sir?" the driver asked.

"Of course. I'm surprised you haven't asked before this."

"Would you like one?"

"No, thank you."

The car filled with the smell of tobacco, and Colonel Skelly remembered those old days, when smoking had been a national trait, not a furtive guilt-trip all intertwined with uneasy visions of growths swelling in the body's dark recesses. Whiskey and cigarettes. The lovely major vices, both enjoyed in the open bliss of ignorance and guilelessness. Today it was shooting stuff in the veins or snuffling some concoction in the nose or washing down pills with absinthe behind locked doors. *What a rotten way to seek fun,* he thought dourly. *What fun is there in freaking out with something you can't taste, alone in a closet? Where are the laughs, the comradeship you can remember?* The whole U.S. Army was a Caesar's legion of junkies and tosspots, and he knew in his gut that it couldn't fight its way out of a Little League awards banquet. His primary solace as a career officer was the knowledge that the Soviet army was no better off. And, if. . . .

"I feel sort of goosy on these runs, don't you, sir?" The driver, obviously, had taken chitchat to be a fringe

6

privilege of the smoking permission.

"Goosy?"

"Riding along these narrow roads, a Squeaky no more than fifty feet behind. It makes a guy think."

"At least you have the assurance that your death, should the bomb go off, would be squeaky-clean. There is absolutely no cleaner nuclear weapon anywhere in the world. You would meet your Maker as an array of immaculate atoms."

"You're joking, aren't you, sir?"

"I suppose so."

The conversation went no further, the driver presumably having decided that there was simply no way to have a decent gossip with someone this weird. Colonel Skelly resumed his catnap, drifting in and out of awareness. Occasionally he would open an eye and, consulting the passenger's sideview mirror, check on the state of things among the weapons truck and its decoys to the rear. Then, after a glance at the escorting helicopter gunship that churned along, discreetly distant over the autumn fields and lacy treelines, he would drowse again.

He could see Gibbons, sitting smugly beside the driver of the weapons truck. The insufferable Major Gibbons; the fawner, the obsequious buttinsky. For weeks Gibbons had dogged him—in the office, at the motor pool, during drinks at the officers' club—for permission to ride a convoy. To have the experience, to feel the vibes, to learn better the needs of convoy personnel, vehicle-maintenance-wise. That kind of gee-whiz crap.

It was during one of these half-awake peeks when Colonel Skelly observed a remarkable phenomenon.

The gunship, an olive-drab insect clacking in the pale sunlight, seemed to fold in on itself and, almost immediately thereafter, to balloon outward, as if it had first exhaled, then taken in an enormous gulp of air. As he sat up, startled, to examine this with concentrated attention, the aircraft dissolved in a flash of white-yellow fire, throwing a cascade of junk and sparks and roiling smoke into a stand of trees to the east. The impression had barely registered when he was thrown forward by a furious slamming of the brakes, and he heard the driver shout, "Holy jumping hell!"

Instinctively, in a kind of throwback to the long-gone time in Nam, the colonel banged down on the door handle and launched himself from the careening car, hitting the frosted shoulder of the highway and rolling blindly down the embankment in an explosion of pain and breathlessness. His mind received, sorted, and identified the shrieking of tires, the stuttering of machine-guns, and the crumping sound of grenades. He clambered up the embankment, his breath coming in great, rasping sounds, and blindly—instinctively again—he scurried to the weapons truck. In the haze he could see Major Gibbons, the ride-along motor-maintenance officer, lying beside the front wheel, face down on the macadam, his hands clasped over his head like a child hiding from a thunderstorm.

Skelly ripped open the rear door, crawled to the inner compartment door, and threw the emergency hatch handle. The door pinged open and the bomb-carrier area was bathed in the white glare of emergency maintenance lights. With two quick strokes of the Dietrich lock, the panel slid and the bomb and fuse were revealed.

8

He clasped the disengagement toggle, pulled the override handle, and began to turn the specifier.

But something hit him in the back, something harsh and cruel and uncompromising in its force, and he felt himself turning and falling. There was an impression, misty and fleeting, of Major Gibbons, of all people who might have been in his last thoughts, and then he was sliding into a whirling tunnel, at the end of which was a light of incredible beauty. . . .

DAY 1

1

The body was lying face-up on the edge of the sea near the Porpoise Point jetty. It lifted and rolled gently from side to side as the waves, breaking, sent seething washes across the hard-packed sands. A small crowd of tourists and local teenagers stood in a semi-circle, shooting glances at the dead man and pretending great nonchalance in the presence of death in public, the ultimate exhibitionism.

Wagner came upon the scene while on the return leg of his walk along the beach, which he'd begun after an afternoon of suffering through the latest best-seller. He had hiked north from his place on the inlet to the big dune house with the Polynesian roof. The overcast and the east wind that stirred it had left the Atlantic pewter-colored—a restless, spray-hazed wilderness redolent of infinite age and depth and distance. Rain was on the way, but it would probably hold off until nightfall, so he had taken his time on the return, trudging barefoot through the hissing ebb and flow and wondering why he was so sure someone had been following him for the past two days.

And now this—this utterly absurd coincidence.

"Has anybody called the police?" he asked the sight-seers.

No one spoke. A kid with knobby knees and acne took an ample bite of a Baby Ruth candy bar and, chewing, shrugged indifferently. A fat lady in a purple bathing suit giggled nervously. The others stood there, looking bored, as if they were above all this.

Wagner knelt and examined the face. It was gray, of course, and icy to his touch; the eyes were closed and the mouth was open, revealing a set of good teeth. He

13

guessed that the body, clad in fisherman's denims and deck shoes, had been in the water at least a day.

"Anybody know when this fellow washed ashore?"

There was another giggle.

"Has anybody searched him for identification?"

After more silence he said, "Thank God for concerned citizens like you. Such warmth and sympathy have made our country what it is."

A squat man in Bermuda shorts nudged the fat lady and said, "Let's go. We'll be late for supper."

"In a minute, Richard," she said.

Wagner arose from his crouch and regarded the group with sadness. To the candy-eater, he said quietly, "Why don't you run up to the restaurant and ask somebody to call the cops?"

"Who are you, Perry Mason, or suthin'?"

"Come on, kid. Somebody's got to contact the authorities."

"You're too old to be Perry Mason, come to think of it." The kid grinned through his candy and winked at a girl who covered her gender with a Bikini that seemed to be made of three eye patches. She patted her hair and looked pained.

Wagner beckoned to the kid with a finger. "Come here. I want to tell you something confidential."

Curious, the youth sauntered across the sand to where Wagner stood, and Wagner, taking his elbow, bent to murmur in his ear: "Get cute with me again, you little squid, and I'll tear off this arm at your belly button. Understood?"

The kid nodded and swallowed the last of his candy.

"Now," Wagner added, "get that scrawny butt of yours up to the telephone before I stop being so polite."

The kid brushed some sand from his swimming trunks, leered at the girl again, then trotted off toward the high dunes.

Wagner waited until the Rescue Squad and a car from the Sheriff's Office arrived, then he edged away from the now-sizeable crowd to make his way to the house. He rinsed the sand from his feet under the outside shower, then, slipping on his clogs, went up the stairs to the deck and through the side door. The kitchen was crisp and silent, except for the purring of the refrigerator, and he lingered there only to take a clean glass from the dishwasher rack before moving on to the living room, where he opened the bar and poured himself a waiting-husband's Scotch. He much preferred a heretical, low-brow rye with beer chaser, but he had been sticking with Scotch in the hope that the habit would catch and thereby add a touch of chic to what Eva most surely must consider his lackluster image.

He stood by the big window, sipping his drink and watching the whitecaps on the inlet, an expanse of dirty green that roiled under the double assault of tide and the freshening wind. The lights of St. Augustine were winking on across Matanzas Bay, and the western sky was a band of orange beyond the storm clouds that scudded, low and fast, out of the darkening ocean void.

Somewhere in that city, with its ancient walls and faded casas and jasmine-scented gardens, was the splendid woman who was his wife—smooth-skinned, level-eyed, and radiant from an inner warmth. He tried to guess her location among the brooding slabs

15

and towers silhouetted against the sunset. She was to have left the college five minutes ago. So where was she now? Walking to the VW? Driving north on San Marco? Turning east on A1A? Crossing the drawbridge? It was a little game of his, the retired civil servant who waited through the lonely days for the homecoming of the school teacher who had crashlanded in his bachelorhood and turned his life around. He would do this every day—trying to see her in his mind as she went her campus rounds, feeling her absence in the silence of their rented house on the dunes.

The game went poorly this evening, though, taken up as he was with the fact of Strasser's body on the beach.

The gray face rolling in the sea wash had evoked images of times and places he had buried carefully in the cellar of his mind. Strasser had been among the best, capable of surprising lapses into grace and compassion in a trade that had no room for either. He'd had a kind of exuberant love for the world which service in the West German intelligence apparatus seemed unable to quench, and perhaps it was this paradoxical quality in him that had virtually guaranteed his assignment to the most delicate and internationally sensitive of the Nachrichtendienst's involvements. Whatever, Strasser had been a first-class human being, whom Wagner counted among the few true gentlemen he'd known in his years of rambling down CIA's murky lanes. He found himself thinking now of the rainy day in 1983 when he and Strasser had followed Baldur Henckel, the terrorist leader, to an apartment in Handschuhsheim, across the Neckar from Heidelberg. Strasser had driven the Mercedes

16

along the boulevard, never losing an inch in his trailing distance from Henckel's Porsche, while all the way regaling Wagner with the history of the Schloss and the role of the Philosopher Weg in Germanic mysticism. In the subsequent shoot-out, Strasser had taken a bullet meant for Wagner, and this had sealed their friendship in a kind of mysticism of its own.

But that had been long ago, and Roger Wagner, the archetypal has-been, was now able to look down on the cold dead face of a former admired comrade and feel no more than mild annoyance over the intrusive memories it brought. There had been too many such faces over too long a time. So few good guys and so many bad. So much transience. So little of substance. Why should he now be expected to mourn anyone but himself and the wasted years?

He stood in the twilight, watching the sky and sea and distant town, thinking, reaching back in his mind for the thread that might tell him what had brought Heinz Strasser to Florida waters and anonymous death. Strasser had worked only on the most imperative and consequential of matters. So what quirk in the unending international con game had put him into work jeans and sneakers?

A shrimp boat appeared out of the eastern gloom, ghostly white and showing its lights, and his eyes followed as it entered the inlet, negotiated the swirling there, and then churned into the bay and a southward turn for the fleet anchorage. As it showed its stern to him, he felt a sense of discord. Something had altered in the generally peaceful scene; something had occurred, or changed, or moved from routine to unusual.

It had been a little more than a year now. He had

been free of the old life of watchfulness and tension and gnawing anxieties for—let's see—fourteen months, and not once in all that time had the Wagner Early Warning System, the absolute inner sureness that something discordant had appeared in the workaday ambience, come into play. His life had been spared many times, thanks to this intuitive capability, but once his life was no longer on the line, even implicity, the phenomenon had ceased to manifest itself.

Until now. Until the car that followed him. Until Strasser.

He was almost certain that something had fallen from the shrimp boat. A darkness had appeared on the pale white flank of the craft, then—well, dropped into the blackness of the bay.

Dropped? What could have dropped?

A net? A rolled tarpaulin? A man?

Reaching, he took the old CIA night-glasses from the bookcase. He pressed his fingers to his forehead and rubbed, seeking to relieve the sudden heaviness there. Then he raised the glasses, and they showed him a light flickering on the strand below the great black hulk of the Castillo de San Marcos—showing where no light should be. Why? Who would be signalling a shrimp boat from an ancient fort occupied at night only by spiders and mice? Or was it signalling? Maybe it was a couple of kids playing with a flashlight.

I must find something to do with my time, he told himself. *I am seeing things. Imagining things.*

He returned the glasses to their place on the shelf.

The wind, picking up, was making unhappy sounds in the eaves, and he felt a chill. Northern Florida in the fall, he reminded himself. Wind and rain and rawness. That's what had made his skin cold.

Not the vague sense of danger gathering.

He was imagining that.

That was from the old days.

He thought he heard tires crunching on the gravel road to the rear of the house, so he turned on the living room lamps and went through the kitchen and out the door and onto the deck. There was darkness below, and, leaning, hands on the railing, he called down, "Eva? Is that you?"

But there was only the wind, with its melancholy sighing and its oppressive dankness, smelling of the sea. He stood there, listening, waiting for something he couldn't name. Eva was not there, of course; but *something* was out there in the damp blackness—a memory, a thought, an ineradicable past that insisted on returning. The body on the beach had evoked years long dead, and with them a nervous restlessness, and, with this, an inner sense of something very close to guilt.

He returned to the living room and, after pouring himself another drink (How easy it was to resort to that . . .), he began to pace, the feeling of cold and unidentifiable dread refusing to abate.

Those days were in the past.

He was now another man, in another time.

What was he worried about?

Crossing the room, he picked up the phone and dialed Universal Information. "The number in Washington, D.C., for the Central Intelligence Agency's operations group. The public number."

After a crackle or two, the operator intoned, "There

is no such listing, sir. Only the Agency's switchboard number."

"Well, let me have that, then."

He dialed again and asked the CIA operator for Operations.

There was another crackle. "Public Information Office; Miss Burns speaking." The voice was creamy, in the airline hostess mode.

"I wanted Operations."

"Well, I'm sorry, sir, but that line doesn't accept public calls."

"Even when a public guy like me has some information about a foreign espionage agent?" Wagner said, uncreamy.

Miss Burns didn't miss a beat. "Have you tried the FBI, sir?"

"Once. But they turned me down. I was too young, and had flat feet."

"Oh?"

"Look, Miss Burns: give me somebody in charge. Somebody in the spy department. Soon. I'm calling long distance. On my money."

"Well, that's nice of you, sir. But I must repeat, I'm charged with taking unsolicited calls from the public."

Truly angry now, Wagner grated, "OK, then stick this in your IBM, baby: A body washed ashore at Porpoise Point near St. Augustine, Florida, today."

"May I ask your name, sir?"

"It's the body of a West German intelligence agent named Heinz Strasser. Heinz, like in pickles; Strasser like in S-T-R-A-S-S-E-R."

"Sir, I must have your name."

Wagner hung up and sat for a long time, staring at the wall.

The least he could do for Strasser was to have him sent home.

DAY 2

2

The room was dappled in sunlight and shadow, and Eva sat by the big window, listening to the surf and feeling the house about her. It was a small house; its furnishings were few and threadbare, in the manner of beach rentals, but among its borrowed boards and glass were her memories—accumulations of thought and experience shared with Roger—and so she cherished the place as if it were her own. There weren't many memories, either, come to think of it, since her life with him had begun such a short time ago, but when taken together with the house itself they authenticated her as a wife.

For how long, she couldn't guess. And the uncertainty was the why of her teaching full time—the rationale of days (and many nights) spent in ancient rooms, expounding the thoughts of men long dead for collegians who'd not yet begun to live.

She and Roger had met in the Austrian-Tyrol, where, recovering from a lover's betrayal, she had been working as a hotel maid to earn the air fare home. He had been about to leave the CIA, wondering what had happened to his life. He had entered his sixties, she was in her early thirties, and the peanut gallery was simply not ready to concede that they could sustain their reach across the difference.

The age thing was nonsense, of course. The true gap was much more difficult to perceive, even at times for her, since it was rooted in her own insecurity. Roger was tough, urbane, knowledgeable in a really astonishing range of things. She was a hillbilly schoolmarm, the product of a puckered frontier ethos that valued insularity, hard work, the three R's, and the subservience of women, suspecting anything beyond these perimeters as being effete or subversive. No one had been more surprised and uneasy than she when she'd run off to Europe to teach at a starchy, well-endowed denominational school: surprised by her readiness to go and uneasy over her reason for going, which was to convince the homefolks that she could be more than a gingham-draped baby-sitter. Unfortunately she had taken her vulnerability—loneliness—with her, a fact quickly recognized by Jean-Paul, the headmaster, who had sympathized her into his waiting sack. After a time he'd begun to see she was serious (the frontier had also bequeathed her the idea that physical privileges demand spiritual commitment). Being as he was, Jean-Paul broke off the affair in a decisive way by seeing that the trustees learned of it. The board's European chauvinism had done the rest: in its collective eye, the headmaster was simply a sportive fellow doing what healthy men do; she was a retread Sadie Thompson, who must be fired summarily for having been "caught up in sin." The only positive aspect of the disaster was an anger that had torn her out of her provincial mind-set. By the time Roger Wagner had appeared in her life she'd begun to see herself not as the wayward girl the homefolks would have deemed her but as a woman who had simply made a bad zig on the zaggy Road to Worldly Wisdom. *C'est la rotten vie,* eh? Fight on, Notre Dame. . . . Ironically, loneliness had done her in with Roger, too. He was very high-power manhood, and this, coupled with the frequently eerie reach of his power of discernment, had proved to be a lot more to deal with than had the limp-wristed posturing of a mission school satyr-in-saint's-clothing. Jean-Paul had, by being such a wart, triggered in her a determination to be self-sufficient; Roger Wagner had, simply by being the man he was, made her wonder if that was such a hot idea after all. She had known instantly that he was someone she needed, but, once their marriage had certified her ability to acquire him, she'd begun to look for ways to prove to herself that she wouldn't need him when she did need him—to depend on him without being dependent.

He came in from the bedroom, pulling a sweater over his head. It was the blue sweater, with worn elbows. His favorite.

"What did you say?"

He smoothed his hair with his hands and gave her a curious glance. "Say? What do you mean?"

"You were mumbling in your sweater."

"Was I? What about?"

"That's what I asked you."

"I never mumble on Tuesdays. You must be hearing things."

"This is Wednesday."

"Oh?" He made a business of going to the window and regarding the morning. "It doesn't look like a Wednesday. It looks more like a Tuesday."

"Do you want breakfast?"

"I'll pick up some at The Corner after I drop you off."

"There's a piece of that coffee cake left."

"I'll have that when I come back."

"You won't be downtown all day, then?"

"No. A little stroll around. Lunch at the Monson.

That kind of thing."

"Wild day, eh?"

"Breathtaking."

They traded smiles, the day's first dose of the ritualistic kidding with which they tranquilized the pain of his idleness. She had a sudden vision of all the husbands and wives in all the cities and towns and farm homes who were at this very moment dealing with the fact of unemployment, forced retirement, or general uselessness. It was a bleak picture, filled with sad people wondering silently where all the golden times had gone, and there was an explosive surge of her determination to learn, to pull on the armor of capability, so that she might protect herself from the stagnation settling over the world. She must not stand still for a second. She must move. Do. Earn. Fortify.

"Ready?"

"Yep."

"Where are your books?"

"In the car. I didn't bring them in last night."

"Too tired to work?"

"Too dispirited."

He took her elbow and turned her to him. "Hey," he said gently, "you're not allowed to be dispirited. It's against the house rules."

"I was having one of my spells of futility. I get them now and then."

"We can't give up. That's for the spoiled brats."

"It doesn't seem to matter. The harder I work, the harder you look for work, the more we seem to fall back."

"We're doing all right. My pension and your salary still carry us. We still have a place of our own. We don't have to live with two hundred people in three rooms, like so many are doing these days."

"But for how long, Roger? I mean, isn't it ever going to get better?"

Having no answer, he held her tighter, for longer than the occasion required. After a time, they locked the house, went down to the car, and drove into town. On the way, she found she, too, had no answers, especially to the question that had truly been nagging her: What had happened to Roger last night? She could not ignore the fact that something had been altered in him—some subtle modification in his eyes, his color, the way he walked—which had returned her instantly to Austria and the bad times. Arriving home, she had no more than reached the top of the stairs and moved across the deck when, seeing him in the living room, pacing and pale, she remembered the days in the Tyrol and the hauntedness he wore about him, as tangible and sad as the dumb old blue sweater. And she'd felt immediate fear, a kind of icy sureness that the time had finally come.

He had tired of her.

He was looking for a way to be rid of her.

For all her yearning for independence, she saw now that the thought of being without him was unacceptable, frightening. She would suffer, not simply from the abiding sense of drifting and rootlessness which most certainly would resume, but mainly from the understanding that she had been so busy protecting herself from being hurt by his loss she had lost him.

The death-wish, restated.

The self-fulfilling prophecy.

He left the Avenida at Hypolita Street and went to Cordova, where he turned south and brought the VW to a stop at the entrance to the faculty parking lane.

"Here you are, Learned One. Get in there and be pedantic."

"You'll pick me up at five?"

"Jawohl-you-all, as we say in Southern Germany."

"Roger—"

"Mm?"

"What's wrong?"

"Wrong?"

"You've been very quiet. Since last night. Something's bothering you. Other than the usual things, I mean."

He gave her a too-ready smile. "I'm a fat and complacent householder drowsing in the sun, reassured by high taxes, a swelling crime rate, unemployment, inflation, pollution, and all other signs of normality. I am Mr. Smug."

"I'm not joking."

"I know you're not."

"Are we all right, Roger? The two of us?"

"Of course we're all right. It's part of my smug scene. The main part. Thanks to you, there's not a smugger bugger anywhere."

"Be serious."

"I am being serious."

She saw she was getting nowhere, so she gathered her books and handbag, and bussed him on the chin, then swung out of the car to stand in the sunlight.

"*Ciao*," she said, solemn with the knowledge that she had indeed lost him.

"Five o'clock."

She turned and hurried along the palm-shaded walkway, her skirt swinging. She did not look back, as was her custom.

Watching her go, he thought: *I've lost her.*

It had been coming for weeks. But now, after the rotten little conversation just concluded, his mind had given it words.

He had never been much good at dealing with females. From high school days, those misty times beyond the beginning of the world, he had known that it was impossible to tell where you stood with women—what they were really thinking behind the smiles or the frowns, the sighs, the ready words. He had been wrong about them so many times his inner gears would automatically fall into *Slow-Forward, With Caution* whenever a new liaison presented itself. Later, in his years with The Company, where wariness was prerequisite to the next salary check, his by-then reflexive suspicion of the other sex had remained in overdrive. So, in a way, it was a minor miracle that he had come as far as he had with Eva. She had proved to be the only woman in his long and wasted life who had expected nothing of him, made no conditions, asked no questions, extracted no price, material or social, for her companionship. By being calm, straightforward, patient, and loving, she had somehow penetrated his defenses and turned him into a house cat.

But he hadn't been much good at that, either.

He'd spent too much time in the alley. And now the alley was calling him again.

3

The night's rain had left the world clean, and a breeze, soft and dry, whispered through the palms lining the Avenida and stirred the bay into restlessness. The sun was warm, and clumps of cotton clouds cruised aloft, daubing the water and the suburban facades of Davis Shores with lazily changing patterns of shadow. Gulls, great swarms of them, circled and called in the brilliance, and a squadron of pelicans glided down the wind, holding an impeccable V formation. Wagner breathed deeply of the sweet air and walked a steady pace, feeling Creation around him and wondering why he had wasted so much of his life, roaming and aching among the alleyways and billboards and gas stations and dirty snowbanks of Cheapsville, when this real world of sun and sky and glittering waves had been here all along, waiting.

He had made a thing of coming into town because he'd really had nothing else to do. First he'd walked south along the bay front, past the Bridge of Lions to the municipal pier, then back north to the great gray hulk of the Castillo de San Marcos, the grim and melancholy fortress the Spaniards had built in the 1670's to command the bay they had called "Slaughter." He paid his dollar and went up to the uppermost level and leaned on the parapet like any old tourist, gazing out at the sugar-white sweeps of Porpoise Point, picking out his house there, and trying to imagine how it all had looked to a homesick cannoneer almost four hundred years ago. All that time, and still the world insisted on grabbing, holding, exploiting, killing in the name of a higher purpose—the euphemism for political power and material acquisitions. Four hundred years, and replacing coquina blocks and drawbridges and moats and the breast-plated barbarians who held it all with pikes and swords were bunkers and hollowed-out mountains and nuclear bombs coming down from the frozen stratosphere.

He thought of ancient Spain and the bandy-legged little buggers with the helmets and beards it had sent here to look for gold and to make Catholics of the Indians and to keep those French and English nudniks out of New Spain, which in the King's eye ran from Cuba to Canada. And he thought of those who had disagreed with this enough to earn a few lifetimes in the moisture-beaded dungeons below, provided they hadn't first been treated to a foot or two of Toledo steel.

Wagner supposed these bloody musings had their root in the murder of Heinz Strasser—identified in the press reports as a tourist, Fred Rowe, of Philadelphia. It was an event his mind refused to let go.

The local newspaper had made much of it, of course, and the incident seemed to have impressed the natives with the truth they had admitted but never before accepted: their small city, so parochial and so eclipsed by the giant shadow of Jacksonville, had gone the way of all American towns and was irretrievably lost to Big and Nasty Crime. But the shock given word in the press and on street corners was curiously qualified. That a vacationer from Philadelphia could be shot dead on a fishing excursion, eventually to wash ashore on the beach in front of a popular family-type restaurant, was cause for concern, to be sure; but Wagner had noted a kind of veiled satisfaction in all the gabble, a barely communicated smugness that appeared to be based in the fact that Big Crime goes only where Big Money gathers. Vandalism, petty theft, juvenile drug and alcohol violations had been St. Augustine's lot for years; but now, the execution-type slaying of a Yankee on the town's seaward hem was the stuff of drama and intrigue—a certification of the fact that the community had left behind the penny ante years and was entering a new, golden, economy-boosting era of Big League Sin. Nothing attracts crowds faster than wickedness, and crowds need food, gas, beer, cigarettes, shoes, hats, soft drinks, tires, magazines, socks, contraceptives, tooth brushes and motel space. So for all the dismay to be heard in saloon and salon there was a notable lack of bitterness. Herb Lucey, a St. George Street merchant, had burbled, "Hell of a thing, tourist fellas getting shot on our beaches. But, lordy, how I did sell sunglasses! Everybody going out to look at the murder scene, eh? Ha-ha."

Wagner sighed, moved among the cannons for the stairs, and told himself once again that it was a rotten world. He went into the rectangular courtyard, through the damp blue shadows of the portcullis, across the drawbridge, and down the lane to the Avenida, where he was nearly overrun by a thundering herd of joggers, all muscled, puffing, snorting, and glistening with the sweat of calories subdued. One of them, a cute little tyke only slightly larger than the Colossus of Rhodes, collided with him, spinning him around.

"Hey, Tinkerbell," Wagner snapped, "you'd better start hanging warning blinkers on those shoulders."

The young man, panting, took Wagner's hand and

shook it, saying, "*Verzeihung, bitte.* Ah—I Eggsguse me, blease. I am sorry to haff struck you zo." Then he trotted off in the wake of his healthy, noisily breathing pals, who continued up the avenue, a blur of churning knees and elbows.

Wagner watched after them for a time.

During his return to the car he thought of the old Charles Atlas ad and the 97-pound weakling who was always getting sand kicked in his face by the beach bully.

He was surprised to find Eva in the kitchen. Eva was never home before five, and to discover that she had broken the custom was somehow unsettling, like finding an IRS communication in the mail box. It could be routine, but probably wasn't, and the unnaturalness created an immediate sense of impending difficulty.

She was engaged in the clattering ballet of a woman preparing dinner.

"Well, you're early," he said warily. "How come?"

"My classes were finished at three. Grabbed a cab. We'll have to eat early if I'm to catch my plane out of Jacksonville."

Wagner felt a swift rise in his wariness, and he realized there was shock and some anger intermixed. "Plane? You're going somewhere?"

"Read that letter," she said, nodding over her shoulder at the telephone stand. "It was delivered to me at school. Special delivery, registered, return receipt requested."

He picked up the envelope, which was ablaze with red-stamped cautions, alerts, and advisories, all under

35

a Colorado Springs postmark carrying yesterday's date. The sender's address, embossed in raised, elegant black letters, was that of Winfield and Lindsay, attorneys at law. "Somebody suing you?" he said, trying for nonchalance.

"Read it." She held a head of lettuce under the sink's cold tap and blasted it with a gush of water, seeming, as she did, to be struggling with a vast excitement. "Read it aloud, so I can understand it, maybe."

" 'Dear Mrs. Wagner,' " he intoned. " 'This is to advise you that you have been named as a beneficiary in the will of the late Enos B. Lawrence and, if you can arrange to be in these offices no later than 4 p.m., January 21 next, bringing birth certificate or other documentation of true identity, a certain bequest will be delivered to you. Thanking you for your attention to this matter, I am, most respectfully, Andrew L. Lindsay.' " Glancing up at her, Wagner said, "Who in hell is Enos B. Lawrence?"

"I haven't the foggiest. I mean, ah, Lindsay has told me who Lawrence is, but I don't *know* who he is, if you follow me."

"No, I don't, as a matter of fact. Told you? When did he tell you?"

"I called right away. From the department office. Mr. Lindsay said Enos B. Lawrence was a business associate of my father many years ago. Lawrence died in 1985 and his will was found only a year ago and he didn't have any survivors and so he had left his estate to my father or his heirs, or whatever they call me, and I'm it, because there's nobody else." There was a tight, exultant tone to her voice, and her cheeks

36

were flushed.

"Let me ask the obvious. Did the man say how much?"

"About a hundred thousand dollars. After taxes."

Wagner, despite his will to the contrary, blinked. "Well, now," he said, "that's a respectable amount. How long did it take you to climb back up after you got that little news?"

She laughed, a high, nervous sound, unnatural for her. "I could hardly breathe."

"Me, too. That should buy you a new dress or two."

"Us. I'll buy us a lot of nice things."

"I always wanted to be a kept man."

She laughed again and came to him, holding him tightly. "I still can't believe it. This makes all the difference, Roger. We can pay all our bills, and save a lot, and get interest, and we won't have to break our backs just to keep up."

"Yep."

"I just can't believe it." There was a pause, and then she asked carefully, "Would you like to go with me?"

He knew she'd asked out of propriety, and he respected her for it. No. Loved her more for it. "I don't think so. You need a complete change. A vacation from things. Me included. You can visit your old friends in Colorado Springs, have a lot of hen talk, catch up on things out there. I'd only be excess baggage."

"Well . . ."

"No kidding, Eva. Go and have fun. I'll be fine here. And when you get back I'll let you take me out to dinner on your new wealth. OK?"

She kissed his ear and said, "Sure. But I want you

37

to be a good boy while I'm gone."

"Oh, heck. You mean I can't have some girls in?"

She laughed again, kissed him hard, then returned to her chores. "I won't be going anywhere if I don't get this supper fixed."

"When's your plane?"

"Nine-thirty."

"You packed?"

"Not completely."

"Well, go do it. I'll make the supper."

"It's a tuna salad. . . ."

"I don't think that's beyond my competence. Now git."

She gave him a grateful glance and hurried down the hall toward the bedroom, calling back to him, "I still can't believe it. I simply can't believe it!"

"You're not supposed to believe it," Wagner called as he finished washing the lettuce. "You're supposed to spend it."

He struggled hard to deal with a very heavy depression that had unaccountably seized him.

4

After watching Eva's plane disappear into the starry western sky, Wagner drove through Jacksonville on I-95 to its intersection with U.S. 1 about five miles south of the city, and, following this older, more direct road to St. Augustine, took his time in getting home. As he headed down San Marco toward the historic district, he considered going on to the Chart House to smother his blues with a drink. But it was getting late and he was tired and he now had an incipient headache to deal with—a task he could handle better in the quiet of his house than at a bar. So he turned east on A1A and was on his deck, rattling the door keys ten minutes later.

He needn't have bothered.

The door was unlocked, and when he flipped on the lights he saw Groot, pudgy in his ill-fitting $800 suit, sitting, feet together in that oddly prim attitude heavy men assume in an easy chair, in the far corner of the living room.

"Good evening, Wagner. The Agency appreciates your phone call of last night."

"How did you get in here?"

"Oh, come now. Isn't that a rather ridiculous question for one ex-Company man to ask another?"

"I'll rephrase the question: How about getting the hell out of here?"

"Certainly. After you've agreed to handle something for me."

"As we used to say in the Hitler Jugend, up your giggy with a hot-cross bun."

Groot's eyes were as flat and dark and expressionless as pond stones. His hair was quite gray now,

Wagner noticed irrelevantly, and the jowls were heavier, giving him the general appearance of a wicked Pillsbury dough boy. "Desperate things are afoot, Wagner," Groot said in his wheezing way.

"I told the Director once, and I'm telling you again: I will not work for you, with you, around you, above you, under you, or in any other prepositional condition. If I would not work with you in the Company after finding you and your foxy friends in the Presidential hen-house, why in hell should I work with you now, when you're no longer in The Company? When I'm no longer in The Company? When The Company's no longer The Company?" He realized he was babbling, and he hated himself for it.

Groot had always had a way of reappearing in the life and times of Roger Wagner, and each time the experience had been as pleasant as a swim in the Niagara rapids. They had joined The Company at about the same time, years and years ago, when the business of espionage had been a business of people versus people, not a mere contest of computers, as it had become. Groot was of German derivation—remote, cold, pasty of complexion and lumpy of body and dark of soul. Wagner was Irene Wagner's little boy, the wide-eyed kid who would persist in the delusion of good guys and bad guys and the happy endings of the Saturday matinee at Shea's Kenmore. Groot, the emotionless pragmatist, had risen to CIA's loftiest heights—the hushed corridors and the expensive clothes and the cultured drawls and the purring IBM's—while Wagner, the marshmallow idealist, had remained in covert operations where for three decades he'd been shot, stabbed, beaten, and, worst of all, ignored, all the while viewing the world through John Wayne-colored glasses and wondering why the cavalry never came clattering over his grubby horizons.

"I'm not kidding. The subject is very serious."

"Tough patootie."

"World War Three, as a matter of fact."

"Oh, come on, Groot. You and all the other nerds in The Company have been using that one for years. Do not expect me to become all a-twitter over your bureaucratic hyperbole, as we used to say at Kelly's Pool Hall and Massage Parlor."

"Even so, it's true. And Strasser's body puts a whole new facet on it."

"And, by the damn-old way, what are you doing, working on World War Three? The agreement was that I wouldn't blow the whistle on you and your sedition if you retired from the Company. Yet, here you are, screwing around at the same old stand."

Groot nodded. "That's a reasonable question. My answer is that I am indeed retired from the CIA, as you stipulated. However, as many retired business men are asked for their opinions from time to time, often by the management of the very firms from which they receive their pensions, I am asked for mine. And, in all truth, there are occasions of very special delicacy and urgency in which mainstream intelligence carries too high a profile to be effective, and in some of these instances my direct participation has been requested. Since I am out of the mainstream, I'm not burdened by attention from alien agencies—from unfriendlies, both foreign and domestic—and therefore I have a special value to the President and other very high ranks in our government."

Wagner humphed. "For which you charge an exorbitant fee, no doubt."

"No fee is exorbitant if it buys the desired result. What price do you put on an avoided war, a saved presidency?"

Wagner was about to mention Eva's bizarre inheritance, but he held off, recognizing it to be a trump he need not play. Why admit that he knew her great good luck was due to Groot's need to clear the decks—to get her out of the way?

Take the money and shut up, Wagner. It was Groot's idea. Let him pay.

For all this, though, Wagner was not feeling especially comfortable. Groot was prime rib of bastard, to be sure, but this was no real reason to take taxpayers' money and run—to be the very kind of person Groot could be.

"You've got a point," Wagner heard himself saying. "I should not let you go back to Washington without I at least listen to your problem. So what's your problem?"

"Now there's the Roger Wagner I know."

"Come on, Groot. Don't try to romance me. Just inform me."

Groot turned in his chair and stared out at the night and the distant lights across the inlet—vexed, but, as always, hiding his annoyance behind a placid brow. It was the woman, as he had expected. The wife. For all his self-righteous postures, his fits of idealism, his living in an irretrievable past, Wagner had been an excellent field agent, frequently exhibiting astonishing levels of competence and courage. There had always been a tenacity there, a kind of rough-and-ready will-

42

ingness to plunge into a puzzle and to hang on until he had worked it out. In truth, Groot had been separated from the CIA mainstream at Langley thanks to Wagner's virtuoso performance in Munich, when certain U.S. officials had embarked on a vulpine scheme to short-circuit the election process by kidnapping the President during a summit meeting. Groot himself had been snookered by the plotters, but Wagner, the Eternal Rover Boy, had tarred him along with all the other miscreants, and the bottom line was this psuedo-retirement, in which his talents were still valued, but only for special problems. And now, when he was needed the absolute most, Wagner was not responding to the old stimuli; since no other factors were evident or likely, it had to be assumed that his marriage to the Whitney girl was the cause. A wife, especially a young and beautiful wife, could be a debilitating disease, and Wagner showed advanced symptoms. Groot was therefore most grateful for her need to go to Colorado—one of those kind touches of coincidence fate was capable of. Even so, he found himself sighing and hoping for the best as he gave it to Wagner from the top.

"Terrorists have stolen one of our most sophisticated nuclear weapons," he said, "and we haven't the slightest idea as to where it might be. It was being convoyed from the depot at Wolfratshausen, in Bavaria, to the airbase near Fürstenfeldbruck. The convoy was hit in a rural area between Weilheim and Landsberg. All the convoy troops but one were killed on the spot, and when investigators arrived, the bomb was gone. We've been turning Europe and the Mideast upside down in the attempt to find it."

"Who was the surviving American?"

"A colonel. The convoy commander. Named Skelly. A highly respected, much-decorated officer."

"Has he been questioned?"

"He's still unconscious. Under intensive care at the U.S. military hospital in Wiesbaden."

"How about satellite scans? Haven't they picked up a radiation glow in an unlikely spot?"

Groot sighed. "That's one of the more rotten parts of this rotten incident. Satellites can readily pick up nuclear concentrations, from atomic power stations to military arsenals, but they're rarely successful in spotting the movement of individual tactical weapons. Moreover, this particular weapon is housed in a transport jacket that further obscures nuclear manifestation. So it can be easily moved from place to place and stored in isolated areas without disclosing its presence. Still, it's my guess that the terrorists have hidden the bomb in an area fairly close to a known radiation center—just in case."

Wagner asked, "Can the satellites spot any increase or decrease in the glow at known centers?"

"Only if large numbers of major weapons are involved. There's no detectable change when one or two bombs are moved from Point A to Point B."

"So the stolen bomb could be sitting in a culvert next to the Cornhusker Corners Atomic Power Plant and our satellites wouldn't report, first, that the nuke had left Wolfratshausen or, second, that it was now in the culvert."

"That's about the size of it."

"Peachy."

Groot sighed again, a deep, disconsolate sound.

"And that means we are faced with a catastrophe of literally cosmic proportions."

Wagner gave him a less-than-awed glance. "We've had nukes stolen before. Once in Albuquerque, another time at that air station in the UK. The bombs were found in garbage dumps—ditches, or something. The thieves apparently couldn't break through the trigger codes. So why all the excitement this time?"

Groot, who had given up smoking, wished he had a cigar. "Two reasons," he said, feeling his pockets absently for tobacco he knew was not there. "First: this bomb is a Squeaky—a drop-projectile, no larger than a watermelon, that kills every living thing in a hundred square miles without any more fuss than a hand-grenade explosion. It does not kill by blast. It kills by intensified X-ray flash. It goes off like a photographer's flash bulb. That's all. There's a small concussion, then a brilliant, momentary light. Then, within a half hour, everything, right on down to tadpoles and caterpillars, keels over."

Wagner nodded, trying for insouciance and not quite making it. "I see. Why is it called Squeaky?"

"It's clean. The trick is in the fuse. With such a fuse, even a standard K-bomb will contaminate no more than two days. After two days, a week, troops can occupy the bombed area and its undamaged structures."

"And bury the dead tadpoles."

"Yes. That, too."

"Any witnesses to the theft?"

"Only three. Two German kids, hikers in a nearby woods. And a dairy farmer."

"Where are they now?"

"The young ones are back in Munich, students at the university. The farmer's back on his farm. All released after questioning."

"So when does World War Three come in?"

"When the terrorists make their exultant announcement that they have acquired a bomb and will use it unless they are given the moon, the stars, and free passes to the World Series. The United States will not hesitate to go in to get it, by force if necessary, no matter who the host country may be."

"Why?" Wagner said.

"Because the bomb is programmed for Doomsday. It's in what the designers have dubbed 'Stage Nemesis.' All Squeakies are in fail-safe condition while in storage or in routine handling, on the ground or aloft. But after commitment to strategic units, they are placed in Nemesis. Which means, simply, that unless the grenade-like fuse is adjusted every two weeks, the bomb will trigger. Which further means that if the U.S. is wiped out in a first-strike war, the surviving Squeakies spotted in hidden depots will go off two weeks later."

"Hidden depots? Hidden where?"

"Here and there, throughout the world."

"God-amighty! We've got little fellows sitting in places around the world who do nothing but keep hidden Squeakies from going off?"

"There are two of them hidden in Moscow alone."

"How much time have we got?"

"Eleven days to trigger time. But only eight for us. We've got to give the terrorists three days to get the bomb back to our control."

"God-amighty!"

"Three days to understand the seriousness of the situation and return the bomb."

"The obvious question at this stage, Groot, is why me? But I'm not going to ask it because I think I know the answer. You need me to chase down the Strasser angle."

Well, then, Groot thought. *Wagner's juices still run.* "Yes. That's quite so. All our regular troops are committed. Need-you is the word."

"Do you think Strasser had anything to do with the stolen bomb?"

"You have just asked the key question. We don't think so, but we can't afford to ignore any angle. Strasser was working undercover, in Germany, to penetrate a secret organization purported to be infiltrating the Chancellor's governing party. It was said to be a long-range effort by political sophisticates whose leader was Siegfried Unger. Objective: to move Germany to the full right. The group eschews terrorism and the hoodlum element. It is said to put a high premium on legality and decorum—to make the system work against itself."

Wagner sniffed. "So did Adolf Hitler. And you see what that got us."

"Do you want to hear all of this? Or would you rather be sarcastic?"

"Go on."

"About two weeks ago, Strasser's case director at the Nachrichtendienst lost track of him. He had been filing clandestine reports via a T-47 out of Nesselwang, a small town at the foot of the Alps in Bavaria. Twice a week, and without a hitch, and. . . ."

Wagner broke in, "What's a T-47?"

"A new high frequency radio, about the size and shape of an electric razor. It sends voice, but the voice is taped, then transmitted instantly at a very high-speed garble. When it is sending, it compacts the time frame to micro seconds. The Gettysburg Address, for instance, would, in its entirety, sound to unfriendly radio monitors to be no more than a bleep. And even if they capture and decelerate the message, it's in mechanical garble—not an understandable word."

"What's Unger's background, Groot?"

"Investment broker, seemingly legitimate. Very rich, having inherited the fortune amassed by his late father, Richard Unger, in West German reconstruction after World War Two. His tie-in with the right-wing group is confusing, since he was for years identified with leftist causes."

"Why Nesselwang?"

"Strasser's reports indicated that the clandestine organization is headquartered there. His last message was the news of his appointment to Unger's leadership council, a development that would have made him privy to the identities of the top echelon."

Wagner rubbed his eyes. "And it also made him a candidate for execution, it would seem."

"Yes."

"But why in Florida waters? What got him over here, all the way from Nesselwang? And what was Unger doing here, renting boats?"

"That's what we're paying you to find out."

"Paying me? How much?"

Groot pushed himself free of the chair and managed to get his heavy frame upright. He crossed the room and, with his hand on the doorknob, paused to return

Wagner's stare. "You will have an advance of $250,000. Any expenses you incur in the pursuit of the Unger-Strasser matter will come out of that. If our searchers in Europe find the bomb and negate it before you make any effective contribution, you will keep ten additional thousand, return the remainder. If you make a substantial contribution, you keep twenty. I decide what is substantial."

Wagner considered this for a moment. Then: "What if I go to Europe and find the bomb for you?"

"In that unlikely event, you would keep the entire amount remaining after your expenses."

"In other words, if I spend $5,000 to visit Europe and bring the bomb back home, I keep $245,000?"

"Your grasp of mathematical concepts is incredible." Groot nodded toward the phone table. "My unlisted Delaware number is on that card there. I'll want daily reports. Daily. No matter what's going on."

"Before you go, Groot, tell me something."

"Well?"

"What led you to me? I didn't give my name to your PR lady."

"Strasser's disappearance has been a matter of intense interest to U.S. and West German intelligence for two weeks. When an anonymous caller claims a dead Philadelphia vacationer is really Heinz Strasser, the machinery hiccupped. Strasser would be known as Strasser only to a very few who have worked on the deep side of CIA. What few in St. Augustine, Florida, where the body was found? We asked our computers and out you came."

"Another question: could the Soviets have stolen the Squeaky?"

Groot shrugged. "Why would they bother? They have a similar device of their own. We're frozen in impasse. Remember?"

"Just thought I'd ask."

Saying nothing further, Groot pushed through the door and into the night beyond.

Wagner spent almost an hour trying to arrange the earliest possible flight from Orlando to Munich. The two daylight connections—both via the Azores and Paris—were booked to the rafters and had standbys for the standbys. So he settled for a seat on the nonstop SST leaving Orlando at eight p.m. the next evening, figuring he'd lose no more than a few hours, all things considered.

Then he gave another hour to rummaging through his old CIA stuff, picking out the items he thought might be useful on this rinky-dink.

Nothing flashy. Just the staples.

DAY 3

5

There were no open parking spaces on King Street, so he gave up on breakfast at The Corner and went on to the Avenida Menendez, where he turned north along the bay front and pulled into the Monson motel lot. After its indifferent beginning, the morning had decided to give the tourists a break, featuring a velvet blue sky, puff clouds, a balmy breeze out of the south, and a yellow sun that sparkled on the water and made the delicate filigrees of the Bridge of Lions glow like a wedding cake. He stood by the car for a moment, breathing deeply and admiring the view and pondering once again the grotesqueness of a world that could accommodate simultaneously the Almighty's elegance and gun-shot bodies on a beach.

The dining room was packed, but he caught Audrey's eye and she nodded him toward a booth by the window that had just been left, heaped with rumpled red napkins and grapefruit rinds, by four gray little ladies in bulging pants suits.

"Thanks, Audrey. You are the crème de la crème, the epitome of empathetical sensitivity to the urgencies of an esurient earthling."

"You can't talk to me like that. I'll call a cop." She cleared the table in what seemed to be three magical swoops of her arms. Then, balancing the tray of clutter with balletic grace, she gave him a wink and said, "The usual, earthling?"

"Over medium, with grits."

"See by the paper you had a murder out your way."

He shrugged. "Is that what the paper said it was?"

"How the hell do I know? I just read the headlines. Gun victim found on beach at Vilano, it said. You want more, call Jessica Savitch."

"Better yet, fetch me a paper, eh?"

"I'll bring it with the coffee."

The *Times-Union* had given the story three terse paragraphs below the fold on its second news front. The body was tentatively identified as that of Fred Lowe, a tourist from Philadelphia last seen when renting a boat in Miami. The cause of death, established by autopsy, was a gunshot wound in the back. The investigation was continuing, according to the Sheriff's Office.

Audrey brought his eggs, and after he'd eaten, he watched the morning again, feeling the sun's warmth on the window pane beside him. The fishing fleet had gone to sea by now, and the bay was busy with cabin cruisers and sailboats, brought out like insects that feel the oncoming spring. The horse-and-buggy tourist tours were clopping about with full loads of fatties wearing funny hats and Instamatics, and two buses bearing billboard-size Vermont Trailways legends on their flanks went blattering by in a cloud of diesel smoke. These vignettes, the spectacular sky, the special awareness of kitchen sounds and subdued laughter and the muttering of the TV in the lounge and the smell of coffee, made him feel keenly alive and oddly liberated from the burden of Eva and the problems she represented. Somehow everything would turn out all right, he felt suddenly; even if Eva left him, it would be all right. In the end it would come around to the good.

"More coffee?" Audrey hovered beside him, holding the pot at the ready.

"A splash or two." He nodded toward a tall young

man who stood in the parking lot outside, holding a large map between widespread arms. "Who dat?"

Audrey squinted into the sunlight. "The guy with the charts and the fisherman's hat?"

"Mm."

"That's Paul Driscoll, a guest here."

"Who he?"

"A young archeologist on a Federal grant. He's fixing to do some digging for arrowheads and old helmets and like that. The eggheads are always digging up St. Augustine."

"I thought he was a tax assessor or something."

"Nope. He's too nice a young fella for that. Cute, too."

"I hate cute young fellas."

"Well, you got a lot to hate these days. The town's crawling with cute young guys from South America. Don't ask me why. Jillions of 'em."

"Maybe it's a dope-smugglers' convention."

"I doubt it. They're too healthy. Clear-eyed. They ain't sneaky."

"Well, St. Augustine's tourists represent the world itself, to quote one of our Chamber of Commerce brochures."

"Ain't it the truth. I kept track this week. Would you believe in three days I waited on two Russians, a Chinaman, four Frenchies, and an old man and his wife from Tierra del Fuego?"

"Where's that?"

"I don't know. Somewhere south of Miami Beach, I think."

They chuckled, enjoying the foolishness.

An Irish-tenor voice announced from behind them,

"All right, let's clear the company street. You got a trooper here who's coming through for some serious eating. Alert the cooksmith, Audrey."

"I swan: Bob Veck," Wagner said. "I'd ask you to sit down, but I know you're going to anyhow."

Veck instructed Audrey, "A number ten, or whatever it is that has the Raisin Bran and the pancakes and eggs and sausage and home fries and juice and toast and apple butter and coffee."

"What'll you have for an entree, sir?" Audrey said blandly.

"Get thee hence, crone." Veck eyed Wagner amiably and said, "How are things in the retired civil servant business, my boy?"

"Tolerable. Anything new in the private-eye business?"

"Insurance cases. Missing kids. Erring husbands. Profligate wives. All that neat kind of fun stuff."

"The world is a sad and disheveled place, to quote the great philosopher."

"Which great philosopher?"

"Roger M. Wagner."

"Curious thing at Vilano Beach, eh?"

"Yeah."

"What do you think? Dope pay-off?"

"Who's to say?" Wagner shrugged.

"Way I hear it, the cops can't put a make on the body. The ID cards he was carrying seem to be phony."

"Not surprising in these perilous times."

Veck nodded his big bald head. "Things are really screwy, all right. The Yanks and Russkies immobilized; Castro running around Central and South

America, warning all the oil tycoons he's going to take them over; the Germans up to their heinies in neo-Nazis; the Arabs ready to nip off the Israelis at the bagels. God. Next thing you know, my eggs will be undercooked."

"Empires may crumble, Veck, but Audrey will never let your eggs be ruined. It's one of life's few immutables."

"My girl friend's sister is just back from Miami. She says Castro's wheeling and dealing in Mexico and his threats against the South Americans have the Cuban exiles hyper. A lot of fist-shaking, mixed with nail-biting."

Wagner humphed. "What do they expect? In this world, every country has to watch out for Number One. With the Big Two impotent, the Soviets are having trouble keeping even East Europe in line, let alone Castro. Castro's obviously decided to go autonomous and tell the Ivans to peddle their borscht. He's a bona fide maverick now in a wallowing world that admires mavericks."

Veck sighed. "The Soviets have the biggest armada in all their big navy parked off Havana, just to make their influence felt. And Castro merely chuckles and lights another cigar."

"Olè."

Audrey brought more coffee, but Wagner declined. "I've got to get along. Big day on the retirement front. Give my check to Mr. Veck. He'll add it to the fee he charges the anti-adultery forces."

Veck laughed, shook his head, and began to read the paper.

From Aviles Street, Wagner cut through the library lane to St. George, heading for King Street and the Plaza. He saw a group of young people bending over a rectangular, grave-like hole in the lawn of Trinity Church, and, curious, he paused to see what was up.

"What's up?" he asked a young man who was wearing a T-shirt that read, I'm A Peach; Pick Me Up and Squeeze Me.

"We got a First-Period Spanish dig here, I think."

"Oh, who's we?"

"Florida State University archeology class. Field work."

"Oh." Wagner peered into the hole and saw nothing but an irate earthworm. "Is this one of the things Paul what's-his-name is in charge of?"

"Driscoll? Naw. He's on a Federal grant. We're undergrads. We're working under Dr. Samuels, the bearded guy in the baseball cap, there by the palm tree."

Dr. Samuels must have heard his name, because he looked up from his notes, nodded hello at Wagner, then sauntered over, smiling amiably. "Help you?"

"Not really," Wagner said apologetically. "I didn't mean to interrupt your work. I'm just a nosy guy asking questions."

"We welcome questions. Part of our PR, and all that. Are you a tourist?"

"No. I live here. Or out at Vilano, to be more precise."

Dr. Samuels nodded politely. "I see. Are you interested in archeology, Mr.—?"

"Wagner. Only at the National Geographic level. You know: paintings of the bare-breasted priestesses

58

of Ancient Razzmatazzia." Because he felt he was expected to, he asked, "What are you guys digging for here?"

The smallish man smiled again and shrugged. "The usual. Our students spend at least half of each academic year unearthing and rummaging through 400-year-old trash and garbage dumps. This is the oldest surviving municipality in what's now the continental United States. Its petrified household throw-offs can tell us a lot. People's cast-offs often say more about them than their words."

"I'll say. I live next door to a deacon in one of our more prominent churches hereabouts. You ought to see the gin bottles piled in his trash cans every Monday a.m."

"Mm."

Wagner felt Dr. Samuels allowed little room for waggishness in his academic world. So, putting a more somber tone in his voice, he said, "What you got here?"

Dr. Samuels looked down at the hole, thoughtful. "A 16th Century water well site. We're finding primitive Indian and Spanish bone needles and corn grinders. Some later period stuff, too: English toys, jewelry, musket parts."

"In the middle of downtown St. Augustine, yet."

"Mm. This town is the only archeological site in the United States that spans in a single, neat package all the time periods and all cultural and occupational frameworks figuring in the colonization and development of North America. And while we're digging into the 1500's, there's a living city around us, struggling like mad to cope with the social and economic demands of the 1990's."

Wagner was about to admit that he was having the same problem but turned instead to find the source of a muffled drumming, a sound akin to a quartet of horses dancing soft-shoe on the cobblestones. It was a gaggle of joggers, all young men in shorts and sneakers, puffing their way toward the Plaza. Watching after them, he asked Dr. Samuels, "Would you, at their age, ever have considered running through the center of town in your underwear?"

"Ah. Do I detect the snarl of envy in your voice, Mr. Wagner?"

"You're damn right you do. If those guys want to be all healthy and sleek and radiant, it's their business. But to be it in front of me is absolutely outrageous."

They talked more about archeology for a time; then Wagner shook the professor's hand and agreed to stop by again some day soon.

6

He had his hair cut at the shop on the corner of King and Cordova. While the man worked on him he gave a trance-like stare to a talk-show on the telly, which, unhappily, had been mounted on the wall facing his chair. Behind his glazed eyes, his mind continued its struggling with the puzzles represented by Heinz Strasser. Outside, beyond the plate glass window, pigeons swirled, traffic purred, tourists laughed and pointed cameras at each other and looked self-conscious and oddly apologetic for riding in horse-drawn jitneys. And with all this there were recollections of Strasser again—little snapshots of him, pondering a road map; eating a *belegtes Brot* at a Tyrolean Gasthof; buying a necktie at Luigi's; swearing the air purple over a flat tire on a mountain road at twilight. Where did such men go when they died? Where did anybody go? Who's on the Celestial First? What Time Does the Heavenly Balloon Go Up?

Who cares?

A gaggle of Flagler College coeds twittered on the corner, all smooth and curved and pressed into jeans that fitted as close as paint. Not a crooked tooth anywhere to be seen. Not an unglossy hair. Not an unshapely rump or a sagging chest or a bulbous nose or a crossed eye. Such factory-like, stamped-out, stereotypical perfection had not existed in his college days. The girls had had individuality. Sexy imperfections. . . .

"How old are you?" the barber asked.

Wagner, rising to the surface of his doleful ruminations, blinked. "That's classified information."

"Don't know how you do it. You sure ain't no kid,

but you ain't got no gray to speak of and you got the build of. . . ." The man groped for a simile.

"The Michelin tire man?" Wagner suggested helpfully.

"No kiddin'. You don't look over forty-five. Fifty, maybe."

"No kiddin'. You just earned yourself a five-dollar tip."

"Hey, I wasn't anglin' for that."

"I know. That's why you're getting it."

The barber fell silent, his scissors clicking busily, and Wagner tried not to watch as the silly hostess asked burbling questions of the silly movie actor who was just so pleased with himself he seemed about to swoon.

"Mind if we switch to the news channel?" Wagner asked the barber. "There's a summary due about now."

"Sure thing, sir. Just punch the selector on the arm of your chair."

"You mean I could've turned off that nerd all along?"

"I was wishin' the hell you would. I can't stand her, myself. All she does is giggle and ask people stuff like, 'Do you hate pain?' or 'Should we respect the American flag?' or 'What's your recipe for rutabaga meringue pie?' "

The news was not new. It was the same old material, rewritten, re-illustrated, and regurgitated by glossy men and women who waved hand microphones in the faces of the same old sources and asked the same old questions to get the same old answers in a manner that suggested it was all breathless and fresh.

The Middle East Coalition for the Conservation of Energy, acronymed "MECCE," was in deep negotiations with the European Ten, a federation of nations whose unabashed and unapologetic aim was collaboration with the Mediterranean oil-producing countries in an entente against Israel. The British were, as usual, urging caution. The Soviets were, as usual, denouncing the entente as a CIA-sponsored plot. The Americans were, as usual, denouncing the Soviets as the cause of all of it. The bottom-line fact, seemingly ignored by all the blabberings, was that the U.S. and the Soviets were immobilized by the greatest Mexican stand-off of all time and MECCE could, if it weren't for its lingering fear of The Big Two, immobilized or not, become the world's center of economic and political gravity. The Americans and the Russians were paying the piper for their many years of mutually destructive one-upmanship; both had painted themselves into a corner—frozen, inert, and unwilling to challenge each other further. Both were additionally debilitated by epidemic alcoholism and drug addiction, by weather aberrations of unprecedented severity, by chronic inflation and unemployment, by housing emergencies, burgeoning populations, crop failures, labor anarchy. The so-called Third World countries continued to flounder in unrealized dreams, leaderless and contentious and bitter with the understanding that they were dying from the germs of superpower paralysis and MECCE's waiting game.

"Same old crap, eh?" the barber said.

"I was just thinking that."

"Those Ay-rabs is going to end up runnin' everything."

"Unless Castro gets there first."

"Well, why shouldn't they? They been crapped on by the rest of the world for a jillion years. Why shouldn't they have their turn?"

"You got something there." Wagner was in no mood to participate in barbershop philosophizing, and so, recognizing that the quickest way to end a discussion is to agree with everything and everyone, he was determined to remain agreeable. It worked. After another few minutes of unopposed declamation, the barber subsided into another silence.

The New York anchorwoman paused, looked off camera a moment, and, after nodding almost imperceptibly, let her eyes go to the script ribbon just above the lens.

"Here is a bulletin," she said coolly, turning her face slightly to present its most flattering angle, "from our desk in Bonn: West German and U.S. military officials have admitted that a small convoy of American army vehicles was attacked by terrorists Tuesday on a rural highway southwest of Munich. Spokesmen for the two governments are unwilling to give details of the assault, and, because of the relative sparseness of population in the area, there were no known civilian witnesses. No casualty figures have been released, and traffic has been re-routed around the section of highway where the incident took place.

"The U.S. Army public information office at Stuttgart would say only that the convoy, originating at the huge Wolfratshausen training base, was on a routine mission, carrying food and maintenance supplies to the army's facilities near Landsberg. They do admit, however, that several vehicles were damaged in the incident. No terrorist organization has yet claimed responsibility for the attack.

"Turning to other news. . . ."

"Do you want more off the top?" the barber asked.

"No. That looks O.K." Wagner stifled a yawn.

The St. Augustine anchorman came on, all cute and scrubbed and glistening of tooth, to read an area wrap-up: The Old City's population, according to the latest figures from Tallahassee, was now thirty-two thousand, counting its annexations; the shrimp industry was expecting a dismal year; the 20-story condominium at Crescent Beach was cited as a disaster-waiting-to-happen by the county fire marshal; Flagler College enrollment, including satellite accommodations, was now twenty-eight hundred; three men were injured in a traffic crash on Anastasia Boulevard; wreckage of a luxury cabin cruiser washed ashore at Flagler Beach and was thought to be a clue in the disappearance of a wealthy German businessman; the forest fires near Bunnell. . . .

"Hey," Wagner blurted, "what did he say about that cabin cruiser?"

"Didn't hear all of it. Something about a German somebody."

"You finished?"

"Almost. What's the rush?"

"I've got to get to a phone."

"There's a pay phone over there in The Corner. Half a buck for two minutes, local."

"I need a replay screen. Dust me off and let me out of here, OK? And here's your twenty bucks."

He drove directly to the house, keeping his eye on a

tan Chevy that hung discreetly behind. After going to the tube and setting the dial at News Band, he telephoned the eight-hundred number for Item Replay. There was two chimes at the other end and then an unctuous male voice came on.

"This is News Band Jacksonville. May we help you?"

"Give me Area Replay. My subscriber number is A-Four-oh-Nineteen."

"One moment, please."

Two more chimes sounded, and this time it was a woman who wanted to help.

"St. Augustine summary had an item on a cabin cruiser's wreckage washing ashore at Flagler Beach. I'd like the root story, please. My set code is thirty-one, eleven, twenty-eight."

"One moment, please," the woman crooned.

During the moment, he cradled the phone on his shoulder and made a peanut butter sandwich. The coffee maker was still on, so he poured himself a cup and sipped at it between bites of the sandwich.

"The item is ready, sir. You may activate your set at any time within the next three minutes."

He punched the button and the screen revealed the toothy Augustine anchorman, cute and scrubbed as always, who intoned: "Meanwhile, the Flagler County Sheriff's department is investigating what might prove to be a link in the disappearance of a wealthy German businessman. Flagler Beach residents this morning came upon wreckage they said had washed ashore during the night. It appeared to be sections of an expensive cabin cruiser. Deputies report that a serial number inscribed on a radio manual recovered at

66

the site is that of a boat leased from Lang's Boat Service in Miami by Siegfried Unger, a Munich investment analyst. West Germany sources say very little is known about Unger, except that he is rich, lives in Bavaria, and travels widely. He has not been heard from since his cruiser, manned by a hired crew, left Miami a week ago. Susy Liggett was at Flagler Beach today. . . ."

Susy came on camera, squinting into the seashore sunlight and trying hard to look as cute as the anchorman. She didn't make it.

"Could Siegfried Unger have died in the explosion that tore through this once-elegant craft"—she nodded toward a clutter of white boards awash in the surf—"leaving no clues as to why he had left his castle in Bavaria for a cruise through Florida waters? We asked the question of Sheriff's Deputy Alvie Cronmiller." Turning, she shoved her hand-mike under the mustache of a portly fellow wearing the inevitable sunglasses, boy scout hat, and air of self-satisfied self-importance.

"Do you think Siegfried Unger died in this shipwreck, Deputy?"

"Somebody musta. No boat blows up that good without somebody dies."

"Do you have any reason to think Unger *didn't* die?"

"Nope."

"Could you be a bit more specific, Deputy?"

"Well, Unger coulda died. But then he might nota."

The girl nodded profoundly. "I see. Is this the Sheriff's official opinion?"

"I dunno. Could be. Nobody's said."

"I see. What's the next move deputy? What will you do next in your investigation?"

"Pick up these boards and put them in the evidence warehouse."

"I see. Will they be examined for further clues?"

"Beats me. That's not my department."

The girl nodded again, terribly moved, as if she'd just heard news of Appomattox. Turning again to the camera, she squinted and said earnestly, "So the probe goes on, with Deputy Alvie Cronmiller and his Sheriff's Office colleagues digging ever more deeply into still another mystery of the sea—a mystery of international scope." A pause, a most sincere gaze into the lens, then: "This is Susan Liggett, News Band Special Team, at Flagler Beach."

Wagner punched the off-button and shook his head irritably. "Ever deeper. God."

He called Lufthansa and cancelled his flight to Munich. Then he reserved a seat on U.S. Air's shuttle to Miami.

7

There was something he was missing, Wagner decided. Something drifting in the deep of his mind—forming, lurking for a split of time, then dissolving until its return a moment, an hour, later. He sought after it during much of the flight to Miami, sensing its importance, but after landing and renting a car and driving to the marina it was still just beyond acquisition.

The afternoon was warm and brilliant, with a damp breeze off the ocean, and all the tired stucco buildings with their sad, 1920's look were like bones bleaching under a malevolent sun. He drove along the littered streets between the orange juice stands and gas stations and billboards and utility poles, wondering why a town that could have been an Eden had been deliberately made into Tritesville, USA. What kind of people could take a subtropical coastline and turn it into junk? Where had been the reward? Money? How much more they could have made by doing things right.

To hell with it.

The whole world was due to become junk.

And if it weren't for Eva, he wouldn't really mind.

It would be worth losing the world just to nail the son of a bitch who'd built that building over there.

The marina was about what he'd expected. Pilings, docks, dirty water sloshing, tacky sheds, and the smell of gasoline and fish and suntan oil and whiskey coming across the bobbing, chrome-glinting decks. This and That for Hire. Eats. Bait. The Pause that Refreshes. Gulf and Exxon. Beer. Evinrude. Women the color of baked chicken lazing on canvas chairs behind

69

insect-eye sunglasses; men shaped like fire hydrants fussing with ropes, their salesmen's bellies hanging over their two-hundred-dollar shorts. All of them bored—glutted with conquest, money, alcohol, and orgasm—and wondering why it wasn't enough.

He went into the blue shadows of the office, and a blonde in a white strapless dress peered up at him from behind the counter.

"Help you?"

"Maybe," he said. "I want to talk to someone about chartering a party boat."

The blonde nodded, pretending the announcement had interested her. "Well, we do run such a boat. But Mr. Lang—he's the man on charters—isn't in right now. And I'm not sure when he'll be back."

"Too bad," Wagner said. "I'm trying to arrange a special do. A few executives weekending during a seminar. You know the kind of thing. Pot-bellied baldies with nothing but money. Ha-ha."

She shaped an appropriate smile. "Sounds like fun."

He nodded toward a sign at the next dock. "That place over there have a charter boat? The place called Ace's?"

"Well, I—It did. But they're about to suspend operations for awhile, I think."

"Why would they do that?"

She hunched a brown shoulder. "Something about a repossession or something. There's a bankruptcy pending. Least, that's the talk around the docks here. I don't know, really."

"I'll go talk to them anyhow." He turned for the door.

70

"What did you say your company is?"

"I didn't. It's the J.W. Brockmiller and Sons Dry-goods Company, Ink. Marcus Hook, P-A. Six guys: Five hundred bucks each is the budget. Could I get a boat for a Saturday for three thou? Or isn't that enough around these parts?"

The woman blinked, and her interest was no longer pretended. "As I say, Mr. Lang is the one. But that figure sounds reasonable."

In the next room somebody faked the slamming of a door. Then a small man wearing tight knit slacks and a polo shirt with a cute little seahorse over its breast pocket came through a canyon formed by two banks of file cabinets. His face was narrow, and his eyes were like ball bearings. "Hi," he said. "Can I help with something?"

"You are Mr. Lang?" Wagner said.

"That's right."

"Hefflefinger. Joe Hefflefinger. Wallingford, P-A."

They shook hands, and Wagner noted that Lang's grip was only slightly less firm than a slab of farmer's-market mackerel.

"What's on your mind, Mr. Hefflefinger?"

"I was telling the lady. A drinking and fishing party. Six guys, drowning worms, or whatever. Budget no more than three grand."

"Mm. I see." Lang turned the ballbearings toward the blonde. "Is Number Four out of drydock yet, Miss Lenowski?"

The woman blushed under her tan and began pretending again. She riffled through a looseleaf notebook on her desk, as if it might really contain the records on Number Four. She paused in the middle of the book. "Friday, Mr. Lang. It'll be ready Friday."

"Mm. Good." Mr. Lang regarded Wagner with a smile that looked as if he were suppressing a burp. "There you are, Mr. Hefflefinger. A boat. A nice big one. Captain. Crew. Wet bar, ice chests. The latest in gear. Ready for any Saturday you say."

"How much?"

"Two thousand, eight hundred and ninety-five dollars. For six hours. Ten percent deposit. Unreturnable."

"Golly, that's super. May I get a look at her?"

Mr. Lang seemed sorry. "I'm sorry," he said, "but that boat's in overhaul at Fort Lauderdale."

"Oh, well."

"Is it important that you see it?"

"Yes. I have my instructions. The boys want me to get a Polaroid of it before we make a reservation."

Mr. Lang and Miss Lenowski were both truly sorry now, Wagner saw. "Maybe I'll just toddle over to Ace's and see what they can do for me," he said, feigning his own disappointment.

"I've got an idea," Miss Lenowski said with sudden brightness. "Why doesn't Mr. Hefflefinger just take a picture of Ace's Seaspray? It's exactly the same as our Number Four, Mr. Lang. He could get a picture and tell his friends that their boat will be just like it. Know what I mean?"

Mr. Lang thought about that for a moment, clearly unsure as to whether that was such a good idea.

"Sounds OK to me," Wagner said helpfully.

"Well," Mr. Lang said, "I won't be able to show you aboard. It's not our boat, and, frankly, Ace isn't exactly fond of us. Besides, I think the thing's in repossession process, and all that."

"I don't have to see aboard. Just show me the boat. I'll take my picture, and if the guys say go, I'll call you the date and send you a check. Two hundred and ninety-five dollars. Right?"

"Three hundred even," Mr. Lang said. "Five-dollar service charge."

"Shoot a buck, I always say. Ha-ha."

The night was sultry, with the same damp breeze that had fretted about the city throughout the day. The palms in the sad little park at the marina entrance swayed in the restless air, clacking and hissing, and the streetlights on the avenue seemed gauzy in the humid gloom. The water made soft splashing sounds, and somewhere a mooring rope creaked. Except for an occasional car passing over the distant viaduct, there were no direct signs of human presence.

Wagner stood in the shadows of a fuel shed for a full five minutes, watching the Seaspray at the Ace dock. Nothing moved aboard it; not a sound; no light. When his watch showed 4:15, he began to walk along the bulkhead duckboards, staggering slightly in the manner of one who struggles to master his drunkenness. At the dock, he turned in feigned indecision, then wobbled to the Seaspray and sat heavily on its gunwale, singing softly to himself and pretending to feel his pockets for cigarettes. Still unchallenged by a watchman, he rolled to the boat's deck and lay there for two minutes even. Satisfied that the Seaspray was truly unattended, he took the small fabric folder from his pocket, selected a jimmy, and opened the lock on the cabin door, or whatever the hell sailors called it.

73

There was a kind of lounge, with cutesy chairs and tables and ornaments made of rope and brass, and, beyond this, a double-bunked forecabin. He went over it all with his hooded flashlight, and it was all a huge bore. From there he went to the bridge, if that was the nautical name for the place where the controls were, and rummaged through the box of charts he found beside the steering wheel. They seemed to be routine: Geodetic Survey and Coast Guard representations of the waters off Miami and around the Keys and even one of the Gulf side, near Fort Myers and Sanibel. The Inland Waterway, as far north as Jacksonville. And Cuba. The Havana harbor and its approaches. Three Playboy magazines, a motel guide, and a pair of sunglasses with a cracked lens. An envelope with Lang Boat Rentals printed in the upper left corner, and, on the rear, some figures that appeared to be course headings. On a hunch, he placed the flashlight on the decking and copied the numbers and letters in his notebook.

Discovering nothing else to write home about, he sat in the darkness for a time, thinking, and during this furious burst of energy he remembered a movie he'd seen on the late, late show.

"Ah, yes."

Bumping around, he finally found a trap door and, pulling it open, he held the flash on a short ladder leading to what appeared to be the boat's cellar. He descended this, and he thought he heard water gurgling under the board flooring. Aft of the dank area was a bulkhead which was entirely without character, but as he was about to return top side his flash picked up something shiny. Certain screws in the bulkhead had

74

lost their paint, presumably during a recent loosening by a screwdriver. He considered this fact for all of two seconds and, using the blade from his burglar kit, began to remove a panel that had escaped his initial inspection.

"Well, now. Fu Manchu strikes again."

He left the area only after careful examination of the dock and its adjacent buildings. Nothing had changed, except the wind, which had grown clammier and more insistent.

Dropping his drunk act, he strode directly to the parking lot, where an outdoor phone booth stood in the chalky glow of a nearby streetlight. He put a five-dollar bill in the slot, dialed Maryland, then opened the door to darken the booth.

"Hello?"

"This is Wagner, Groot."

"My God. What time is it?"

"Time for your briefing."

There was the sound of yawning at the other end. Then: "Where are you?"

He was about to answer when, weirdly independent of his will, his body slammed against the wall of the booth and the phone flew out of his hand. There was an instantaneous inability to breathe, since the shock of the bullets seemed to crush his chest. And his head spun and rang with cruel, inner clanging, and he fell through the open door to the asphalt, rolling and kicking.

Then he was still, face to the damp, oil-smelling pavement.

He thought he heard someone hang up the phone,

but he was too tired to turn his head to see. Or to care.

DAY 4

8

Eva had dozed intermittently, using the wakeful periods to call St. Augustine. She hated hotels, with their box-like walls and bargain drapes and plumbing that smelled of disinfectant, and for all the time she had spent in them, sleep had never been easy to come by. This one had proved to be even worse. The night-long buzz of traffic in the street below would alone have been enough to keep a junkie awake, but her problem had been more than the noise and the institutional loneliness pressing in: The phone ringing in the Florida distance, a far-off warbling that went on and on, had filled her mind with numb images of her home, dark and sad in the night. Where had he gone? Why was he not answering?

Who was he with?

She remembered seeing the dawn-glow on the eastern facade of the great gray mountains. But when she turned her head on the pillow and looked again, they were in full daylight, and her watch told her it was almost nine.

"Damn."

She rolled from the bed and hurried to the bathroom, where she set the shower to roaring and steaming. She stepped in, sputtering self-condemnation. Her appointment with Mr. Lindsay was for nine-thirty, and his office was four blocks from the hotel—too near to warrant a cab. When she had finished and was rubbing herself with one of the harsh, inflexible towels, there was a ringing. Padding quickly across the carpet, she lifted the phone, praying it was Roger.

"Hello."

"Mrs. Wagner?"

"Yes."

"This is Andrew L. Lindsay. I'm glad I caught you before you left."

"Oh. Yes. I mean, well, what's the story?"

"I'm downstairs in the lobby. I wonder if I might take you to breakfast. One of my cases is in court this morning, and so I won't be going to the office—"

"Sounds fine to me, Mr. Lindsay. Can you give me ten more minutes? I overslept."

"I'll be waiting in the dining room. Just give your name to the maître d' and he'll show you to my table."

"All right. Ten minutes."

Andrew L. Lindsay was small, with sandy hair and eyes as flat and gray as old dimes. He wore a tan suit cut close to his dancer's figure, and a carnation presided over his left lapel. Eva wondered if he had selected his silk necktie to match the color of the flower or the flower to match the tie. He looked to be the kind of man who would go to that trouble with his clothes. He also looked to be a man who would be dangerous to cross. Small men who tried to stand tall were always dangerous. He was standing now, taking her hand and helping her into the chair held by the obsequious headwaiter.

"It's very kind of you to do this, Mrs. Wagner," Lindsay purred. "I'm sorry I couldn't have given you more notice."

"No need to apologize, Mr. Lindsay. This works very much to my advantage. I was running terribly late."

Settled, and with coffee poured, they made polite conversation, trailing from the gathering snowstorm,

80

which sent large and restless flakes against the tall window beside them, to the difficulty of finding parking places these days. As he talked, Lindsay's delicate hands toyed with the necktie, smoothing, straightening, touch-testing the precisely centered knot. Eva decided that she did not like him.

"Now tell me, Mr. Lindsay," she said during a small pause, "just who was Enos B. Lawrence and why he was so good to me."

Lindsay smiled. "In all truth, I can't say. My office received a letter one day recently from Norton-Colorado Bank and Trust. It told us that Mr. Lawrence, who died on December first seven years ago in a nursing home in Nome, Alaska, had filed a letter with them for safekeeping—not to be opened until seven years after his death. The letter instructed them to forward the sum in his safe deposit box to your father or his heirs. You are your father's only survivor, and so the sum, less inheritance taxes and fees, goes to you. It comes to one hundred and two thousand, six hundred and fifty-seven dollars, and thirty-eight cents. The money will be made available to you as soon as the necessary transferral papers have been processed."

"How long will that take?"

Mr. Lindsay smiled again and shrugged daintily. "Oh, I'd guess two, three days. Certainly no more than a week."

"Well, my gosh. Can't they do it faster? I mean, I've got a job, and a husband, and a house—I can't just sit around Colorado Springs for a week." She felt anger penetrating the pleasure she'd felt at hearing the precise numbers. *Thirty-eight cents.* How beautifully prosaic, down-to-earth, supermarket-real thirty-eight cents sounded. The larger sum took on believability when thirty-eight cents were tacked onto it. But then the glow had subsided to make room for annoyance and, if she would only admit it, anxiety. She did not want to be away from Roger for a week. A hundred thousand were fine, but. . . .

"I'll do everything I can, of course. Did you bring your birth certificate?"

"Yes. You want it now?"

"I might as well take it. I'll keep it in the office safe until the processor of wills needs it tomorrow or the day after."

"Well, be careful with it. It's the only birth I've had."

Lindsay's perpetual smile became a soft laughter. "To be sure, Mrs. Wagner. In these days of runaway population growth, it pays to know who you are—to prove to others you really exist."

"I suppose so."

"Population is the greatest problem the world has today," he said, seeming to gather an intensity about him. The amusement had left his narrow face, and his coin-like eyes appeared to stare at the snowfall without focus. "We are propagating ourselves out of existence. Every day there are additional millions arriving, expecting to be fed, clothed, housed. But the world can barely feed the people it has, can hardly provide shelter. And, even as they face starvation and exposure, countless millions continue to copulate without the slightest consideration of even rudimentary birth control procedures. We are drowning in people. We must do something to save ourselves."

"Well," Eva said, suddenly tired of this dreary little man and his fastidious clothing and tiny hands and precious inflections of voice, "there are those who look at you and me as the problem—as some of the people *they're* drowning in. I guess what I'm saying—asking—is 'Who are *we*?' 'We' always includes Number One and the person he cares about. All others are 'they.' "

"I'm talking about all the drones, the people who consume and don't produce," Lindsay said self-righteously. "There are millions of them, all over the world. All they do is eat, sleep, and copulate."

"Yep. But, since you've brought it up, Mr. Lindsay, what kind of birth control do you use?"

"Oh," he said with sudden contrition, "I've offended you."

"Yep. But not irreparably. I just think everybody—even you Colorado lawyers—ought to keep things in perspective."

"Yes, of course."

For some reason she missed Roger now, wanted him with her, more than ever. *Some* reason? The reason was this man across from her, who, without the slightest awareness of the fact, represented everything that Roger wasn't. Roger was blunt and wry and funny and tough and tender and brave and cowardly and capable and dumb—human. Up front. What-you-see-is-what-you-get. A supersmart idiot, a hard-as-nails marshmallow. A pain in the behind and a pain in the heart. A dear man who should never, in a million years, have had anything to do with the cruelty implicit in secret intelligence. A man, unsuited, who had striven for thirty years to prove to himself he was suited. An absolute singleminded idiot. But a singleminded idiot she wanted more than anything, anywhere, world without end. God, how she *missed* him. . . .

She and Mr. Lindsay went through the motion of breakfast, falling once again into indirections, inanities, as if each was on guard against a new assault on his private sensibilities. The charade came to an end at last, and, after thanking him and presenting him with her birth certificate, she strode away quickly from the tan little man and went to her room and put in a call to St. Augustine.

There was no answer, of course.

9

"Groot?"

"Wagner—is that you?"

"Yeah."

"Where have you been? Your phone call was cut off—I've been trying to call you back. All night. At your house. . . ."

"I was interrupted."

"Well—How?"

"Somebody shot me. Four times. With a .38 Magnum."

"My God! You are still alive?"

"No. I'm speaking to you from the spirit world. Houdini sends his best."

"That was a ridiculous question, of course. I meant, are you all right? Where. . . ."

"I was wearing the Kevlar underwear I stole from the Company."

"I see."

"You wouldn't believe those magnums. Straight out of Otis: They lift you up and put you down."

"Mm."

"And you don't breathe for two hours."

"Where are you now?"

"At Orlando International. On my way to Germany."

"Why?"

"I need a good beer."

"Wagner. . . ."

"I want the names of those Germans who witnessed the theft."

"Right here in my pad. Just a moment—Here. Kurt Münser, Nikolai Hotel, München-Schwabing. Loni

Riess, same address. Apparently living together. The farmer is Ludwig Schattner, Weilheim-Landsbergerlandstrasse, Oberbayern."

"All right. I'll call you collect this evening."

"Well...."

"Meantime, I learned something in Miami. Besides the fact that somebody down there doesn't like me a bunch, that is."

"Tell me."

"I looked into Lang's Boat Service, the outfit that owned the cruiser lost off St. Augustine with the mysterious Siegfried Unger aboard. There's something out of plumb there, and you might get an accountant to make like an IRS guy and go in and do a study of their records. My instincts tell me they're into dope at least, maybe more."

"All right. Anything else?"

"Yeah. I made a little unannounced call on a nearby boat owned by Ace Boat Rentals. I found a cache of Soviet small arms in its basement, or whatever."

"Oh?"

"With the guns and ammo were maintenance manuals. Printed in Spanish."

"Castro?"

"Probably. He's the only South-of-Border type into the import and distribution of Russian weapons these days. All the others prefer American, German, or French, according to Bob Veck, an old pal of mine who's a private eye and has sources among the Castro and anti-Castro people in South Florida."

"Your friend is right. Anything else?"

"Yep. A map of Bavaria and Baden-Württemburg."

"Aha. Why would a map of southern Germany be in

a boat tied up at a marina in Miami?"

"They were going sailing through the Alps, maybe?"

"Be serious, Wagner."

"Why the hell do you think I'm going to Germany?"

"Well. . . ."

" 'Wiederseh'n.' "

10

Wagner knew the Nikolai. It was a twenty-bed hotel in the Schwabing section of Munich, the bohemian quarter inhabited by show people, artists, the demi-monde, young men living off old ladies, young ladies living off old men, and everybody living off each other. The shops were slick and gaudy, like the people, and the pensions and hostelries were staffed by inscrutable mutes who suffered chronic neck pains from looking the other way. The archetype of these was the fat man who presided in the Nikolai's lobby—if that was the word for a dingy little hallway graced by a stairway, a check-in counter backed by mailboxes, a dusty potted palm, and a floor whose carpet runner had last been cleaned in celebration of Bismarck's graduation from military school. The fat man sat by the counter as usual, his slitted eyes feigning a doze, his belly supporting a yellow cat that went up and down with his breathing.

Wagner dinged the desk bell and the fat man, opening an eye, said, "You again." The cat said nothing.

"You have a student living here, name of Hans Münser. What's his room number?" It felt strange to be speaking German again.

"Münser. Münser. Hm."

"Maybe these fifty pictures of George Washington will help."

"You're not going to cause trouble, are you?"

"Only if you don't give me the number."

"I try to protect my guests. I protect those who pay me. I don't like you, though."

"So I've just bought fifty dollars worth of protection. And I'm sorry you don't like me. I adore you.

And your cat."

"Room Eleven."

Wagner climbed the stairs, weary from sore ribs and a wretched sleep on the SST and dispirited by his inability to reach Eva by phone. He'd placed calls from Miami, Orlando airport, and München-Riem, even one from the plane itself over the Atlantic—but without success. Mr. Richards, the hotel desk man, had assured him she was registered but simply not in at the moment and that he would be glad to tell her Mr. Wagner had called.

He tapped on the dark green door with the faded white 11, and after a moment it opened to reveal a tall young man wearing a skindiver's wet suit.

"What you want?" the young man asked, not very friendly.

"You're expecting the river to rise?"

"Oh. You're a nightclub comic, and you're trying out your new ones on me. Well, in my opinion, you're in the wrong business."

"I'll say. Meanwhile, though, I'm looking for Kurt Münser."

"Look, friend: I've told all I know to every cop between here and Praetoria, and I'm in no mood to talk to another one."

"Even for five hundred Yankee dollars?"

The young man's gray eyes blinked. "You're the first cop I've ever heard speak good sense. When do I get the five hundred?"

"Half now, half after I hear your answers."

"What if you don't like my answers?"

"You still get paid. I'm a philanthropist by hobby."

"Come in, then."

The room would have been stunning if it hadn't been for its cracked ceiling, bare-bulb illumination, frayed curtains, sagging bed, moth-eaten overstuffed chair, and peeling wallpaper. Constrasting with all this beauty was the girl who sat in the chair and looked at him indifferently with enormous blue eyes. She, too, was a conservative dresser, favoring a red bikini, army boots, and a World War II German helmet.

"You're Loni Riess, I take it."

"Mm. What's this about five hundred dollars?"

"I want to ask some questions."

Loni glanced at her room-mate. "Is it all right, Kurtchen?"

"It's all right. But make it fast. We're already late for the party."

Wagner sat gingerly on the edge of the bed, which was piled high with blue jeans and newspapers and paper plates bearing the remains of a pizza. He gazed appreciatively at the girl's ensemble and said to her, "You're a lady with little to hide, obviously, so let's start with you. What do you remember of the incident on the Weilheim-Landsberg highway?"

"The shooting thing?" She took off the helmet and shook her blonde hair.

"From the beginning, please." Wagner took out his note pad.

"Well," Loni said, her large eyes level, "Kurt and I were on a hike. He thought it would be good for us. We'd been spending a lot of time here in the room, studying and things. Cold air, a walk through the leaves. Get rid of the cobwebs."

"What time of day was it?"

"A little after noon, wasn't it, Kurtchen?"

Kurtchen, who had been admiring his smile in the fogged wall mirror, patted his hair into place and nodded. "About that." His eyes meeting Wagner's in the glass, he said, "Where's the first half, friend? You're already behind in your payments."

"I was waiting to see what you'd do with it, pockets being in such short supply and all."

"Ho-ho." Kurtchen held out a hand. "Two-fifty, please."

Wagner took out his wallet, counted some bills, and placed them in the hand. To Loni he said, "Go on."

"We drove to the Ammer country, parked the VW near Rott, I guess it was, then began walking north, through the woods and fields. Sort of following the road but not on it, know what I mean? After awhile we reached a kind of hill covered with thick pine forest, and we were tired, and like that, and so Kurt made a thing with pine needles and we rested. Then, a little later, there was the sound of a lot of trucks, going fast, down on the highway, and there was a helicopter buzzing, and I looked down and saw these Yankee trucks and cars, all olive and mean-looking, and, over them, this helicopter. Just as I was watching I heard a popping sound from a hedge down in a field, and there was this rocket thing that went up and hit the helicopter, and it blew up and was burning and falling. You know."

"Did you see who fired the rocket?"

"No. Not really. I sort of had other things on my mind."

"How about you, Kurtchen? Did you see anybody?"

"I wasn't watching them. I was busy."

"Busy? Doing what?"

"Have you ever tried to make it when you're both in parkas, ski pants, and long-johns? Man, that's busy."

"I'll admit the concept is dazzling," Wagner said, nodding thoughtfully. He cleared his throat. "With no intent to probe into your private lives, may I ask, ah, when you *began* to watch?"

Kurtchen shrugged. "Pretty much right away, I'd say. I mean, you sort of climb down from the edge when guns start rattling and grenades start blowing up and trucks and cars burn and people are yelling. I mean, it would take a cool type to burrow into a ski suit and roll over the edge with all that going on around him. Wouldn't you say?"

"It's never caused me a problem," Wagner said. "But then, my generation was different."

"There were two bunches," Loni said, buffing her nails with a yellow washcloth. "One on each side of the road. They blew up the helicopter, then the lead jeep and the sedan that was behind it. The trucks sort of squeezed up and halted because of the explosions, and when the men came piling out, the people in the woods began shooting them with machine-guns. They kept shooting until nobody moved. And then they ran up to the biggest truck, opened its back door, and took out a box, which they ran with across a field and out of sight behind some trees. That was when the other helicopter went up."

Wagner held up a hand. "Wait. How were the shooters dressed?"

"In black ski suits. Or coveralls. Like that. Knit caps, scarves. All black."

"Did they all carry machine-guns?"

"I think so. Hard to say, really."

"What did the machine-guns look like?"

"Short. Sort of like grease guns. Metal stocks. Curved magazines."

Wagner showed him a photo of a Soviet K-07. "Like this, maybe?"

"Yes. Like that. No maybe at all."

Returning the photo to his raincoat pocket, Wagner asked Loni, "Did you hear anything said? Anything at all? A word, a phrase. . . ."

"Not specifically, no. A lot of yelling. But like at a soccer match, you know? A lot of noise, but who knows who's saying what?"

"You, Kurtchen?"

"No. Same thing for me. Nothing clear."

"You understand English?"

"You bet your life, Joe. I have as a waiter in a GI club worked. I am English like a native speaking."

"I can see that, all right," Wagner said, holding to German. "You, Loni?"

"I studied it in school, but I'm not very good at it. I heard one of the Amis yell something like, 'Stop shooting.' Something like that. But that's all."

"Could the attackers have been speaking German?"

Kurtchen nibbled a piece of pizza crust. "Can't say."

"What color was the second helicopter?"

"Gray. No numbers, no insignia. Just gray."

"Which direction did it fly?"

"Straight west. Toward Kempten."

"Was it large, small, medium-size?" Wagner made a note.

"Medium, I'd say. Wouldn't you, Loni?"

"Medium. Yes." She kicked off the army shoes.

"How about the attacking groups? What did they do after the shooting stopped and the second helicopter left?"

"They all sort of lined up on the road and the man in charge said something to them. Then they split up, ran off in all directions. A few minutes later, I heard a truck start up—a big truck, from the sound of it. A tractor-trailer, I think. It drove south, and we couldn't hear it any more."

"Was there snow on the highway?"

"No. Too early in the season for any real snow. Just blacktop road."

"The tractor-trailer: could it have left tracks anywhere?"

Kurtchen sniffed. "I have no way of knowing. But you don't think a bunch of people who pull off a frisky one like that would be so careless as to leave tracks, do you? Besides, that's the kind of thing you cops are supposed to know, isn't it?"

"I know what the cops know. I want to know what *you* know."

"Well, friend, you've just got the last of it. Two-fifty more, please."

"Loni?"

"I don't know any more, either, Mister. Honest."

Wagner placed the money on a pair of blue jeans which had Kiss Me stitched on the seat. Giving Kurtchen a long, steady stare, he said, "There are five thousand more of those if you can give me anything you haven't told the other cops. Anything of substance that I can eventually act on."

There was a protracted silence while the young couple assimilated this announcement. Then Kurtchen, his eyes showing a slyness, said, "What's to keep us from just making up something and taking the money?"

"Two things. First, I wouldn't pay the money until after I'd acted on your information. Second, if your information proved to be, ah, made-up, as you say, I'll find you—wherever you are—and use that wet suit as a sling shot and send you to the moon."

"Oo. Tough guy, eh?"

"I have my moments."

"No need for that kind of talk," Loni murmured. "We don't know anything more to tell you, no matter how much you pay."

"All right. Just thought I'd ask." Wagner stood up, wincing with the pain that the .38's had left to lurk in his rib cage. "Well," he said through clenched teeth, "it's been charming to meet such fine young people who represent our leaders of tomorrow."

"What's your name, Mister?"

"Schwarz. Otto Schwarz. Landespolizei."

"Where do you Landespolizei types get so much American money?"

"My dear boy," Wagner clucked, "West Germany has been built on American money."

"Sure we can't dream up something else to tell the gentleman, Loni?" Kurtchen said, amused.

Loni, her attention span already beyond its limits, yawned and curled her bare legs under her in the chair.

"So, then," Wagner said, going to the door. "I'll be on my way. I'll call if I have further questions."

"Call? On what?"

"I'll have the fat man downstairs call you to the house phone."

"Hah. To do that, he'd have to leave his chair. And he hasn't been out of that chair since 1922."

In the hallway and on the stairs, Wagner smelled pipe smoke. It reminded him of something he couldn't name.

After a quick snackbar lunch, Wagner went to the public telephone center on Ludwigstrasse and put in a call to the U.S. military hospital at Wiesbaden. The switchboard would not put him through to Colonel Skelly's ward, and so he asked to speak to the medical director.

"Colonel Venable speaking."

"Colonel, this is Roger Wagner, on special duty for the CIA. To check my authenticity, call this number in Wilmington, Delaware. Collect." He read off Groot's office number.

"Very well," the colonel said warily. "What can I do for you?"

"I must interrogate Colonel Skelly as soon as possible, and I need to know when that might be."

The colonel cleared his throat, then spoke even more carefully, choosing his words like a husband talking to a divorce lawyer. "Well," he said, "I don't know how exactly to answer that question, Mr. Wagner. Colonel Skelly's case is now under the complete control of the Army Criminal Investigation Division and Military Intelligence. I. . . ."

"Why is that?"

"Well, ah, there has been an attempt on Colonel Skelly's life."

"I know that," Wagner said impatiently. "That's

why he's in the hospital."

"I mean someone tried to kill him this morning. In the hospital. With a fatal injection. Two doctors walked into the colonel's room during the attempt and the intruder fled."

"O.K., Doctor. Thanks. I'll be back to you."

Wagner hung up and lingered in the booth, thinking hard.

11

His next stop was at District Seven, where he asked a haughty sergeant at the reception desk if assistant detective inspector Georg Klatt might be available.

True to his profession, if not to his post, the sergeant managed to look even more disdainful now that a question from hoi poloi had obtruded upon his hibernation. "Who should I say is asking?"

"Wilhelm Koenig," Wagner said, heavy with an unspecific resentment.

"Care to state your business?"

"No."

The sergeant did not like this unembellished answer, presumably because it suggested that Wagner was not awed. A poloi unawed by a policeman is a poloi that must be taught a lesson, and so the man frowned, tapped his fingers on the desk for a moment, and then, nodding toward a metal chair, snapped, "Take a seat."

"Thanks. But I'm in a hurry. Would you give him a buzz, please?"

"Take a seat."

"This is a matter of considerable urgency."

The sergeant frowned again and showed great interest in some papers on his desk. He then half-turned, picked up a telephone with an officious sweep of his hand, and dialed. After a moment, he murmured into the mouthpiece, "Hugo? Ulrich. Have you finished your weekly summary yet?" Pause. "Well, be sure to include the Korneliushaus incident. Nothing came of it, of course, but it should be part of the report." Pause. "Very well. Right." He hung up and resumed his study of the papers.

Wagner sighed, crossed the sterile room to a public phone affixed to the wall near the drinking fountain. He selected a coin, inserted it in the slot, and dialed the police Zentrum.

"Police headquarters," the voice said. "May we help you?"

"Connect me with Inspector Klatt at District Seven, please."

"One moment."

There was a faint buzz, a crackle, another buzz, and then the phone at the other end lifted. "Klatt here."

"Putzi? This is Koenig."

"Koenig?" There was a ring of genuine pleasure in the metallic voice.

Wagner could feel the sergeant's stare, and so he met Klatt's delight with slightly more effusiveness than his mood would otherwise have allowed.

"It's good to hear your voice again, Putzi," Wagner said.

"Where are you? My God, it's been years—!"

"I'm in your reception room. I'm using the pay phone."

"Well, tell the sergeant to bring you in."

"I asked for you, but the sergeant doesn't seem to be disposed toward helping me. He's too busy with some forms to call you and tell you I'm here."

"Oh, is he." The phone clicked, then went to dial tone.

Wagner hung up and turned slowly toward the sergeant, whose face was a remarkable shade of magenta.

"You didn't have to do that," the sergeant said throatily.

"I enjoy doing things for you. Don't deny me the pleasure."

The sergeant's phone purred, and he picked it up, his expression that of a man outrageously put upon. "Sergeant Senker here." He listened for an interval to a series of snaps and raspings. Eventually he said, "Yes, sir. At once." Replacing the phone, he gave Wagner a solemn, indirect stare and said, "Would you follow me, please?"

Wagner settled in the chair Klatt held for him, his mind going back to the time when the two of them had been friends. As with Strasser, too much had happened since, too many faces and events and tests had come and gone for Klatt and him ever to pick up the relationship again, but there was a kind of lingering after-sense of life lived and danger shared that was warming, as riffling through a high school yearbook can be warming. They sat, beaming at each other, groping for the dangling ends of their mutual past, each hoping not to give offense by his forgetfulness, his inability to find the words or to evoke the incidents that had once made them close.

"So then," Klatt enthused, "what brings you to Munich?"

"Business."

"You're still with the CIA?"

"No. I'm retired now. It got to be too much for an old klutz like me. It's a different world now, Putzi."

"That it is, that it is."

"Aren't you about to retire?"

Klatt spread his arms in a gesture of goodnatured exasperation. "Me? My God, man. I'm still a child. I only *appear* to be a hundred ninety-three years old. You should know. You attended my christening."

"I attended Kaiser Wilhelm's christening, as a matter of fact."

They laughed together, glad to find that they hadn't lost their relish of nonsense.

Klatt said, "I know it sounds false, but I think of you often. Our department owes you a great debt. If it hadn't been for you, Hans Trille could still be with us, still using a great police organization as a cover for his rotten political schemes."

"If I hadn't found him out, somebody would have. The Machiavellian types always get found out, sooner or later."

"You're too modest. Tell me something."

"Sure."

"Is Koenig your real name? I've often wondered."

"No, it isn't, Putzi. But it's the one you—all the others—know me by. So I use it whenever I come to Munich. It makes things easier."

Klatt made the question sound casual: "What kind of business are you in these days?"

"I'm a researcher for a New York periodical. An obscure publication that goes in for obscure themes, causes. I'm working on an article they plan on neo-Nazis. Nothing garish. That's not their style. Just a thoughtful, plodding piece on Where Have All the Nazis Gone? Or, Hitler's Reich Revisited. That kind of thing."

Klatt nodded. "Well, between you and me and the dining table, there's something funny going on within our Nazi populace right now."

"Funny?"

"Mm. As you know, there's been a very strong right-wing sector in German politics for years. The Führerprinzip is still with us, my boy, and the number of Germans who are willing to be counted among the so-called Resurgents is growing by the day. But what's queer is the recent disappearance of so many of the more outspoken ones—the more overt ones. For the last several years they've been on the very edge of illegality, what with their Nazi-type speeches, their rallies in the woods, their torch parades. And now, all of a sudden, they're all quiet as mice. No evidence of their being around at all. Very strange."

"How many of these overt types are there?"

"Oh, a dozen or so. The obvious leaders. As I say, there are thousands who are sympathetic to the idea of a strong, centralized, national-socialist government, but it's only a dozen or so who organize, lead, speak. Wave fists."

"You're talking about people like Siegfried Unger?"

Klatt winked. "Especially Unger. He sort of personifies the movement. Or did. The word now is that he's in smithereens on the bottom of the Gulf stream, or whatever. Which is where he belongs, I think. Along with all those stomping-boot types."

"You mean," Wagner asked with mock incredulousness, "that you don't approve of Unger and his Nazis?"

"I was a kid during Hitler's war. I'll never forget or forgive. I saw what the Nazis did," Klatt said darkly.

"Hey, I was only kidding. I know how you hate them."

"It's the one thing I can't kid about."

Wagner sat for a time, listening to the muted traffic

sounds beyond the room's only window. Dusk was falling, and already, above the restless, naked tops of the courtyard's trees, brilliant stars were showing— hard, unchanging, remotely cruel. He found himself wondering what day it was. How many days were remaining? How many hours until the click of a fuse, the concussion of a grenade, the chalky flare of light that would begin the end?

"Do you," he muttered, "think that Unger, the others, could be the victims of the Red Brigade or some other left-wing terrorist group?"

"Who's to say? But it's logical. The communists have been very active, world-wide, since the early '80's. Worse this year than ever. Kidnapping. Assassinating. General hell-raising."

"I've read about Unger. What do you know about him, Putzi?"

Klatt humphed. "Precious little. Only what I read in the papers. I'm not one of the bigshots in the department, so I'm not privy to a lot of stuff, especially in the political area. But I suspect there's some kind of underground war. And the Reds are winning. Unger tried to run to the States but the commies caught up with him, is my guess."

Wagner thought about that, watching Klatt light up a fat black cigar. "Any famous commies missing these days?"

"Not so you'd notice."

"Then that rather shoots down your underground war thing, wouldn't you say? There are casualties on both sides in a war."

"No," Klatt sniffed. "The Reds have famous types, overt types, I could count on one hand. They are a

103

very private bunch, I'll tell you, and if one comes a cropper the public rarely hears about it. At least in Germany. The public hears about everything only in your country. But, all in all, my guess is that, behind the scenes, the Reds are killing a lot of Nazis and the Nazis are killing a lot of Reds."

Wagner decided to launch the balloon he'd come here to float. "There's a rumor," he said blandly, "that Red terrorists have stolen a nuclear weapon from NATO. Have you heard anything about it?"

It wasn't Klatt's answer he considered to be important, since a cop as well-trained and conscientious as Putzi would never, in a thousand years, say anything—even to an old pal—that might in any way compromise confidential police information. If a nuclear device had indeed been stolen, or even if there was no more than a rumor, it was highly unlikely that Putzi would admit it. But Putzi had an idiosyncracy, a physical peculiarity that betrayed him. Wagner had noted many years earlier that Putzi would rub his nose when confronting a delicate situation. In the Kosmer sting; in the talks with the kidnappers of the West German security chief; in the stakeout of the Mueller Gesellschaft robbery plot; in each of these, as well as in some others time had dimmed, Putzi had rubbed his nose with the back of his right hand vigorously, as if attacking a nagging itch. So now, with the question asked, Wagner watched Putzi's nose.

Not once did the right hand make a move toward that pink, rather bulbous construction.

Wagner accepted this as confirmation. The theft of the Squeaky, while the subject of an intense, clandestine, international search, was not yet known beyond the circles of covert intelligence. If anyone had talked about it to anyone outside, a cop as good as Klatt would have picked it up.

"Not a peep," Putzi said, showing interest. "But I wouldn't be surprised if somebody did steal one of those babies one of these days. You wouldn't believe the rotten security they have around those NATO installations. I think I could steal a tank at midnight from most of them."

"Well, no accounting for rumors, as the saying goes."

The phone on Klatt's desk made its little clamor.

"Excuse me, Koenig."

"Sure."

Klatt lifted the phone, identified himself, and listened to the rasping. He made a few notes on his pad, shifted the cigar to the other corner of his mouth, and said, "Right. Mm. Very well. I'm leaving at once. Yes, sir."

He hung up and made a gesture of apology. "Sorry, Koenig, but I've got to run. Business is picking up."

Wagner pushed himself from the chair, wincing again. "Sure, Putzi, I've overstayed my welcome anyhow."

Klatt came around the desk and ushered Wagner to the door. "Come on. I'll walk you to the street. Need a lift anywhere?"

"Where are you headed?"

"Schwabing. There's been a double killing there, and with so many people out sick with the flu, I'm needed there to lend a hand."

"Oh? Who was killed?" Wagner, suddenly terribly depressed, instinctively knew the answer.

"Young couple. Students. Living together. Both shot."

"Any suspects?"

"In Schwabing? You're kidding. Nobody knows anything about anything when blood flows in Schwabing, my boy."

"I guess so."

Klatt shook his head, muttering. "Schwabing. The only place in the world where a girl would wear army boots with a bikini."

"It's a kooky place, all right."

Depressed to the point of numbness, Wagner put in another call to Colorado Springs. It was one of his dreary characteristics to seek out a trusted voice when the world hurt too much. In his line of work it had rarely been easy, because the world always hurt the most when he was the farthest from someone he could trust.

Trust?

Who had he ever really trusted?

Let's see. There was Mom. Dad (a peculiar guy, but always meaning well). Eva.

Anybody between?

A couple, here and there. Some sometimes. Nobody always.

The connection was completed finally and the stereotypical switchboard voice came on.

"Hotel Allison."

"Room eight-oh-four, please. I'm calling long distance."

There was a series of flutings.

"Eight-oh-four doesn't answer."

"Give me the desk, please."

A click and a snap.

"Reservations; Mr. Richards speaking."

"This is Roger Wagner, calling long distance. My wife is registered in eight-oh-four."

"Oh, yes, Mr. Wagner, how are you?"

"Has my wife left any messages for me? She's seems always to be out when I call."

"One moment, please." After an interval, Mr. Richards came back on. "Yes, there's a message, Mr. Wagner. Shall I read it to you?"

Of course you should read it to me, you permanent-press idiot. "Yes, please."

" 'Roger, dear: Sorry I've been out when you've called, but I'm so busy you wouldn't believe it. Meetings, meetings, meetings. And when I call home, you're never there. Stay put for awhile, will you? I'll call you at four a.m. if I have to. Love, Eva.' "

"That's all?"

"Yes, sir."

"All right. Tell her I called, please. It's important that she knows I've called."

"Very well, Mr Wagner."

"And, Mr. Richards—"

"Yes, sir?"

"Tell her the reason she hasn't been getting me is I've been walking the beach a lot. Day and night. She knows it's my habit. But tell her anyhow."

"Of course, sir. Anything else?"

"No. Thank you. Good-bye."

He hung up and left the booth, more downcast than ever and hating himself for having explained himself to some oily-voiced desk clerk in Colorado Springs,

Colorado, U.S.A.

That was worse than anything: letting a stranger hear the loneliness, the vulnerability.

12

As he drove into the lake country, south of the great treed expanse of the Forstenrieder and toward the featureless Alpine wall, it began to snow. The evening sky, its lowering clouds under-lighted by the setting sun, reminded him of a dying wood fire—black, laced with restless gold. And out of it came large, soundless flakes, whirling and somehow malevolent. He thought of St. Augustine and its warm hues and soft scents and gentle facades, and he was filled with a yearning for home.

His mind went again to the young people and the violence that had claimed them. He had spent some thirty years in one of the most intrinsically violent of professions; yet today, as at the first, he abhorred violence, and since leaving Klatt he had suffered horrid little visions of the boy and his nutty lover and how they must now look. He'd long known that his aversion to violence had been the subject of much scoffing among his peers, and in private moments he could admit the absurdity of a dirty-tricks undercover agent who eschewed the use of muscle except in times of exceptional need. He had learned, though, that enemies were much more fearful of economic disaster or banishment or disgrace than they were of physical injury—even death. Guns, knives, explosives were tangibles a man could comprehend, deal with, thwart; but how do you prevail over humiliation, impotence, lost prestige, professional exile? So for him the killing of Kurt Münser and Loni Riess had been a personal affront; it had been an unnecessary squandering of youth and—for all the far-out costumery and laid-back talk—human promise. Whoever had killed them must surely have overlooked, or not considered, another way.

Whoever had killed them. . . .

Who? Who was the whoever?

The whoever who had shot fourteen American soldiers. The whoever who had shot Heinz Strasser. The whoever who had blown up Unger's boat. The whoever who had fired four bullets into his own vest.

The whoever who had stolen a bomb.

He followed Highway 2 all the way to Weilheim, cutting diagonally southwest between the twin graynesses of the Ammer and Starnberger lakes. Then he turned his rented Audi northwest on the road to Rott, slowing about half-way there to watch for the lane that led to the farm of Ludwig Schattner.

It was an Einhaus, the typical Bavarian farmstead in which several generations of a family lived with their cows and geranium bulbs. Brown timbers; white plaster walls; great, spreading roof topped by a bell tower to call the men in from the fields; the sweet smells of hay and ancient manure and a wood fire and bread baking. He drove to its entrance and, huddling against the freshening wind and its darts of snow, trotted from the car to the house, where he pounded his fist against the door and waited, identifying the smells and feeling a deepening of his homesickness.

The door creaked open and a man in Lederhosen, knee socks, and mountaineer's jacket stood in the rectangle of yellow light and said, "What is it?"

"Herr Schattner?"

"Yes."

"My name is Koenig. I would like to ask you a few questions. Most confidentially. Secretly, actually."

110

"Are you a policeman?"

"No. I'm an insurance claim adjuster. The American army has referred me to you as one who can verify certain aspects of the destruction of some vehicles near here."

The man began to close the door. "Go away. I'm sick of answering questions about that sorry mess."

"There's a fee. You will be paid."

The door's motion halted. "How much?" Schattner asked.

"One hundred dollars, American, or the equivalent in marks, if you wish."

"All right, then. Come in."

Schattner was stocky, blunt-featured, and clear-eyed. He was as brown as the timbers of his house and appeared to be as tough. He was not pleased, even by the prospect of money. "Ask your questions," he grated, his voice heavy with Bavarian inflections.

"May I sit down some place?"

"You may not. It's dinner time, and my wife is waiting."

"Well, then," Wagner said, blowing on his hands, "I want to know what you saw that day. The day of the, ah, altercation."

"Altercation? What means that? It was a slaughter. Fourteen men ambushed and killed. I've already given a number of secret statements and I'm not about to give another. Tell your insurance company to read the U.S. Army reports of what I said."

"Well, Herr Schattner. . . ."

"Anything else?"

Wagner felt a stir of anger. The world coming to an end and this squarehead cow plop was going to dinner.

"Yes, there's something else. I need to know if you saw any of those attackers, the men in black. Did you see their faces?"

"That's all in the reports. The answer is no."

"Did you hear anything that was said?"

"I heard a lot that was said. But I didn't understand a word of it. The Amis yelling to each other in that impossible English of theirs— The men in black talking in Spanish— How am I supposed to report on what was said?"

"Spanish?"

"I said Spanish. How many times do I have to say it?"

"Are you sure?"

"Of course I'm sure. I may be a mere farmer, Herr Insurance Man, but I've done my share of traveling, both in Spain and in South America. And I assure you I know Spanish when I hear it, even if I don't understand it."

"Ah." Wagner thought for a moment. "Did you see which way the helicopter flew? The gray one, I mean."

"Yes, I saw."

"Well?"

"Well what?"

"Which direction?"

"Full west. Toward the Bodensee."

"You mean Lake Constance?"

"Whatever you want to call it. Toward Friedrichshafen."

"I see. What. . . ."

Schattner held out a hand and broke in, "The money. Give me the money and leave. I've had enough, and my wife is waiting."

"I have a few more. . . ."

"Out, I say."

Wagner gave him a hundred dollar bill and went out the door, filled with the anger that had been building. As the door closed behind him, he snapped, "Heil Schattner," and gave the stiff-armed Hitler salute. It was a silly, infantile thing to do, but it made him feel better.

He arrived in Friedrichshafen quite late, because rain had mixed with the snow and the roads had become nightmarish. He paid for a room in a small Gasthof overlooking the lake west of town, and then went to the bar for a bit of restoration. The room, a low-ceiling affair with huge oaken beams and leaded glass windows and a tile corner oven, was unoccupied except for the barmaid and two old men playing checkers in an oriel alcove. He was well into Eine Halbe of authoritative Württemberger when the old-timers yawned and snuffled and, with no little clatter, packed away the board and pieces and ambled into the snowy night, leaving him alone with the chesty blonde.

He would have liked to have had more time to develop his moves, but a renewed sense of time racing prodded him into sighing, patting his lips with the cocktail napkin from the bar before him, and saying, "Can I trust you?"

The blonde gave him a polite but wary inspection. "I'm not sure what the gentleman means."

"I'm sorry. I didn't put that very well. What I meant to ask was whether I might ask you some questions in confidence."

She looked from left to right, her big blue-button eyes probing, as if the shadows concealed Malevolent Forces. "Well, yes, sir. I assure you that I'm the soul of discretion. One learns to be so in the innkeeper business."

"I dare say. And I'd really appreciate your help. You see, I'm the advance scout for a major motion picture company, and I'm looking the town over for possible locations. We've scheduled a rather large-budget espionage thriller, and the producers believe that Friedrichshafen, with its central position on the lake shore, with its great scenery, would be ideal for some of the more important footage."

The blonde's face flushed with sudden excitement and pleasure, and she gave the bar a few hefty swipes with her spotless cloth. "Oh, that's wonderful. Wonderful. Who will be playing in the film?"

"The star, you mean?"

"Yes, yes."

Wagner wasn't too familiar with recent films or those who were favored in them, since he rarely visited movie houses, and those pictures he did occasionally watch on television were antedeluvian. But his memory flipped through some of the display ads he'd seen for the St. Augustine houses and settled on a full-page promo for something called "The Vindicator."

"Allen Brand," he said, offhand.

"Oh, my God. Allen Brand is coming *here*?"

"In time. He's just finished up on 'The Vindicator,' you know."

"Oh, how wonderful!"

Wagner sipped his beer and looked wise and powerful, a mover of men and circumstances. With a touch

114

of sadness, too, so as to suggest the loneliness at the top. "You'll like Allen," he murmured. "He's a good fellow, along with being a good actor."

"What can I do for you, Herr—"

"Wagner. Buzz Wagner. I've registered as Fred Hermann, from Cleveland, Ohio. That's just to keep all the exploiters, the hangers-on, from complicating my life. But I do need some information, and you appear to be a very trustworthy young lady."

"Oh, I am. I *am*, Herr Wagner. You can trust me completely."

"What's your name, dear?"

"Gisela Feder."

"Pretty. Handle yourself well, and we might be able to place you among the line-speaking extras."

"Oh, my God!"

He placed his notebook on the bar, clicked his ballpoint importantly, and gave her a sincere gaze. "Now then: Is there anybody in town who rents cars? I mean, other than Hertz and Avis and the other majors? I'm looking for someone with specialty vehicles, like World War Two-period Mercedes-Benzes, Horchs, and so on."

"Mm. Let me see. There's Freddo Kolmann. He has a garage on the Lindauerweg. I've seen him driving around in a big, shiny, old-fashioned car. I think it's a Mercedes. But I'm not sure. Anyhow, he'd be a place to start. He knows a lot about cars and who has them and things."

"Good." He made a note. "K-O-"

"K-O-L-M-A-N-N. On the Lindauerweg. Want his phone number?"

"I'll get it from the directory, thanks." He leafed

through the notebook, humming to himself in the manner of a self-satisfied physician checking his golf dates. "Now, Gisela, how about boats? Boats of all sizes for rent. Power boats."

"That's easy. The Sigmund Marina. You can see their sign from the Bahnhof."

"O.K. I'll want to talk to some food caterers, too. . . ."

"The Eugenstrasse Verpflegung. Without question."

He jotted another note. "All right. Good."

Gisela stood behind her barricade, moving her cloth across the oak, preoccupied with visions of impending glamor.

"One more item, and probably the toughest to find. Would there, by the remotest chance, be anybody in the neighborhood who rents helicopters?"

"Helicopters?"

"Helicopters. For aerial photography. Air-to-air. Air-to-ground."

"Oh, my. . . ." Her eyes grew thoughtful. "I don't think so. We have a seaplane service here. You know: flying boats. Regular planes with two motors that can land on the water. But no helicopters. Not that I know of."

"I see."

"The only helicopter I've ever seen close-up was the one that landed on the freight pier at the seaplane base. Several days ago, that was. It just came and went, so it doesn't belong to anybody from around here."

Wagner nodded, pretending to be busy with his notes. "I see. Ah, what did the helicopter do? Anything special?"

"No. Two men got out of it, talked with Herr Kessel for a moment, then took a box from the helicopter and put it in the seaplane. Then it took off and flew. The seaplane flew south."

"Who is Herr Kessel?"

"The owner of the seaplane service."

"Do you know him?"

"Not really. He came here a year, two years ago. From Munich. He bought the service from Olga Rieder's father—she's my girl friend—and he takes passengers and freight and things to the different towns along the lake. You know."

"I'll probably have a chat with Herr Kessel. Where do I find him?"

Gisela made motions with her shapely arms. "Take the street out front until you come to the big white house with the red shutters. Turn right to the lake. The pier is right there. You'll see several airplanes tied up beside it. Herr Kessel's office is in the small metal shed."

"Good." He snapped the notebook shut. "I guess that's enough for tonight. Time for some much-needed sleep."

"I hope I've been helpful, Herr Wagner."

"More than you have any idea, my dear."

"I'm so thrilled at the chance to see Mr. Brand in real life. He's so marvelous. Marvelous!"

"I'll see to it, Gisela, that he comes by to say hello to you."

"Oh, dear, dear Lord. Oh!" She clasped the bar cloth to her breast, which was, as they said in the novels, heaving.

117

"Good night, my dear."

He paid his tab and left, hating himself as a deceitful wretch who played on the vulnerabilities of innocents.

DAY 5

13

He really needed sleep, and so he went to his room and, after a stinging shower in the immaculate bathroom at the end of the hall, climbed into the feather bed and was instantly unconscious.

At four, the alarm on his wristwatch hummed, and he fought his way to the surface of a bog-like dream, heavy and thick and without form. Out of habit, he dressed in the dark as quickly as his aching body would permit, gasping once when his ribs protested his efforts to pull on the Kevlar T-shirt.

A glance out the window showed him a town and lakeshore dark and silent in the clammy aftermath of last evening's weather. He was about to turn on the bedside lamp when his gaze, lingering on the night outside, caught a discord.

Nothing moved in the scene below. Even the trees, reflecting the cheerless glow from the streetlights, were motionless, and smoke from the chimney pots rose straight for the stars. But a man stood at the end of the driveway. A man in a parka. He simply stood there in the damp night, smoking a cigarette.

Night watchman?

For a third-class inn in a sleepy lakeside town? Don't be ridiculous.

Local cop?

No. Any local cop on duty would be by a phone, toasting his tootsies by the tile oven.

State police stakeout?

Too big a coincidence.

A tail?

Mm-hm.

But if there's one, might not there be two?

Oh, jeez, Roger. You're so durn clever.

With one man watching the window, Roger, where would you put the other, if you were on the bad guy's side?

Down the hall by the stairway, so he could keep one eye on my bedroom door, the other eye on the lobby below.

Right.

He closed his overnight bag, checked the room with his pen light for anything he might have forgotten, then went softly to the door. Turning the knob gently, he let the door swing inward, creaking on its ancient hinges, until it was slightly ajar. Standing in the shadows directly behind it, he waited.

Eventually there was a sound on the stairway, followed by the slow and barely audible shuffling of shoes on carpeting.

The footsteps halted outside the door, and Wagner could hear the man's guarded breathing.

Curiosity is one of mankind's most demanding masters, Wagner's mind told him. *It had better be*, he answered back, *or I'm in a real crack.*

After at least a full minute, a hand touched the door and eased it open, slowly, carefully. When light from the hallway fell short of the bed, the door swung wider, and the man moved partially into the room for a better view of things.

Wagner stepped out of the darkness and, delivering a karate chop, dropped the intruder, who went down almost gracefully, like a tango dancer doing a dip.

He wrestled the sleeping beauty to the bed, threw him down, and, breathing hard, pulled off the fellow's trenchcoat. Next he took a roll of bandage tape from his traveler's first-aid kit and strapped the man's wrists to the bedposts, twisting the final turns into a rope-like binding. He used the last of the tape to tie the ankles together and plaster a gag across the mouth; then, finished, he threw the feather quilt over the head.

"Nighty-night, sweetums."

He hurried down the stairs, through the deserted lobby, and along what seemed to be a service corridor. This led him to a glistening kitchen, where a woman in a white cook's dress fussed busily with a coffee urn. He moved behind her and into a kind of rear foyer without her notice, and, grateful for little favors, found the back door to be unlocked. Stepping into an alley, he pulled on his visitor's trenchcoat, placed the man's Tyrolean hat on his head, and, taking a deep breath, trotted to the street.

From the corner he could see the driveway, and the tail was still there, sending little tobacco clouds into the night air. Wagner took another breath, then moved into the light of an overhead wall lamp, one of those cutsey Alpine things.

He whistled, low and soft.

The other man turned, dropping his cigarette to the street.

Wagner motioned, quick little sweeps of his gloved hand that beckoned.

"Here! Quickly!" he stage-whispered.

"Is that you, Rolf?" the man whispered back.

"Of course! Come here! Something's happened!"

The man in the parka came at the quick-step, muttering, and when he arrived at the alley Wagner dropped him without a sound and dragged him into the dark, bricklined cul de sac. This fellow he tied with strips cut from his own scarf.

Making for his car, Wagner said to no one in particular, "Welcome to beautiful Germany."

A Grumman Albatross sat in the gloom, aloof to the black water that sloshed indifferently at its weathered flanks, and Wagner wondered how early in winter the Bodensee froze over, and, when it did, where Herr Kessel kept his flying machines and the daring young men who flew them. It was one of those countless irrelevancies that forever nagged him—he had spent a whole wakeful night in his childhood wondering how Santa Claus kept his white furs clean in all those chimneys—and yet he was now cheered by the phenomenon, recognizing that if he could be thinking such nutty things in such nutty times then he surely must still be sane.

He used a jimmy to spring the lock on the metal office shed, and stood inside for a time, adjusting his eyes to the darkness and feeling the vibes of the place. He had learned to do this in his Company days, discovering as he had that buildings and rooms, like people, have personalities, and if you stand and listen and feel a place you can somehow sense its attitude toward you. One night in Augsburg he had absolutely flabbergasted Strasser when, for no discernible reason, he had told the German to pull up some flooring in the vacant factory they had entered. There, between the joists, had been the map case they'd spent two weeks searching for. And, moments later, he'd assured Strasser that Mikki Blom had to be hiding behind that door, right over there, and, sure enough, the

124

little toad walked out, blinking and holding his hands to his head like some little old POW of April, 1945.

This place, this shed, was full of malice.

To rid himself of the oppressiveness he felt suddenly, he began a systematic search, starting with the desk drawers and running through the file cabinets, chart boxes, supply bins, and maintenance racks; fine-tuning, he studied by the pen flash cash ledgers, bank statements, check stubs, bills, receipts, and phone message slips. Once, while reaching for the telephone list finder on the desk, his coat sleeve caught and knocked over a rack of rather nice-looking Meer-schaum pipes. They made a clatter that must have been heard in Athol, Mass., and he waited, frozen, for at least two minutes, listening for the approach of a watchman. None came, though, and he spent another quarter-hour rummaging through the office without effect or reward.

"It's too damned normal," he told the darkness.

The darkness did not disagree.

Giving up finally, he made certain that everything he'd moved had been restored to its original position or condition—except the pipes, which he had failed to observe for placement and for which he'd simply have to trust to luck. He let himself out, carefully relocking the door behind him.

He returned to the Audi, which he had parked in a municipal lot near the Postamt, and drove through the dawn light to München-Riem, where he bought a ticket for Orlando.

He put in a call to Eva, but the desk clerk read him a message: *Roger dear: Settlement is taking longer than expected, so I've run up to Denver to spend a day or two with Millie Oglethorpe, an old school chum. I'll be back by Thursday, but will try again to call you at the house. Where have you been, anyhow? Love you. Eva.*

"Thanks, eh—What's your name again?"

"Mr. Richards, sir. Desk clerk."

"Appreciate your help, Mr. Richards."

"Any return message to Mrs. Wagner, sir?"

"Just tell her I've been helping a friend do a job and haven't been home much. She'll understand. Have you told her, by the way, how many times I've tried to call her?"

Mr. Richards chuckled. "Oh, yes indeed, sir. And, although you two haven't gotten together on all these calls, she seemed to be very pleased that you've tried."

"Good. Hell hath no fury like an Eva Wagner unphoned."

"Oh? Ah. Yes. Ha-ha."

"Thanks again, Mr. Richards, and have a nice day."

"It's almost midnight here, sir. Ha-ha."

"Oh, yeah. Well, have a nice midnight."

He hung up and went into the new restaurant and had a breakfast of Spiegeleier und Schinken á la Tyrol, which turned out to be no more than ham and eggs á la McDonald's.

Ah, well.

"Hello, Groot."

"Where are you?"

"München-Riem. Waiting for Lufthansa to zoom me over the sparkling Atlantic to the sunny delights of Orlando and nearby Disneyland, where the whole family can laugh together and play together and spend money together."

"Be serious. You have only three more days."

"Correction: *We* have only three more days."

"Have you turned up anything?"

"I'm not sure, Groot. But there's a very strong link to Castro's Cubans."

"How so?"

"One of the people I interviewed said he heard the terrorists speaking Spanish during the bomb-ambush."

"Oh?"

"Yeah. My question to you is: didn't he tell you guys that during your interrogations?"

"Not a word of it. You're talking about Schattner, I presume."

"Yep."

"Why would he not tell us and then tell you?"

"I'm not sure, but I think I know why."

"Well, why, damn it?"

"I paid him. People—even hardnosed bastards like that Bavarian clodhopper—get remarkably cooperative when you slide them some green. But you wouldn't know that. You're a CIA executive, all proper and pressed and with a neat little hanky peeping from the old Brooks Brothers."

"No need to get sarcastic with me. I've paid my dues."

"Well, obviously you never thought to do something so grubby as to pay an informant."

"What else have you learned?"

"Somebody's been following me. I interviewed that pair of kids in Schwabing, and I hadn't left them more than five minutes when somebody cooled them."

"Oh."

"And, when I made a little run down to Friedrich-shafen, two bad guys were waiting to watch me."

"Did you elude them?"

"No. I talked to them, long and seriously, about their wasted lives. They have given up their evil ways and have become Benedictine monks."

"Come on, Wagner. . . ."

"My plane's loading. I'll call you from St. Augustine. Bye."

As he crossed the concrete apron toward the waiting SST, a flurry of wind tore his boarding pass from his hand, and he turned to chase it.

As he did so, there was a sharp, snicking sound in the air directly adjacent to his ear. He knelt quickly, and another snapping sounded.

But then the other passengers were milling about, obviously unaware of the shots having been fired, and one of them handed him his pass.

"Thanks. I was afraid it would get away from me."

The little fat lady gave him a broad smile and said something pleasant in what sounded to be Polish, and he took her arm and helped her up the boarding stairs.

From the platform at the passenger entrance he paused to examine the airport buildings, but there was simply no way to determine where the shots had come from.

"All aboard, sir," the stewardess said in her school English.

"Oh. Yes. Sorry to hold you up."

The flight to Orlando was without incident, and he slept again.

14

The day was bright and fresh, but the pale fall sun gave it the aluminum look of deep winter. The city was dusted with the early snow, and the skyline, out where the most distant buildings seemed to become part of the Rockies' steep rise, was a hemstitch in smoky blue. Eva had waited much of the morning for the phone to ring—whether it announced a call from Roger or Mr. Lindsay no longer mattered, since the waiting had become so intolerable she would have welcomed a wrong number. At last beyond any suggestion of patience, she had pulled on her boots, bundled up in the red topcoat, swirled a scarf around her head, babushka-style, and set out for a walk. She had left the main traffic arteries for an aimless wandering through the older residential streets, with their trees and frowning Victorian facades and stained-glass windows. Colorado Springs had, for her, the sense of the Old West frozen, a kind of *Bird's-Eye* view of the times when men strode the unpaved lanes, their spurs clinking, their clothes smelling of horses and whiskey and sweat. Even downtown, where the high-rises and the traffic lights and the diesel smells and the honking were indistinguishable from those in Passaic damn-old New Jersey, she had always felt it to be no more than Gold Rush City Updated. She liked it. She wished more American cities could have kept the essence of their beginnings this way; it was the main reason she was so utterly daffy over St. Augustine. So she walked, breathing in the mountain air and wishing indefinable wishes.

Mr. Lindsay was proving to be a royal pain in the caboose. Not just his mincing ways, his fancy clothes, his lawyer's obliqueness; they were bad enough, to be sure. But the worst was his open indifference to the inconvenience to which he was putting her, to her homesickness and lonely idleness. She would tell him of these things only to have him purr some abstraction about the law and its immutable ways, leaving her to feel somewhat the maudlin fool, and then another day would have passed without discernible progress in the mysterious inheritance procedure.

Virtually in mid-stride her resentment, smoldering, flared into the flame of anger, and she turned and made for an intersection, where, in a lucky matter of moments, she had acquired a cab. She gave the driver the address of Andrew L. Lindsay, attorney-at-law.

The address was in a suitably respectable part of town and was affixed to the end section of a squat pile of stone, timber, and glass in the Hollywood Modern mode. Potted plants and pebbled walks and a half-hearted atrium fountain, squirting on a patch of tired ivy, compounded the plastic effect. There were signs for dentists and realtors and insurance agents in the lobby, and Musak murmured discreetly from overhead grilles, and she stood for a moment, sorting and absorbing, before climbing a flight of plank stairs and pushing through the plate glass gateway to juridical delights.

"May I help you?" asked the plastic blonde at the plastic reception desk.

"I'm Eva Wagner, one of Mr. Lindsay's clients. I'd like to see him."

"Mr. Lindsay is in conference right now, Mrs. Ah. . . ."

"Wagner. From St. Augustine, Florida. Regarding

an inheritance.''

"Oh. Yes. Well," the blonde said, forming The Smile of Gracious Forebearance, "perhaps you'd take a seat. He shouldn't be too long."

Eva crossed the commercial-grade rust carpeting to take uneasy possession of an overstuffed chair beside a reading table. The wall clock showed 10:50. By 11:45 she had leafed through eight *Newsweeks,* two primordial *National Geographics,* a three-day-old copy of the Denver *Post,* and a *Reader's Digest* reprint of "Let a Lawyer Do It for You!"

At 11:46, she stood up, smoothed her skirt, and strode purposely down the hushed corridor that prefaced a flush door whose gilt letters spelled Andrew L. Lindsay. Without knocking or even pausing, she opened the door and went directly to the glasstop table where Lindsay sat in deep conversation with two men, one a bald fellow who looked bored, the other a pipe-puffer.

Startled, Lindsay tried unsuccessfully to smile. "Well, now. Isn't this a nice surprise. . . ."

"I simply wanted to let you know, Mr. Lindsay, that I'm sick and tired of waiting around for you to get off your tort. I'm leaving on the earliest plane, and you can mail me my inheritance."

The bald man—Eva felt a fleeting sense of something familiar about him—stood up and went into what seemed to be a lavatory. The pipe-smoker stirred, and in a heavy bass asked Lindsay, "Who's this?"

"Mrs. Roger Wagner. She. . . ."

"She is getting out of town," Eva snapped. "And I'll thank you, Mr. Lindsay, to be quick about settling my affairs. And if you can't do it, let me know, and I'll ask the Colorado Bar Association for the name of an attorney who can."

The blonde flustered from the doorway, "Oh, Mr. Lindsay, I'm so sorry. She got away before I could stop her."

"Butt out, blondie," Eva grated. "Go do your nails."

"Mrs. Wagner, please." Lindsay stood up, his delicate hand adjusting the hang of his necktie. "You can't leave now. Your presence is required. To sign papers, swear oaths. . . ."

"I'm all sworn out, Mr. Lindsay. Good-bye."

She turned on her heel, pushed past the blonde, and marched down the corridor, past the reception desk, through the glass doors, across the lobby, and into the brittle outdoors, throwing her coat about her shoulders and feeling very good.

This was her day for cabs. A Yellow was waiting practically at the bottom of the steps, and she was at the hotel in minutes.

"I'll be checking out," she informed Mr. Richards at the desk. "Will you meanwhile ask your travel desk to get me a seat on anything—a Sopwith Camel, if need be—that's flying to Jacksonville today?"

"Ah, yes. Yes, of course, Mrs. Wagner," the round little clerk said, obviously perplexed. "I'd thought you'd be with us a bit longer. . . ."

"Nope. Hibernation's over. It's back to St. Augustine to see why that husband of mine hasn't called in all the time I've been here."

Mr. Richards clucked sympathetically. "He's probably been busy."

"It's not like him not to call," she said, mostly to herself.

She headed for the elevator bay but two men sidled up beside her, took her by the elbows, and, lifting her from her feet, carried her, sputtering and powerless, out the rear entrance and into a waiting car.

"Stop," she managed to blurt. "You—"

But then someone had her skirt up and there was a sting in her exposed thigh and she felt the car begin a series of slow barrel-rolls. The spinning accelerated, and her mind hummed, and she dropped into an enormous, black pool.

15

"Good evening, Mr. President. You know Mr. Groot, I believe."

"Hello, Ben. Yes, I know Mr. Groot."

"I'm sorry we had to see you so late this evening."

"Quite all right. Any news on the missing Squeaky?"

"Well, nothing definite, really, Mr. President, but Mr. Groot has been coordinating the investigation, as you know, and we thought you might want an update."

"Good thinking, Ben. I'm due a phone conference tomorrow with the West German chancellor, and I'm afraid I'll have to bring up the subject. God knows I hate to, what with all the domestic heartburn he's been troubled by lately—leaks of state secrets, left-wing sedition, right-wing counter-sedition. God. Everybody's got problems."

"Yes, sir."

"Well, Mr. Groot, what can you tell me?"

"We have fairly good evidence, Mr. President, that the bomb was not stolen by German leftists, as first feared."

"Praise be. That'll help the Chancellor's dyspepsia. Who did, then? Do we know that?"

"Not for certain, sir, but indications are that it was stolen by the Cubans."

"Cubans?"

"Yes, sir."

"*Castro* Cubans?"

"Yes, sir."

"Oh, my God."

"It's only an unconfirmed suspicion, Mr. Presi-

134

dent."

"I'd rather it be Germans, Ben. Left *or* right."

"Well, sir, our agents have scoured Europe and the MECCE countries. We've done every possible computer scan; we've had the new Sherlock satellite do deep-spectrum analyses of Europe, Eurasia, and North Africa, on the off-chance we might pick up a glow in an uncharted locality; our orbiting laser probes have revealed not a jot of unusual activity in any of the Soviet zones of interest; we have even done a deep-dish surveillance on Cuba itself."

"What did that tell you, Mr. Groot?"

"Nothing as yet, sir. There are very mixed signals coming from Cuba. The laser probes are fuzzed by the presence of the Soviet fleet units anchored off Havana and Santiago de Cuba. The fleet includes atomic powered vessels and nuclear missiles in its armament, so we get fuzz on the read-outs."

"Lord in heaven, do you realize what would happen if we confirmed a Cuban theft of a Squeaky? Do you, Mr. Groot?"

"Yes, Mr. President. It was clear to me at once. We would have to pinpoint its location and then go in and get it."

"And with half the Soviet fleet sitting in the crossfire. It would be general war."

"Yes, sir. I'm afraid so."

"God. What are we doing about it?"

"We have Morgan, one of our top agents, and his team concentrating on the matter, Mr. President. If the Squeaky's in Cuba, he'll find it. If it's not—if it's really somewhere in the Middle East as we've suspected all along—his investigation will point us back that way."

"But, for hell's sake, Groot, we have only three more *days* to keep the lid on all this! After that, it's universal panic."

"Yes, sir. But Morgan's good. He's renowned for speed and accuracy. And we've got another good man—Roger Wagner—running a parallel probe by way of backstopping Morgan."

"Surely two men can't do what your combined CIA and NSA and NDA and G-2 and ONI haven't been able to do."

"When it comes to Cuba, Mr. President, two good agents and backups can do more than two hundred. The Cubans are very sensitive to numbers. A pair of agents stands a much better chance to penetrate their screens."

"But, God above, man, we're facing Armageddon!"

"It's our single best shot, sir. We have no other options."

"So what's your game plan?"

"Wait. We wait, Mr. President."

"*Wait?*"

"For the three days, sir. If our agents don't come up with something in those three days, we'll have to go public. We'll have to let the terrorists know about Nemesis and what technical steps they must take to avoid a wipe-out of themselves and the hundred miles around them."

"You're continuing your European and Asian searches, aren't you?"

"Yes, Mr. President. Africa as well. We honestly believe the bomb to be in the Eastern hemisphere."

"All right. What can I do to help in the meantime,

Ben?"

"Draft a statement which I, as Secretary of State, can use in a press conference. A statement that announces the theft of the Squeaky, instructs the thieves how to deactivate it, and asks its return to us in the interests of humanity."

"I'll have to get Crisis Management on it, too."

"I was rather hoping you could delay such a move, Mr. President. There are, as you know, serious leaks in that group."

"We've got some good people in Crisis Management, Ben."

"Of course, sir. The best. But the overriding need at present is to keep an absolute lid on the matter. To avoid world panic. To give us a chance to work. Unhappily, to talk to Crisis Management is to talk to the networks."

"Well, get with it, then, gentlemen. Three days. *Three.*"

"Yes, Mr. President."

DAY 6

16

St. Augustine was at its best when Wagner arrived. The sky was deep blue, with enormous cauliflowers of cumulus cruising sedately before the westerly wind. The palms swayed and whispered, and there was that unspecific fragrance exuded by dim gardens and ancient wood and dampness. After the cold grayness of southern Germany, it seemed a piece of Eden, and he enjoyed it with the pain that comes with the understanding that today is the only day there is.

He turned left from King onto Charlotte Street and then west again on Hypolita to the municipal lot next to the Pan American Center. After popping his dollar's worth of quarters into the meter, he locked the car and picked his way through the platoons of tourists to Bob Veck's house, a Second-Period Spanish thing that loomed over St. George street and looked adorably historic for the gapers from Des Moines.

Veck wasn't home, of course—private eyes are never home—but Wagner let himself in with the help of a jimmy. With things getting as sticky as they were, he was in no mood for more derring-do. In the past five days he had found a friend dead on a beach; he had been followed; he had been re-hired by the CIA; he had been shot at twice—once in Miami, once in Munich; he had two informants killed in his tracks, and he'd had to deck a pair of German hoods. It was not unreasonable to expect that his own house had become a hard-hat area.

He took a can of beer from Veck's refrigerator and went into the living room and plopped on the sofa and put his feet on the coffee table and, struggling against jet-lag, sipped and brooded.

Strasser had been investigating a group of neo-Nazis for West German Intelligence. *Check*. He had disappeared while doing so, eventually turning up dead on Vilano beach, thousands of miles from where last seen. *Check*.

Siegfried Unger, wealthy German identified with the group Strasser had been watching, likewise disappears from the German scene, possibly as the result of an intense, secret war between communist and Nazi terrorists. *Check*. He, too, surfaces briefly in Florida, only to vanish again, leaving only the wreckage of the boat he had rented from a Miami marina. *Check*.

A visit to the marina reveals a boat carrying a cache of Soviet automatic weapons and a map of Southern Germany. *Check*. The visit is annoying enough to someone to bring a fusillade of .38 bullets into his Kevlar long johns. *Check*.

His questioning of two German kids gets them killed. *Check*. His questioning of an arrogant German farmer tells him that the bomb thieves spoke Spanish and, therefore, could have been Cubans stealing the bomb for dear old Fidel. This informant does *not* get killed, according to a phone query to Klatt. *Check*.

The thieves' helicopter is traced to Friederichshafen on the Bodensee, the large lake lying between Germany and Switzerland. *Check*. What could have been the bomb was transferred to a waiting seaplane, which flew off toward the south. *Check*.

The visit to Germany is annoying enough to someone to bring a couple of parting shots at his head while strolling toward Lufthansa's SST for Orlando. *Check*.

He put down the empty beer can and thought about that.

He was missing something. Not seeing something. He knew it in the same way he had known—still knew—he was overlooking a tiny nugget of basic information that could lay the whole thing open. He had known it on his way to Miami. He knew it now. All along it had been there, at hand but beyond reach. Recognizable but unseen.

He had first sensed it when returning home from the beach on the afternoon Eva learned of her inheritance.

It had been stronger after his chat with Putzi Klatt in Munich.

It had been even stronger after his questioning of that quintessential pain in the kiester, Farmer Ludwig Schattner. And stronger still in the dark of the seaplane office in Friedrichshafen.

Why?

What?

Something.

He was still noodling all this when Veck came home, clattering up the porch stairs, rattling keys in the lock, and swinging in with a huge suitcase that looked as if it contained four locomotives.

"My God," Wagner said over the rim of his second beer, "you sure do travel light. What you got in the suitcase—four locomotives?"

"A week's dirty underwear and a correspondence course on How to be a Successful Private Detective and Make a Living Anyhow. May I, in passing, ask what in hell you're doing in my lavish home?"

"Waiting for brunch. And hiding out."

"Oh?" Veck sat on the edge of a chair, sighed an

143

enormous sigh, and pulled off his shoes. "Who from?"

"I don't know."

"Say, that's avant garde. Not everybody hides from people they don't even know. Did you leave me any beer?"

"There are three cases—one in the fridge, two stacked in the hall."

"Well, that's enough for openers, I guess." Veck pushed himself erect and headed for the kitchen, yawning. "No kidding, dad, what's going on?"

"I can't really tell you that because I don't really know. But I do know that somebody's been tailing me for the past few days and I'd like to get out from under. I thought maybe you'd let me stay here for a night or two. They've got my house staked."

"Didn't they see you come here?" Veck returned with his beer.

Wagner shook his head. "No."

"I know you used to be one of those CIA hotshots, and all that, but are you sure?"

"I'm sure. I picked up my VW from long-term parking at Orlando International, then drove to a gas station in the city, where I pulled up to a pump. While the guy was filling my tank I went to the rest room, climbed through the back window, toddled down to the next block, hailed a cab, went to the Avis office, and came home in my rented Belchfire Six. I suppose the tail is still watching the VW, which is no doubt being held as collateral by a rather irritated gas station owner."

"You're lucky that men's room had a back window. Most of them don't."

"Why do you think I went to that particular gas

station?"

"You'd checked it out before, then."

"You'll probably find it written in that correspondence course of yours: 'A Head that Thinks Ahead Never Gets Behind in Bind.' "

Veck sniffed, took a large pull at his beer, and said, "So what can I do for you? Other than room and board, that is."

"I need a name."

"What's wrong with Wagner?"

"I need the name of somebody who knows what's going on these days among our dope-running brethren to the south."

"Good guy or bad guy?"

"Makes no never-mind."

"Reason I ask is, I'm sort of pals with a Coral Gables fella who just got his Mafia 25-Year pin. If something happens in drugs he doesn't know about, it didn't happen."

"Will he talk to me?"

"If I tell him to. He owes me a couple."

"Will you tell him to?"

"Why not? I owe *you* a couple."

"You don't really owe me anything, Robert."

"How about the tip on who to see in the Department of Justice on that Puerto Rican caper? Or the use of your car that afternoon when I had to sneak up on the child-support defaulter in Ormand Beach?"

"Heck, you could've found the Justice guy in the phone book. And you used my car while I was doing eighteen holes at the Ponce with Al Humboldt. Big deal."

Veck shrugged. "It was to me, pal."

"OK, so who's the Mafia guy? I'll have to see him very, very soon. I'm racing the old Timex."

"Can you tell me what it is? Maybe I can help."

"Buddy, you could help a real bunch, believe me. But it's a confidential thing involving another old buddy, and I'm under Scout's Honor. Besides, you're already helping me by letting me use your guest cot and drink your guest beer."

"All right. So, while you get a couple of steaks out of the freezer, I'll go see a guy and set it up for this afternoon, if we're lucky."

"You can't just call him up?"

Veck put on his veddy British act. "Please, Roger, old chap, don't be so gauche. One can't just dial up the Mafia as if it were in the Yellow Pages, can one?"

He didn't have to go to Coral after all. The contact set up by Veck was in Eustis, a medium-rare town on one of the Central Florida lakes. To make better time, he drove Route 1 to Bunnell, then southwest on 11 to the Deland by-pass and a straight shot on 44 into Eustis. The roads were mostly two lanes, rarely patrolled, and thinly traveled, so he kept the rented Ford at about Mach Ten all the way. He was at the rendezvous point in the municipal parking lot across from the hospital at 3:57, three minutes early.

The lot was packed with cars at that time of day, he found, so he made two circuits of the perimeter lane and, instead of parking near the exit, as instructed, he had to leave the lot and pull into a metered slot across the street. He waited until 4:05 and had begun to worry that he'd missed the date when a shadow filled the window beside him and a wheezing voice said,

"Let's use your gas."

"OK. Hop in."

The man opened the rear door and climbed into the back seat, out of range of the rearview mirror. "All right," he said in that soft hoarseness, "go to the lake, turn left, and then to the light at Route 44. Left on 44 and keep going until I tell you otherwise."

"I just came in on 44."

"Oh? Gee whiz. What a coincidence."

Wagner blushed, realizing how silly he must have sounded. He drove as directed, resolved not to say another word until spoken to. He tried to get a good look at the man behind him, but the best he could manage with the corner of his eye was the impression of squatness wrapped in a flowered sport shirt.

They continued straight east on 44, into orange grove country, where the terrain was rolling and sparsely populated and somehow bleak in the dusty afternoon light. As they descended a long slope, the man in the back said, "Pull over at that fruit stand at the intersection down there."

Wagner did, and the man got out of the car, to be replaced by another, this one wearing sunglasses, a Panama hat, and a seersucker suit.

"Drive up the side road, then turn right into the grove on the dirt lane," the new fellow said. "Go straight for a quarter of a mile, then stop the car and turn off the motor."

"You're Dom?" Wagner said.

"I'm Dom."

When the car was finally parked in the grove, surrounded by rustling trees aligned like a Roman legion, Wagner had the brief feeling that he was at the end of

147

the world, lost forever in a restless nowhere.

"So what do you want to know, pal?"

"Veck says you're familiar with the dope-running scene."

"So?"

"So I'm not into dope. I'm working something for the Feds that has to do with national security. I'm not interested in snitching or busting or any other thing that might interfere with your, ah, activities. I'm after information only."

"What kind of national security?"

"I can't tell you that."

"Spying?"

"I said I can't say."

"Terrorists?"

"Look, I'm not asking what you do. Why should you ask what I do?"

"Don't get smart-ass with me, pal. I'll have you hanging up there with the oranges."

"And don't pull your Marlon Brando crap with me, pal. I'll have you up to your pizza in indictments."

"You Feds don't have anything on me."

"Want to bet?"

There was a moment in which the only sounds were the dry rustling of the orange trees and the distant grumping of a truck making the hill on the highway. Finally Wagner said, "Now that we have all the schoolboy my-old-man-can-lick-your-old-man out of the way, maybe we can get back to the subject."

"Which is?"

"For openers, what do you know about the Lang Boat Rental Company and Ace Boat Rentals in Miami?"

"Squids. Noods. The whole bunch shouldn't be let out without their mamas."

"What whole bunch?"

"The owners. The operators. That goober, Lang, especially. He's the big-piece owner. The others are his wife, that ginch that sits in the office and fluffs her hair, and his brother-in-law, name of Sammy Hudson, a grifter whose brains are in his pants. They pretend to rent boats for parties, fishing, that kinda crap, but they really run boat-pickups from island way-stations. And. . . ."

"What island way-stations?"

"In the Bahamas and Antilles chains. Marijuana, cocaine, ludes, other dope are shipped out of Cartagena and Baranquilla in Colombia to islands in the chains and then flown from there to airstrips in Florida, Louisiana, Alabama, sometimes Georgia and the Carolinas. U.S. pilots do the airplane chores, coming in under the DEA radar screen. But creeps like the Langs pick up the leavings, the second-rate junk that doesn't bring the Big Green and usually goes to shadow-dealers working the back alleys with kids and basket-cases. This is usually done by boat, because the cargoes are small and the enforcement not worth the time and trouble for the Feds and the state anti-drug noods. Squids like the Langs don't make any more than a hundred, two hundred a week—table crumbs."

"Hundred, two hundred whats?"

"Thousands, dummy. Thousands. Any self-respecting, so-so organizer does a coupla mill a week. The big, cool guys do hundreds of millions a year."

"Oh."

"You don't seem to know a hell of a lot about the racket, do you, pal?"

"That's why I'm here, Dom, sitting at the master's feet."

The man in the back seat sneered audibly.

"How about gun-running?" Wagner asked. "Are the Langs into that?"

"Sure. That's what Ace is all about. Lang Boat Rentals does the dope tricks, Ace runs the guns."

"From where to where?"

"You name it. But mostly small arms stuff—rifles, pistols, light and heavy machine-guns, grenades, bazookas, plastique. Russian stuff; from Cuba to Latin American and South American leftists, revolutionists. Castro, for all the years on him now, still has the yen to be the Third World's answer to Tito. You know: use the Russians, but don't play their patsy; talk peace, but knock everybody into line behind you. That crap. So the Cubans are still shipping guns around all over the place, and it's the noods like Lang who do the running. If the noods get caught, the Cubans can play real innocent."

Wagner inched into riskier territory. "What was all that flapdoodle about the German rich guy—Unger, or whatever his name was? Did you people ever get a line on that?"

"We get a line on everything, pal."

"So what happened?"

"The way it comes down is, there's a hell of a war going on between Castro and the anti-Castro forces—Cuban right-wing expatriates, mostly—based in Miami, New York, Mobile, and Panama City. It's been a thing since God knows when, but the heat is really hot now, with lots of gang war stuff. Well, Castro was supposed to get a very special delivery of some kind of special weapon—an artillery piece useful for city fighting, the way I get it—from Germany. The drill was that the piece was to be flown to a rendezvous in international waters off Miami, from where Ace would take it aboard a small boat for a fast night run to Havana. The. . . ."

Wagner broke in: "Why didn't the Cubans send one of their own boats?"

"Because," Dom said, exasperated with such stupidity, "half the U.S. fleet is watching the Cuban and Russian navies. The move of a Cuban government boat out of Havana or Santiago de Cuba is—how do they say in the papers?—a matter of great interest. But a small pleasure boat going *into* Havana? Yawnsville."

"OK. So Ace kept the rendezvous. What then?"

"So the anti-Castro people also kept the rendezvous. Bang, bang. The Ace boat goes down. So does the airplane. So does Unger and some other people. A real mud-fight. Then the antis go back to Miami."

Wagner asked the obvious. "What happened to the weapon?"

"Davey Jones-ville. With the boat and the plane and assorted noods."

"Who says?"

"Lang. Who was watching from another boat at a distance."

"Lang says. Who the hell can trust what Lang says?"

"I can," Dom purred. "He's on my payroll. He lies to me and he swims across the Atlantic in a concrete wet-suit."

"So he told you all this, eh?"

"Mm-hm."

"Well, I'd check him out if I were you. Don't you know that Siegfried Unger was about as likely to deliver a new weapon to Castro as I am to kiss your fevered brow? Unger was a notorious rightwinger—a certified Nazi."

Dom laughed, a soft, deep-in-the-belly sound. "Mama mia! You sure are a naive bastard, ain't you? Unger was a Nazi like I'm a Presbyterian deacon. Unger's been working for Castro since Castro threw Batista out of Cuba in the Sixties. Unger's a Commie of the old school, pal. Where you been?"

"So let me get this straight: Some German Reds offer to sell Castro a hot new weapon. They deliver it by plane to a Lang boat near Miami for undercover delivery to Havana. But anti-Castro rightwingers intercept the delivery and blow all the Cubans, and their hot new weapon, out of the water. Right?"

"You got it."

"Another question, Dom: Where can I find somebody in the anti-Castro group? Somebody I can get some answers from."

"The meter's run out on you, pal. I promised Veck I'd talk some with you, not give you the social register. Take me back to the fruit stand. The interview's over."

"I'll give you ten grand for a name."

Dom laughed again, this time with genuine amusement. "Honest to God, I never thought for a minute they still make them as dumb as you. Ten grand? Hell, I carry that around for lunch money, you

152

dumb sumbish."

"All right, then," Wagner said, improvising in a kind of absolute submission to pure intuition, "I'll give *you* a name. You give me a name of an anti-Castro Cuban I *can* trust and I'll give you the name of one of your people you *can't* trust."

There was an interval, and then Dom said, with a touch of bravado, "You can't give me any such name, pal."

"Oh?" Wagner's mind raced. "How long have you had your personal driver?"

"Lou? For three years. Ever since he got out of the slammer."

"He goes everywhere with you? Sees everything? Hears everything?"

"He goes a lot. Sees some."

Wagner said nothing.

"What you got on Lou?" Dom said, husky-voiced.

Wagner remained silent.

After a time, Dom said, "The guy you want is Carlos Garcia. He lives over the Bon Vivant bar and grill in Daytona. Now take me to the fruit stand."

"Sure, Dom. Sure thing."

He was back in St. Augustine by nine, but Veck was gone. So he had a TV dinner, placed another unsuccessful call to Eva, then went to bed for three hours of sleep.

DAY 7

17

The local joke held that, if you stood on St. George Street long enough, you'd see everybody you ever knew. Wagner thought of this when he glanced down from Veck's fancy Spanish porch and saw the two archeologists strolling among the after-breakfast joggers. What were their names? The older one, the man with the beard, was a professor from the university. Dr. Samuels? Yes. The other was the cute young smarty who gave Audrey the hots. Driscoll. Paul Driscoll. They were in deep, unsmiling conversation, and it struck him that they didn't like each other much.

But who in hell did, in the great wonderful world of push and shove and snap and snarl? Wagner was suddenly overwhelmed with renewed understanding: he was living in a world in which just about everybody hated everybody else for reasons as unspecific as the wind, or the wash of the sea. And he had spent virtually his entire adult life on the cutting edge of that hatred, and he was so sick of it, so gorged with its melancholy and tawdriness, he could only return to the living room and sit down and sigh. It was as if he'd been stabbed.

The phone rang, and he picked it up. "Hello?"

"You Veck?" the man's voice wanted to know.

"No. He's out of town. He'll be gone the whole week."

"You Wagner?"

"Yep."

"You want to see a man in Daytona?" The accent was Cuban.

"Yep."

"Be at the Bon Vivant on Ridgeway at nine-thirty. Tell the cashier you from Joe's TV Repair."

The dial tone came on, and Wagner hung up. He checked his watch and saw that he had an hour and a half to keep the date. Just about right.

He went to the parking lot by way of Cuna Street, and came upon the young archeologist—Paul Driscoll, was it?—standing near the Straw Market, pondering the inevitable map.

"Hi, there," Wagner said. "You're Paul Driscoll, right?"

"That's right," Driscoll said, showing mild surprise.

They were within handshaking distance, so Wagner held out his hand. "I'm Roger Wagner. I'm a friend of the president of your fan club. Audrey."

"Audrey?"

"Yeah. The Monson waitress. She admits to admiring you vastly."

Driscoll's brown eyes showed recognition. "Oh, yes. That Audrey. She's quite a character. I like her, too."

"Best waitress in town." Wagner nodded at the map. "What are you up to this gorgeous day?"

"This is a copy of a 1603 map. It says there was a bakery around here in those days. If there was, there had to be a well. And a disposal area. And if we find it, we could have something."

"Four-hundred-year-old Hefty bags?"

Driscoll laughed politely, showing his splendid teeth. "You'd be surprised what we find around old wells and dumps."

"I thought you were concentrating on the fort. At least that's the scoop I got from your buddy."

"Buddy?"

"The guy with the beard. Dr. Samuels."

"Oh. He's hardly my buddy," Driscoll said easily and with no apparent malice. "I'm working under a Federal grant, and he's from Academe, and I gather that he disapproves of those who eat at the public trough."

"I see. Professional jealousy, maybe?"

Driscoll smiled again and shook his handsome head. "I can't see where that would be true. In fact, I seriously question Dr. Samuels' professionalism."

God, Wagner thought, *there is no escape from the old office-cooler politics, the bureaucratic backbiting.* "Ouch. I didn't realize I stumbled into a war. Sorry I brought it up and ruined your day."

"You didn't ruin my day at all, Mr.—"

"Wagner."

"Yes. Thank you. Wagner. There's no war. It's simply that Dr. Samuels seems to be peculiarly amateurish in some of his digs, naive—archaic—in some of his thinking. I'd have thought the university would have a very well-informed man in charge of their field studies and undergraduate practicum. But Dr. Samuels is—well—dated. That's the word. It's as if he were from another age."

"Well," Wagner said diplomatically, "that's what my wife says about me. And she's right. I'm only now catching up with Elvis Presley's music."

"What line of work are you in, Mr. Wagner?"

"I've retired after seven hundred years of eating at the public trough." He glanced at his watch. "Got to run. See you around. Meanwhile, I hope you get down in the dumps."

"Um. Yes. Ha-ha."

He went all the way to Daytona on A1A because he wanted to see the ocean. It was that kind of day, and, besides, he rationalized, he could make better time with the lighter traffic. Dunes and sky and sea to the left, palmetto spikes and scrub trees and trailer camps and Eats to the right; the edge of the universe, overlooked by a bleachers built of schlock, and the strong presence everywhere of some gluttonous, Gatsby-like insistence that everything, from the smallest seashell to the sun itself, must someday be owned, controlled, denied to others.

He wondered what Eva would do with her hundred thousand dollars.

Get a divorce, maybe?

It seemed almost a sure thing by this time, now that his ineptitude with the telephone had been so well established with her. No matter the excuse; no matter the reality of his having tried, she would only see the failure of it and probably, in the bizarre chemistry of the slow-burn, escalate it into willful rejection. Marriages, like wars, are won or lost via perceptions.

Eva would be doing nothing with her hundred thousand dollars, he reminded himself dourly, if someone didn't find that bomb. He tried to imagine the world as it might be after the fact of such an explosion. Or after the fact of preventive war. But the image wouldn't come, as if, in the pinball machine he called a brain, the idea caused an enormous, game-cancelling tilt.

It was fairly clear by now that the bomb had been stolen by Cuban commandos and flown to the sea ren-

160

dezvous. But he didn't accept for a moment the Mafia hotshot's suggestion that it was now on the bottom of the sea. Castro, if he were indeed behind the caper, would not permit such a weapon—such a coup—to lie wasted, even if he had to draft Cuba's twelve million citizens and put them to work in scuba gear. The fact that Groot had received no reports of treasure hunts or salvage-diving at the map coordinates Wagner had retrieved from the Ace boat was testimony to Cuba's lack of interest in the sea bottom there. With India, Pakistan, Iraq, Israel, and Libya now possessing homemade basic nuclear devices, Castro was not about to let go his chance for a massive one-up on them via his captured Squeaky. Nukes were one thing, but Squeakies were another, as the Pentagon liked to say, and, with one, Castro would have moved not only into ascendency in the Third World but total freedom from his Soviet overseers. No, Castro was not likely to abandon a Squeaky once he'd had his hot hands on one.

The question, then, the question Wagner had to resolve, was where *was* the verschlugginer thing?

He wasn't sure, what with all the heavy traffic, but he seemed to have picked up a tail again. A blue Plymouth.

The Bon Vivant was a two-story yellow stucco monstrosity that fronted on Ridgeway and tried to look prosperous. The first floor was given to a restaurant which, presumably, sought to justify the name. The upper story featured two-pane double-hung windows of the 1920's style that bore cracked gilt letters speaking of real estate and economy dentistry and loans, and the whole sat in a kind of isolation, thanks to the sandy, weed-stubbled lots to its flanks. He parked the car at the front door, locked it, then went into the interior gloom, where a fat lady wiped down plastic-topped tables and a kid in denim shorts ran a vacuum cleaner.

"I'm from Joe's TV Repairs," Wagner told the bosomy brunette behind the cash register.

Her eyes, heavily ringed by makeup, showed no sign of joy at his announcement. In fact, they showed no sign of anything. She simply slid off her stool and waddled, waggle-bottomed, to the rear of the place, where she disappeared down a short hallway lit only by signs that said Stallions and Mares. She reappeared after a time, materializing like some gitano ghost. "This way, mister," she beckoned.

She led him to a dank back stairway that climbed behind the kitchen to an upper foyer. Unfriendly doors were spotted around this, their plastic signs bearing the same doleful messages spelled by their flaking brethren on the windows out front. She tapped on the one marked Regency Real Estate Corp., then stepped aside and motioned Wagner through.

A large man with black hair, a pencil-line mustache, and a gold front tooth sat behind a desk that appeared to have been last dusted circa the Boer War. He considered Wagner with neutral eyes, which were not the customary deep brown of the Hispanic but a discordant hazel.

"Sit down, Mister Wagner," the man said in a voice entirely devoid of accent or ethnicity. "Dom has instructed me to talk to you."

162

Wagner saw no need to spar. "I'm a Federal agent working on a most urgent matter. It has certain elements that link it to the struggle between Cubans who support Castro and those who oppose him. Dom says you fall into the latter category and will probably answer some of my questions."

"I see. Where do you stand on the Cuban question, Mr. Wagner?"

"I'm not a political person. In the matter of Cuba, I'm nonpartisan."

"I have only contempt for men who do not take sides. A man who remains aloof from the passions of his times is not truly alive. He is a moral and political eunuch."

Wagner shrugged. "I don't really give a good damn what you think of me. I'm after information, not apotheosis in Omega 7."

"I am not with Omega 7, Mr. Wagner. Nor am I with the more conservative anti-Castro forces, such as the Cuban Nationalist Movement. I am a force apart from those and other segments of the strife. I am founder of 'Cuba for Cubans—Today.' "

"Well, whatever. I just don't want to argue politics with you, Mr. Garcia."

"That's a pity. You'll be involved in the Cuban political question very soon now, whether you like it or not. You and all the other Americans. The war between Cubans will soon break out in the open and turn much of southeastern United States into a battlefield. It is inevitable. Inescapable. Already Florida is filling with Castro commandos and guerrillas. Thousands of them, all posing as South American tourists. My group, Cuba for Cubans, as well as Omega 7 and the

CNM, are the only organized forces standing between you nonpartisan Yankees and open Castro assault on your territories."

"I rather imagine our Defense Department would give you a razzberry on that one, Mr. Garcia."

"Your Defense Department is composed of dilettantes and dreamers. With the impasse between America and the Soviets, they play electronic war games and dream of conquest. But in real war they will fall apart. Real war will result in the ultimate inheritance of the earth by the poor, the meek—just as the Holy Bible says. Who will lead the poor and the meek is the question being debated with considerable ferocity both in Europe and in the Americas—right here in Florida, for that matter." Garcia sat back in his chair and folded his hands on his belly, like a potentate who had delivered himself of a decree and felt pretty good about it.

"Be all that as it may," Wagner drawled, "my concern is not so big-scale. I'm looking for a missing box—a container—that was aboard a boat sunk recently off Miami during a skirmish between opposing Cuban forces. I'd like you to put me onto at least one survivor of that fight. I absolutely need to know what happened to that box."

Garcia smiled, a sardonic twist of his thin lips. "Oh," he said easily, "you mean the Squeaky."

Despite his years of inurement to shock and surprise, Wagner was simply unable to absorb this without physical reaction. He started, and felt himself leaning forward, his eyes widening. "You know about it, then?"

"Of course I know about it, Mr. Wagner. I was in

164

charge of its interception. I, personally, removed it from the airplane and placed it aboard my boat. I, personally, sank the airplane and the Ace boat sent to meet it. I, personally, supervised the execution of the enemies present at that little event."

"The Squeaky is here, then? In Florida?"

"Why do you think Castro is sending in all those people? He is sending them in to retrieve, not the Squeaky, but its fuse. He plans a sweep of all the Cuban exile communities. He is planning to hold Florida hostage until the Squeaky's fuse is turned over to him."

Wagner shook his head in genuine incredulity. "You've got to be kidding."

"No, Mr. Wagner. I'm not kidding. Look at it from Castro's point of view. Castro hopes to become the recognized leader of the hundred-some nations that compose the Third World, or the so-called non-aligned axis that has no allegiance or political indebtedness either to the Soviets or the Americans. He is altogether disenchanted with the Soviets himself, and he yearns to formalize his maverick image with a complete cut away from them. But to do so effectively, he needs nuclear capability—or at least to be recognized as posing a nuclear potential. The Russians control tightly all nuclear weapons stored in Cuba, and the Third World knows it, so Castro needs—demonstrably—to show he has his own capability. So he has arranged the theft of a Squeaky, whose fuse he can adapt to a standard K-bomb, which anybody can make in his cellar, practically. But the only problem with that is that we, the people who will free Cuba from the Castro yoke, have intercepted the Squeaky, stolen it from under his nose.

165

And so now he plans a series of countermoves. He plans to cut off southern Florida. He plans to drop overpass bridges on all key north-south highways, thus interdicting traffic and symbolically sealing off half the state. He plans to close all major airports south of Jacksonville. He plans to occupy a major nuclear power plant in a major city and will blow it up if the U.S. attempts to retaliate while he's conducting his sweep for the Squeaky. For good measure, he plans to hold the city officials of Tampa, Orlando, and Fort Lauderdale, killing them off if any move is made to interfere." Garcia paused, taking a deep breath.

"This is absolutely the nuttiest thing I ever heard of," Wagner managed.

"Almost as nutty as a handful of students holding the United States at bay for a year by way of a humiliating seizure of its embassy in Tehran. Wouldn't you say?" Garcia chuckled softly.

"But this is *too* big. *Too* humiliating. The Americans are committed to fighting acts of terrorism no matter where they occur—even Florida. This thing you're talking about is guaranteed to trigger a major war."

"Castro is gambling that it won't. He simply does not believe the U.S. will destroy millions of Floridians merely to keep him from getting back his Squeaky and/or its fuse. If the U.S. faltered for a year, fearing a wrong move that might kill a handful of diplomatic personnel in Iran, why would the U.S. move precipitously when Florida and its entire population are being held nuclear hostage?"

"Well, for God's sake, then where do you come in?"

Garcia smiled that infuriating smile again and nodded. "Good question. We, my friend, are the people who will do America's fighting for her. While Castro prepares his sweep of Florida, we will be smuggling the Squeaky into Havana. When he learns that any effort to pursue his mad course will cause the destruction of his own capital city, he will desist—become sweetly reasonable."

Wagner barked, "You are absolutely out of your perishing mind! There are the Soviet fleet elements in Havana, the Soviet determination to protect its interests in Cuba, the Soviet readiness to believe that this is all a CIA plot from the beginning, the Soviet willingness to nuke everything in sight. But worst of all, you dumb son of a bitch, none of us—absolutely *none* of us—has any time for all this crap. The Squeaky is. . . ."

There was a crash below, a tinkling of glass, the splintering of wood. Then the rasping tear of a submachine-gun. Shouts. The pounding of feet on the stairway.

"Dear God," Garcia said, pushing away from the desk and yanking a pistol from his shoulder holster. "Get out of here fast, Wagner! The window there. Quick! We've got a raid going!"

Wagner, his mind overloaded with the enormities of the Cuban's revelations, felt as if he were moving in a giant vat of syrup. Every motion seemed to be that of a stop-action camera, and, as he threw open the window and prepared to drop to the shed roof below, he looked back into the room and saw Garcia, seeming to be cocooned in a welter of gun sounds, spin around twice and fall backward across a collapsing chair.

He completed his drop then, and rolling down the

slant of shingles, swung over the eave and onto a pile of cartons in a garbage bin. In a great heaving, he was in the clear.

He ran.

Two blocks away he found a phone booth partially hidden by a billboard, and he stepped into this and pretended to hunch over the phone while he thought things over. His car was beyond retrieval, parked as it was in front of a place that would soon be swarming with cops and ambulances and various hoods who'd be looking for the guy who went out Garcia's window. In fact, merely walking around anywhere in this neighborhood could be a dicey thing.

"I thought that was you," an amiable woman's voice said behind him. "What the hell are you doing here?"

"Audrey?"

She grinned at him from the little red Honda Civic poised at the curb, its motor chortling. "I was coming along and saw you pop into the booth, and I told Harriet, 'That's Roger Wagner, by golly.' And I was right."

"Who's Harriet?"

"My car, dummy. Best friend I got."

"As of now, that's changed. As of now, I'm your best friend. Will you take me to the Hertz office?"

"I've got a date in twenty-minutes. But hop in. I can make it."

Wagner ran around the car and folded his bulk into the tiny passenger area, managing after a struggle to get the door closed behind him.

"Harriet ain't much for big fellers like you. Push the seat back."

168

"If I pushed it back any further, I'd be in the trunk, or whatever they call it in these roller skates."

The car got under way, and Wagner gave Audrey a fond sidelong glance. "Glad to see you, Audrey."

"Glad to see you, too."

"What brings you to Daytona? Isn't this a work day at the Monson?"

"Not for me," she said, her eyes darting about in the watch for the leapers and swervers in the traffic flow. "I'm only a part-timer there."

"Oh? I thought you'd been there for two hundred years."

"Nope. Came up from Lauderdale not too long ago to stay with an aunt who's been ailing. I've finally got her into a nursing home here in Daytona, and so we're renting her house in St. Augustine and I'm trying to get something here so I'll be closer. Came down today to check out a hostess job at a place called the Bon Vivant."

"Have you been there yet this morning?"

"No. Just on my way when I saw you. Why?"

"I'd stay away from there if I were you. They had a shooting there. No more than ten minutes ago."

"Oh, God. That's all I need—a job in a shooting gallery. What happened?"

"I don't know. I parked my car in front of the place, just by chance. Then all hell broke loose, and I ran. I was trying to figure out what to do when you came along, you gorgeous, marvelous lady, you."

Audrey laughed. "This is a weird day for both of us."

"Do me a favor?"

"Sure."

"Let me ride back to St. Augustine with you. You are going back there, aren't you? After you see your aunt?"

"I'm not seeing my aunt today. She's in intensive care and not with it. And now that the job interview's out, there's no place else to go."

"Good. I don't want to go back where my car's parked. So I'll take the keys to the St. Augustine office and ask them to pick it up."

"Righty-tight. Glad to have the company."

18

The cloying, sick taste would never go away, Eva decided. She slumped in the pale red chair, legs out-thrust, arms to the side, hands hanging like leaves on a dying plant. Her eyes ached, and there was nausea, and she felt the desperate need of a bath. Beyond the window, the sun was lowering over the blue, shadowed scarp of the western mountains, and the flatlands between, a desolation dotted with brush, were turning gold and lavender in the softening light. It was cold out there, brittle and inhospitable, and she had a sense of the distance between her and home and reality.

She was in a bedroom of what was obviously a very expensive house. The patio beyond the glass wall was terrazzo, edged with large, costly plants that seemed to have been prepared for the winter by expert hands. She thought she could make out the corner of a pool house, with awning racks and neatly folded lawn furniture, and a serving cart, alone and somehow forlorn. Music was playing somewhere, low and dreamy. She wanted to stand up, pull herself together, stride to the door, fling it open, and run across the rolling, desert-like plain—to a road, a house, an anything where there might be someone who would help her. But she sat, immobilized by an invisible weight and feeling this sickness and fear.

She thought of Roger, but even that failed as an enabler, because she was angry with Roger for letting her come to this unfriendly country without insisting that he come, too. For not calling her. For not being home when she called.

For not loving her.

The dirty rat.
She slept again.

When she awoke she was on the bed, still dressed, still sick, and still feeling the need of a bath. But the aching had diminished, and her eyes, although they seemed to have an inner soreness, could make out detail and could turn in her head without feeling as if they would fall out and bounce across the carpet.

Swinging her feet to the floor, she sat for a time, struggling with the uneasiness in her stomach and the tendency of her head to wobble. *My head is like a golf ball glued to a rubber tee,* she thought, *and somebody keeps pushing it, trying to knock it off.* She considered this, and the absurdity of it caused her to laugh, a bitter, single syllable of sound.

You will walk now, Eva. You will stand up and walk from here to those boots beside the chair. If you do not throw up, and if the golf ball remains on the tee, you will win an all-expense tour of the stockroom at Rieglmaier's Plumbing & Supply Co. in Boilersville, Indiana.

She retrieved the boots and thanked God they were the low-heeled walking style; she had worn them for her morning's stroll around town (Morning? Which morning?) and the idea of trying to make a getaway in spike heels was too much even to contemplate. She tried to slip them on without stooping, but her feet had swollen some, and, after enduring the torture of kneeling and retching, she gave it up as hopeless.

The door did not lead to a closet but to a bathroom, complete with sunken tub, sauna, basking bench, sunlamps, bidet, and a cutesy-pie stall shower disguised

172

to look like a rose trellis, or something equally ridiculous. It was a woman's bathroom; and while the woman might have had money, her taste was kitsch, circa 1935. But the water was good. She found that out by throwing off every stitch and standing under the rose trellis for what had to be an hour.

After drying with a yellow towel and dressing, she considered herself in the mirror, discovering there a young old woman, or was it an old young woman, and a hairdo that could have been created by Genghis Khan. A brush and comb that had been placed in the lavinette drawer sorted out this damage and, returning to the bedroom, she realized that she might now survive.

The sliding glass doors to the patio were locked, as was the Spanish-paneled door to what had to be the interior hallway. Deep twilight had gathered outside, but, deciding that she would rather see than be seen, she did not turn on the lamps. Standing in the dusk, she peered out at the patio, straining for a clue as to where she might be. She had a momentary vision of what she might look like, a girl with her nose to a window—the girl of a long time ago, on a Saturday night in Charleston, hesitating at the window displays of candy and toys and dresses and being tugged along by her father who had no time for any of it. She had a sudden need to cry, to mourn the lost years, but she managed to keep it in check and instead stood in the sad and fading light and whispered the dirtiest, angriest words she could think of.

The Spanish door opened with a quick, small noise and the lights went on. A woman in a maid's uniform swung in with a dinner tray, holding it before her as if the aromatic contents were a bomb about to explode.

"Who are you, and what is this place?" Eva demanded.

The woman—lean, blonde, hard-looking, with blue eyes, and with hair brushed straight back—suggested a woman's concentration camp guard in one of those late movies on TV. She did not answer the questions. In fact, she did not so much as glance at Eva.

"Who brought me here? Why? Why am I locked in?"

The woman placed the tray on the desk.

"Say something, damn you! Why am I here?"

The maid turned and strode stonily to the door, went into the hallway, closed the door behind her, and, in a moment, rattled a key in the lock.

"Damn. *Damn!*"

She began a systematic search of the room, the bath, and the double closet, which contained nothing but her red topcoat, her purse—its money, its credit card, driver's license, and keys precisely where she had put them—and, surprisingly, her suitcase, carefully repacked.

Sipping some of the coffee on the tray, going easily, because she wasn't sure how much her stomach could accommodate, she thought about this. Whoever had brought her here wanted no traces to be left at the hotel, obviously, and it was evident that they had been watching her, probably searching her room even before the kidnapping. She put down the cup and went to the closet, pulled out the suitcase, and went through it.

It was as she'd suspected: everything was there but the manicure set; scissors, files can be used

174

as weapons.

With this thought collecting, she hurried around the room, looking for things—anything—that could conceivably be used as a tool to break out or to support an attack. There was nothing, not even a candlestick, a paperweight, a letter opener, a nail file, a bookend, a massive vase. She eyed the lamps scattered about, but they were either too ungainly to swing or too delicate to make a difference. There were no coat hangers in the closet; her topcoat hung from a wooden peg. Even the drape cords had been removed and the hangings were suspended from a plastic rod with plastic hoops.

The poshest jail in the West.

And she was in it.

She sat in the red chair, exhausted again.

She looked at her hands. The hands that had touched so many things. Apples high in the tree behind Old Man Ranski's barn; algebra books and crayons and chalk erasers and tin lunch boxes and gingham; flower petals; the spiky ears of Allen, the cat, and the wet nose of Llewellyn, the pooch; corn husks and potato peelings and snap beans and cherries and purple grapes from Aunt Ida's arbor. God almighty! Where those hands had been since those times! Steering wheels; passports; panty hose; cocktail glasses; sheets. Roger.

Roger.

Hands.

How had he shown her?

You needn't hit someone with a fist to spin his eyes, Roger had said. *Hold your hand flat, palm down, and swing it from the elbow—fast. The edge of the hand is like a hammer. Few guys can stand the edge of a hand across the face. But when you do it, do it. All out. Hard as you can. Anything less won't work. Same with elbows. Bring your elbow under a chin, real fast, and the chin's owner snoozes.*

There had been other things about toes and heels and knees, but she didn't remember them.

She went over to the door and, resting her back against the wall on the opening side, she waited. She had no idea how long it would take the maid to come for the tray, so she had to be ready for any time.

It was eleven minutes by her watch.

Footsteps in the hallway, the faint clinking of a key ring, the rattling in the lock.

The maid stepped in, officious, prim. Then her eyes showed an instant of awareness, in which she must have felt the difference in the room, the peculiar absence of the prisoner from the ambience.

Eva gave it all she had. Perhaps more, because she was very frightened, and her heart was pumping.

Her hand made a short, mean little arc, blurred, and she felt its edge connect with the woman's face just below the nose, and it was as if every bone in the hand—and in her arm, her shoulder, her rib cage, her backbone, and her legs—had been broken. There was an immediate, intense numbness, and she stood in a kind of detachment, watching, as the maid went down, arms and legs flapping like a ragdoll's.

Nothing at all had been broken. Eva discovered this when she knelt, seized the woman's arms, and pulled her unconscious weight to the foot of the bed. Struggling, she pulled off the maid's uniform and shoes, then, with a nylon stocking from her suitcase, she tied

176

the woman's wrists to a leg of the bed frame. She used the other stocking to tie the blonde's ankles together.

The woman's mouth was bleeding rather heavily, and so Eva hesitated, wondering if a gag might cause choking or—oh, God!—drowning in the blood. She decided that the maid would have to do her breathing through her nose, because Eva Whitney Wagner was about to leave, and if the goddam blonde was going to strangle, it served her right because this had all been her verschlugginer idea, as Roger would say—hers and whoever she was working for, the dirty bastards. She pulled a pillowcase from the bed, rolled it into a rope, then jammed it between the blonde's teeth and tied it behind her head.

She dressed in the maid's uniform, her fingers fumbling because of her excitement and anxiety. She retrieved money and cards from her purse. She also wanted to keep her boots; if she did get free of the house, boots would help a lot in a cross-country run through the darkness. But her best chance of getting out rested in her passing casual observation, and a pair of boots under a maid's skirt would call for second glances. It was her only chance, and she was taking it, by God.

She had to have a coat, though.

The blonde must have one, somewhere.

Easing into the hallway, she held the tray with one hand, waitress-style, and locked the door with the key. Then she looked about her: three closed doors, no sound from any of the rooms they represented; a beige carpet leading to an archway opening on what seemed to be a kind of atrium, where she could hear a fountain splashing gently. There was music, still soft, and she thought she recognized it as Mozart.

She took a deep breath and began to walk toward the atrium, not too fast. Business-like, with the tray held as the blonde had held it.

In the atrium, water gurgled from a rock formation and made ripples in a lily pond girded by sand-colored bricks. Beyond and to the right was a spacious room, mostly glass; at the far end was an enormous fireplace, where the glow from lazy flames merged with that of the lamp behind a great arc of sofa. Two men were talking in low tones. One sat on the sofa, his legs crossed, one hand holding a large, Sherlock-Holmes kind of pipe. The other man, Lindsay, was sipping a drink between irritable bursts of words. A third man was at a desk, on the phone.

She recognized the pipesmoker and the telephoner as the men who had been in Lindsay's office.

She crossed the reception area, keeping a screen of potted plants between her and the living room. As she moved along, not too fast, not too slow, she heard the telephoner say in his light voice, "The Chimes. That's right— No. Well— O.K. I understand. But don't muff it, you hear?" He sounded very annoyed, and one of the others mumbled something that didn't seem to ease matters much.

"Look, damn it," the man snapped into his phone, "we haven't got time. It's got to be now. *Now.* The whole thing has been upset by what you've just told me. It's now or never. If it doesn't work now, we won't get another chance. I. . . ." Pause. "O.K., then. The— Right. Across from the Chimes. Right. Yes. We'll be there. All right. Yes." There was a soft clatter as the phone went back to its cradle.

178

"Dumb bastard."

"He's all right," Lindsay said, placatingly. "You shouldn't be such a perfectionist."

She continued on to the kitchen, a large square of glistening cabinets and appliances done in gold and white. Placing the tray on the serving bar, she hurried into a utility room off the kitchen, where, hanging next to an outer door, was the maid's dark blue trenchcoat. She pulled this on, the white scarf, too, and, turning the knob quietly, opened the door and went into the bitter night.

Three cars were standing in the half-darkness of a parking apron. One was a Mercedes sedan, another a Lincoln. The third car was a Ford, which, she guessed, would be the maid's.

She headed for the Ford, fingering the keys she'd found in the trenchcoat's pocket, but then paused in mid-stride, stopped by an idea. Turning, she went first to the Mercedes, and, stooping, removed the cap from the tire valve and inserted a twig taken from the flowerbed beside her. Eight times she did this, and, satisfied that both cars had been immobilized by flat tires, she hurried to the Ford and climbed behind the wheel. The key fit, and the motor started.

Flicking on the lights, she drove off down a blacktop driveway, fast.

Somewhere there was a shout, and a lot of lights flared on, turning the house, the plantings, the driveway to a chalky white.

A man jumped out of the bushes ahead to stand in a half-crouch, his hands leveling a gun. She flipped on the high beams and leaned on the horn, and the glare, combined with the outrageous noise, seemed to rattle him. He leaped aside and disappeared behind the car.

There was a series of shots, but none could have struck the Ford because no glass broke, no metal clanged, and the motor didn't falter a hair.

At the end of the driveway was a two lane highway.

She turned right on this, the tires squealing, and she drove until she came to a town-limits sign reading Ellicott.

19

Groot poured himself a cup of coffee he really didn't want and carried it to his desk. He sat in the leather-backed swivel chair and, gazing out the window, considered the wintry night and the clammy haze it had lowered across the shopping center—a complex of pseudo-Colonial islands in an asphalt sea. Sipping absently at the coffee, he wondered what hateful god had doomed him to spend so many hours of whatever remained of his life on the shore of a parking lot offering a view which, as a breathtaker, was on a par with the southeast corner of O'Malley's Brickyard.

The phone rang discreetly and he picked it up. "Yes?"

"Dieter Kaulbach in Bonn on Line Two, Mr. Groot."

He punched the button and said in German, "Hello, Dieter. You're working late. I mean early. It's almost dawn over there."

"Ah, yes. I thought I'd better call you before leaving for the office."

"Is something wrong?"

"Well, not exactly. It's the Minister again. He's wondering if there's any news on the Squeaky."

"No. I'm waiting myself."

"The Minister is most anxious that we get some answers on this thing. The media have begun to sense something is wrong, what with all the frantic searching. They are beginning to hammer the government."

"I understand. I'll call you the very moment there's anything to report, of course."

"You have my home phone number?"

"Certainly."

"Don't hesitate to use it. At any time, day

or night."

"It'll be a while yet, I'm afraid."

"What's your guess, Groot?"

"A day or two, at least."

"Oh, God. So long?"

Groot felt annoyance stirring. "I assure you, Dieter, this business is no more pleasant for us than it is for you. You and the Minister are not the only people concerned about the Squeaky, I assure you."

"I suppose so. But you will call me as soon as possible, eh?"

"As soon as possible."

"So then. Good night, Groot."

"Good night, Dieter."

He replaced the phone, only to have it make its little sound again. "Yes?"

"Mr. Morgan is on the Omicron viewer, sir."

"Thank you. Connect him to my screen." He punched the button, and the gold-framed painting above the sofa moved aside to reveal the glassy face of the television plate.

Groot liked Morgan. In Groot's opinion, Big Business was the epitome of wizardry and socially acceptable avarice, and it was fitting that CIA be called The Company because it was likewise guided by the precept that, if handled adroitly, people could be sold (or were willing to sell) anything. The intelligence industry sold politicians on the idea that Secrets Win Elections and Other Kinds of Wars in much the same way Amalgamated Breakfast Foods, Inc., would sell the masses Bliss Through Crunchiness and Regular Elimination. Business saw mankind's love of money, prestige, and self as a boundless field to be tilled, gentled

182

along, cultivated—while Intelligence deemed such love a vulnerability to be exploited ruthlessly. People like Morgan were welcome in Intelligence because they understood this linkage, this similarity of perceptions and goals. Filled with a militant zeal, the Morgans of Intelligence would nonetheless use the facades of Business—three-button suits, piety, and pseudo altruism—to chew up, swallow, and grow fat on less cunning competitors. And, because Groot considered himself a businessman, he esteemed those agents who demonstrated like characteristics. Morgan, graying and slightly pompous and bearded, was among his favorites.

The plate glowed, and Morgan's head and shoulders appeared.

"Hello, Morgan. You're in Jacksonville, I take it."

"Yes, sir. I decided to use Omicron because I'm not certain of the St. Augustine phone security."

"So how are you progressing as the eminent archeologist?"

Morgan smiled politely. "That's what I want to talk to you about. As Dr. Floyd Samuels, professor of anthropology and archeology at Florida State University, my time might be running out."

"Oh? What's your problem?"

"The usual—the invariable—problem in our business: coincidence. Wretched, destructive, unpredictable, damnable coincidence. In my cover as an archeologist on a field dig with my 'students'— Masterson, Bolinsky, and Fawcett, of our Cleveland office—I've had the rotten luck to pick up a real archeologist. A rather smug, self-satisfied young man named Paul Driscoll, who is working under a special

183

Federal grant. He's pursuing a study of the Castillo de San Marcos—St. Augustine's old fort. Which would be all right, but he keeps sticking his nose into what we're doing, and I think he's beginning to suspect we're not all we're cracked up to be.''

"How so?"

"He keeps asking what we're doing, and why. And, as you know, the four of us were able to do only a fast, superficial study on the archeology cover before we plopped down in St. Augustine. I'm afraid our answers are growing a bit thin for him and he'll be checking the university for our credentials."

Groot sighed. Why were things always so complicated, so difficult? "Do you know which agency has given this Driscoll fellow his grant? And his St. Augustine address?"

"The Interior Department, I believe. He's staying at the Monson Motel."

"All right. I'll take care of it."

"That would be very helpful," Morgan said with just the right amount of appreciation—a hair short of obsequiousness.

"Do you see anything of Wagner?"

"Very little. He's on the run a great deal, as you know. I do believe, however, that he's staying with a friend, a private investigator named Robert Veck, while his wife's away. Presumably he feels it's not safe to stay at his own home."

Groot sniffed. "He's probably right. It was one of the good sides of coincidence, by the way, when his wife was summoned to Colorado."

"What was that all about?"

"I don't know, really. Something about an inheritance. Whatever, it worked to our advantage." Groot stifled a yawn and reached for his coffee cup. "So how about your mission? What do you have to report?"

Morgan touched his beard with his fingers, gently, as if assuring himself it was still there. Groot detected a strain of vanity in Morgan, a trait he had never understood, since he himself had such a poor self-image. "The influx continues," Morgan said in his professional way. "A rather impressive number of aliens has entered surreptitiously, and the rendezvous area is, according to Fawcett, who I've sent out as a probe, south of Palatka, near Lake George. There's an old resort camp on the west shore, and the aliens are gathering there, ostensibly as a Christian evangelist international conference kind of thing. At least that's what they've told the owners of the camp when it was rented."

"They're coming in by boat?"

"Mm. I can't prove it yet, but they come up from the Antilles on tramp steamers, transfer to shrimp boats at sea somewhere off the northeast Florida coast, then come in under cover of darkness and are dropped off in the Matanzas Bay in St. Augustine. Pretending to be tourists, they are staged and briefed at the Frawley Motel and then moved by car to Palatka."

Groot thought about this for an interval. Then: "They're all Cubans?"

"They certainly seem to be. The ones we've watched. There may be some Central Americans, South Americans in the lot, but they seem mostly to be Cubans."

"How many would you estimate by now?"

"Close to a thousand. Not counting those who might've sneaked in via the Inland Waterway and the West Coast of Florida."

"God! Can't we send in troops to round them up?"

"It would cost a lot. Fawcett tells me that Castro has already placed a high-yield nuke in Miami. The slightest move against Palatka sets it off. Meanwhile, teams are being sent out to snatch key public figures as an additional assurance against any countermoves the Yankees might make."

"We have no options then. We have to find the Squeaky. Failing that, we've got to go public, instruct the custodians of the bomb how to negate the Dooms-day setting, then, perhaps, give Castro a Squeaky."

Morgan said, "There's another option."

"What's that?"

"Nuke Cuba."

"No. We'd be at war with the Soviets in minutes."

"Looks to me as if we will be anyhow," Morgan said gloomily.

Groot fought his monumental depression by deliberately moving on. "Anything else to report?"

"No, sir. Just the thing with Driscoll. It could really complicate things if he were to tumble our cover."

"As I say, I'll take care of that."

"Fine, fine. Much obliged."

"What are your plans now, Morgan?"

"To go back to St. Augustine, of course. The Jacksonville office is loaning me some long-range listeners for use at the evangelism camp. I want to hear what our Cubans are saying to each other."

The phone chirped again, and Groot said, "Well?"

"The President on the Harrisburg relay, sir."

186

Groot glanced at Morgan and dismissed him with an eyebrow. Morgan nodded goodbye, and his image faded to black. Groot returned the painting to its place and activated the Harrisburg connection. He leaned toward the speaker, as if in an unconscious bow toward the Diety in Washington.

"Good evening, Mr. President."

"Hello, Groot," the patrician voice drawled amiably. "Are you still alive and well in Wilmington, Delaware?"

"Yes, sir."

"Good. I haven't been in Wilmington in ages. There's a restaurant there that serves the most extraordinary quiche. I forget what it's called. . . ."

"Margaret's Place."

"Yes. That's it. I'd like to go there again some day. That's one of the rotten parts of this job—not being able to go where you want to go."

"Yes, sir. I imagine so." Groot waited politely for the President to finish his it's-so-lonely-at-the-top routine.

"About this Squeaky thing, Groot: I received a call from the West German chancellor a few minutes ago. He's deeply concerned over the hijack in Bavaria and the likelihood the device is still somewhere in Germany. He wants our assurance there'll be no nuclear blast."

Because he didn't know what else to say, Groot said, "Please inform the chancellor, sir, that we have traced the bomb to the Western Hemisphere and that the situation is under control."

"I've already informed him we have things under control, Groot. My question to you is: Do we?"

"It's touch-and-go right at the moment, Mr. President."

"Well, we've got to do better, of course. We have a major catastrophe in the making. Are you sure we shouldn't have more people on it?"

"I'm sure, Mr. President. To swamp it with people would almost guarantee a leak—a tearing of the secrecy envelope we've established. One word of this to the public and we'd have a major panic. My God, sir, do you remember the public flap—the evacuation of towns and the hue and cry when the Californians heard we were going to spray the med-fly? That was insecticide. Can you imagine what'll happen when the people hear that a Squeaky is bashing around among some loose nuts?"

"Well, keep with it, Groot. We're counting on you."

"Yes, sir."

"Call me direct on this relay at any time. This matter has absolute top priority. Over everything."

"Yes, sir."

"War is vey close, Groot."

"Yes, sir. You have my absolute commitment, Mr. President."

"I know that, Groot. Good luck."

"Thank you, Mr. President."

The connection was broken, and Groot sat for a long time, staring at the glistening mahogany of his desk. Then, sighing, he pushed himself erect and crossed the deep carpet to the lavatory door. He went to the medicine cabinet, opened the mirrored panel, and rotated the aspirin bottle through two complete turns. The rear wall of the shower stall slid aside with a hissing sound and he passed through to the communications room.

"Hello, O'Malley."

"Mr. Groot."

"I want you to set up some correspondence for me."

"Yes, sir."

"It must go out this evening. Speed is an absolute essential."

"From where, sir?"

"The Department of the Interior. On the appropriate letterhead for Study Grants, archeology, signed by the appropriate executive. To Paul Driscoll, Monson Motel, St. Augustine, Florida. Make it a Dear-Mr. letter, summoning Driscoll to a meeting of grant recipients in the Mayflower Hotel in Washington. Include airplane tickets and hotel reservations. An expense voucher. He must be there by noon, the day after tomorrow. Arrange to have Fred Gilway's people meet him and stall him for at least three days. Any questions from Gilway, refer him to me on the Beta circuit. OK?"

"Yes, sir."

"How's your wife?"

"Better, sir. Thanks."

"Good. Well, then. Get that letter out pronto, my boy."

"Yes, sir."

"And date it and postmark it three days back so Driscoll will think it came straight mail."

"Sure thing, sir. I'll send it facsimile to Jacksonville within the hour for hand-delivery to the St. Augustine post office. The letter will be delivered by lunchtime tomorrow."

"Speaking of which, I'm ready for some breakfast.

If you need me for anything, Louise will know where I am."

"Yes, Mr. Groot."

When he returned to his office, a call from Wagner was waiting.

"Where are you now, Wagner?"

"St. Augustine phone booth. I have a report."

Groot pressed the recording button on the flank of his phone set. "Go ahead."

"I have made contact with the Florida Mafia and the anti-Castro Cubans. My investigation shows that the Squeaky was stolen by Castro Cubans, hijacked en route to Havana by anti-Castros, and is being hidden, presumably in the Miami area. The original plan, it seems, was simply to deny Castro his Squeaky. But now Castro is planning to seize key Florida locations as hostage until the Squeaky's fuse is returned to him. The bomb we can keep. The fuse he wants."

"Florida? *Hostage*?"

"Yeah."

"You've got to be kidding."

"That's what I said. It turns out nobody's kidding."

"I can't believe it."

"I don't either," Wagner said.

"What do you mean?"

"The whole idea's too heavy-handed. Castro's a cool man. Invading Florida is just not his style. He'd send in a few people. Highly trained, dedicated agents with excellent contacts. He'd do everything very quietly. A thousand troops? Seizing atomic plants? Airports? Holding mayors hostage? I don't buy it. Castro wants to be a statesman, not a suicide."

Groot sat back in his chair, his chest feeling devoid

190

of air, his hands cold. "It's just crazy enough to have some validity, though."

"That's what worries me, too, Groot."

"Any particular reason?"

"Yeah. A bunch of people in Daytona beach just got shot up over the whole thing. Who's going to risk a first-class gun fight in a tenderloin beanery over a mere silly rumor?"

"Daytona?"

"Mm. That's where I found my anti-guy. With the help of a godfather type in Eustis."

"These are reliable people?"

"What's reliable, Groot? Are you reliable? Am I reliable?"

"So what are you getting at, Wagner?"

"I think we ought to have the Secretary of State, or somebody, call up Castro and tell him flat out to get his people out of Florida or we'll start rounding them up."

"We can't."

"Why not?"

"Because I've just learned that Castro has already planted an atomic device in Miami to preclude our doing so."

"Where did you learn that?" There was anger in Wagner's question.

"From one of our people working another angle of this thing. To confront Castro openly, to move against his people here, would be to launch an international panic."

Wagner snorted. "What in hell's name do you think you'll have when Castro goes public on his own, announcing that Florida's closed until further notice?"

"That's precisely why we must find the Squeaky and recover the fuse or destroy it. We must find it before Castro is ready to move openly. And we must find it in two days, or it'll go off. And then everything will be academic anyhow." Groot ran a hand through his thinning hair. "Now: do you need any help—any people—equipment?"

But he'd asked the question of a dial tone.

20

Eva had just crossed a river called the Black Angus between Tomville and Foley when she became aware of the helicopter. The night was cold, and so she had the car windows closed tightly, but after a time she was aware of the thumping sound—a rhythmic overhead vibration. It came low, and a brilliant light suddenly swept the area and eventually settled on the car itself. She thought she heard shots, but she couldn't be sure.

The road was very straight and virtually devoid of traffic, so she kept the accelerator to the floor and hoped determinedly that she could reach Foley before the helicopter came close enough to do real damage. Then the light went out as suddenly as it had appeared, and the thumping was gone, and she was driving again by the headlights alone.

She wondered what had happened to her fear. It was as if the act of steering a speeding car, her eyes straining into the flat light ahead, glimpsing the blacker blacks rushing past her in the flanking blackness, had moved her out of herself, beyond herself. The danger was all around, but her blood had cooled, her breathing had subsided, her heart had resumed its anonymous work; she was Baron von Richthofen, guiding his triplane through the crackling tempest, impassive behind his goggles.

She was capable, by God.

That was the word. She was capable of defending herself, out-thinking enemies. She was a warrior.

A truck loomed ahead, a mountain of glare and red lights, vooming past with a thunder that shook the Ford and the adjacent night. And then she was alone again on the arrow-like highway, the humming motor and rushing wind and the blackness marking the perimeters of her existence.

She had learned to drive in the summer of her sixteenth birthday. Uncle George, the farmer with a spread of boulders and tree stumps that never produced anything but moonshine and chickens, had always been overly fond of her, in a slyly erotic, kissin'-kin way that embarrassed her even to remember. She'd been a tease, pretending to discourage him while in truth enjoying his lusting as one of the few real compliments she had ever received from that side of the family. And so, when he had offered to take her up to the meadow and show her how to drive his 1954 pickup truck (which he loved more than his slatternly little wife and almost as much as his "shine"), she readily accepted, knowing as she did that the old coot would use the occasions to sit too close and pat her knee and otherwise make a fool of himself. For all of that, she developed an instant affinity for the art of driving, and within a few weeks even Uncle George had agreed that there wasn't much else he could teach her. Which must have disappointed him considerably, because he had clearly thrived under her hypocritical postures of innocence, her subtle participation in his libidinous games. He had smiled more than she'd ever seen him, talking a blue streak, showing open interest in the things she'd had to say, and even taking on a healthier color—presumably because, having heard her say how she hated the smell of alcohol on people, he had practiced a level of abstinence never before achieved by him or anyone else in his rotten little clan.

So she was a good driver, a fact acknowledged, too,

by Pete Upton, the son of Gladys Upton, the grade school teacher, when he'd come home from Nam and won the county fair stock car race the first afternoon and tried to get her into a motel that very evening. But she had flattered his driving and persuaded him to show her how to accelerate into a curve, and after two hours of showing off, he'd passed out, leaving her unviolated and drunkenly praised as a good ole gal who sure knew how to drive.

Her problem now was which direction to drive.

The initial compulsion had been to go due east as fast and far as possible, pressing for mileage toward Florida and Roger and safety. But logic moved in to replace the incipient panic, and with the new self-image of competence, she was able to analyze the situation. Behind her was Colorado Springs and its commercial airport, busy with beautiful planes leaving in abundance for all points east. But the field was probably also very busy with people looking for her. Kidnappers who could afford rambling luxury homes and maids and Mercedes-Benzes and helicopters could most certainly afford a watch on airline ticket counters and loading gates. Another problem was the Ford: the kidnappers had probably already reported it stolen so that the police would present another reason why she shouldn't continue driving. Money she had; credit cards; licenses. All right, then: Find an airport they couldn't possibly be watching. A small municipal airport, say, where a plane and pilot could be hired. And find it before either the helicopter or the cops found her.

She cleared a slight rise and the headlights picked up a grove of scrub trees to the right of the road. As she allowed the Ford to decelerate, her mind examined, then approved an idea for action.

The Ford followed her touch and swung off the pavement, its tires crunching gravel and throwing stones against the undersides. Pulling among the trees, she turned off the lights and sat in the sudden, overwhelming darkness. She rolled down the side window so that she might hear better.

There was only the sound of the restless wind, sighing in the naked branches. And the cold, coming through the window like a tangible fog.

The helicopter was gone.

But she waited a full three minutes by the dashboard clock, just to be sure. It was a difficult thing for her to do, because something in the darkness and cold and muttering wind got to her core and replaced her earlier confidence with uneasiness. No. Dread. More than uneasiness, less than genuine terror. Dread. And the feeling, oddly, was heightened by the absence of helicopter sounds, as if she could be more threatened by her aloneness than by the presence of enemies.

Satisfied at last, she started the motor and got the car moving again, wheels spinning, rear end fishtailing. Only after returning to the highway did she turn on the lights.

Two miles later, the road arced over another rise and into a gentle turn to the right, falling away then into a shallow descent toward a two-lane bridge over what appeared to be a dry creek bed.

Between her and the bridge, the helicopter.

Poised on the highway, crosswise, its rotors windmilling, its drab flanks glinting dully in the headlight glare.

Three men standing to one side, their legs bent at the knees, their hands cupped around pistols.

End of the line, Eva-baby.

Maybe.

But for them, too.

She pressed her foot against the pedal, hard, and crouched behind the wheel, head held high enough to permit her to see over the hood.

Under the tail. Go under the tail, Eva.

Three holes showed in the windshield glass, small round things, neatly drilled, radiating thousands of tiny cracks. The wind sound became a keening, and the steering wheel trembled in her hands, and she threw on the high beams and leaned on the horn, as before.

The little wedge of men broke finally and there was a scrambling to get clear of the onrushing Ford.

"Run, you bastards!" She heard herself shouting this.

She drove the car at full speed into the helicoper's lazily spinning tail rotor. The crash was explosive, filling the night with clatterings and tinklings and the shriek of violated metals. The Ford careened from side to side, and she fought to keep it from slewing into a full skid and overturning. The windshield was gone, leaving a great openness that filled the car with a booming, blinding rush of dust and wind and splinters.

But she kept on.

The motor still hummed, and the steering was still taut and responsive, and only one headlight was broken, and she murmured thanks to an unspecific god for all of it. Beyond the bridge the road straightened

again, and squinting against the rumbling, gritty slip-
stream, she was able to keep going, despite running
eyes and stinging cheeks and the inability to breathe.

Aberrantly, her thoughts went to Lindsay and his
self-righteous speech on the population explosion and
the need to control it. His necktie, and the way he kept
fussing with it; his prim little suit with its prim little
boutonnière; his talcumed cheeks and barbered hair
and glassy shoes and his smell of bay rum. He was a
kidnapper, of course. A killer, too, since he and his people were trying to shoot her, and he believed in doing
away with populations.

But what she really didn't like about him was his
polished fingernails.

A man who polished his nails was a man who
couldn't be trusted. He might even cheat on his in-
come tax.

She laughed, feeling the touch of hysteria.

21

The bars had closed at last, and the parking lots—asphalt arenas for after-hours squabbles and clutching, back-seat liaisons and mini drag-races and drug parties—had fallen mercifully still. A gentle rain had begun to patter on the deserted town, and Wagner sat in the cold darkness of Bob Veck's porch, looking down on St. George street and missing Eva very much. It was absolutely not right that he'd been unable to reach her by phone. There was a fundamental injustice in this, a gross irony; a man who lived by speedy, sophisticated communications should be able to pick up a mere telephone and get through to his wife in a Colorado hotel. But now she wasn't even in the hotel, having checked out, according to the desk clerk—What was his name?—for a trip to see a friend in Boulder, and, no, she'd left no forwarding address. What was with her, anyway? Where did she get off, going all this time—How many days?—without even a facsimile postcard?

He wasn't meant for marriage, after all was said and done. He sipped his beer, and it tasted sour, perhaps in concord with his bitter acknowledgement of what had been obvious from the start. He was a man who wanted to love and was afraid to love because it might break something in him when it ended. Everything ended, always; and he had spent much of his life trying not to start things that would hurt him when they came to nothing. And, despite his absolutely appalling vulnerability to heartbreak, he'd done the most heartbreaking thing of all: love a woman and marry her. And now it was ending, and he was alone and lonely in a world that would itself be ending soon.

He was very tired, and sleep—a long, uninterrupted time of oblivion—would have been a gift of rare value. But this would have to do, this sporadic dozing in a Boston rocker, sipping beer and watching the rain on nighttime streets and wondering what had happened to the giant toughness, the singleminded wariness, of Fidel Castro that would induce him to launch a major commando invasion of the United States. It was the largest discord in history, a contradiction of the character and canniness that had kept the resilient Cuban alive and well through decades of court intrigues, bush-country wars, dicey collaborations, and economic catastrophes. After all the years of his calculating, intuitive, stubborn going, it simply made no sense at all for the Premier to plunge into a delirious attempt to recover a mere appliance. A Squeaky in Cuban hands would be a matter of great uneasiness and discomfort for the Yankees, no doubt about it; but a Squeaky was no more than another doodad, a piece of machinery, a Sears-Roebuck hardware item that would, if it didn't go off and begin the end of the world, be soon replaced by another gismo of even more horrendous capabilities and which, conceivably, could be coveted by the Cubans with even greater heat.

It didn't wash.

Somebody was putting somebody on.

Castro would in no wise benefit from a shooting war with the United States. And yet that was precisely what he was inviting.

Why?

And what was it that kept tugging his mind toward Germany? There was something there—a strand, a link, that represented great significance. What had he seen or heard or felt? Why did his mind keep going to the murdered kids?

He crumpled the empty beer can, pushed himself erect, and made his way to the kitchen. Taking the phone from the wall, he dialed the operator and set up a call to Munich, placing the charges on his home number.

Klatt was in his office, and his voice came through so clearly and crisply he could have been in the house next door.

"This is Koenig, Putzi," Wagner said in German.

"Good morning. Where are you?"

"In Florida."

"You sound as if you're next door."

"You probably couldn't hear me at all if I were, the way the phones work these days."

"I assume this isn't a social call, since it's about three o'clock in the morning where you are."

"You remember my call of the other day? When I asked about a farmer named Schattner?"

"Mm. The one you wanted to know was he still breathing."

"Could you arrange to facsimile me via satellite a biography on Schattner? Plus ID photos of those murdered college kids, Schattner, and Siegfried Unger. Good, clear, head-and-shoulders shots."

"Sure. What's your charge number?"

"A-four-oh-thirty-seven-hundred X."

"Where do you want it all sent?"

"General Delivery, Post Office, St. Augustine, Florida, USA, thirty-two-oh-eighty-four plus ninety-one-seventy-two."

"All right. I'll have it out to you by this afternoon. Anything else?"

"Yes. Whatever happened to Hans Trille?"

There was a moment of hesitation. "Trille, the police inspector who turned out to be head of the infamous Terror Alliance?"

"The one who resigned after the U.S. President almost got shot during a summit meeting in Munich. That Trille."

"I know very well which Trille," Klatt said, slightly testy. "You mentioned him before, too."

"Yes. But I never asked you where he is, what he's doing these days."

"I don't like to talk about renegade cops."

"I don't like to talk about piles, either, but I mention them now and then to my doctor."

"You're a smart-aleck, Koenig. I don't know why I put up with you."

"Because I'm a winsome tad, all full of bubbly good cheer."

"Fah."

"So where's Trille?"

"Last I heard he's running some kind of aerial delivery service in the Friedrichshafen area. He was a war flyer, you know."

"Ho."

"What does that mean?"

" 'Ho' is an old American colloquialism that means, no wonder I was so itchy about Germany—the thing was right in front of my nose all the time and I should have seen it."

"What a strange language. All those words, all that meaning, from one little syllable."

"Get me an update on Trille, too, will you, Putzi?"

"I'll do it, but I won't enjoy it."

"Send it along with the other stuff."

"All right."

"I thank you, Putzi. I really do."

"Ho. Which is an old German colloquialism that means it puzzles me all to hell and back when you Yankee fellows ever get any sleep, running around Florida at three o'clock in the morning and phoning Europe and complicating life for diligent, handsome, charming, and hardworking German police inspectors."

"I've never phoned a diligent, handsome, charming, and hardworking German police inspector in my whole life."

"Bah!"

Klatt hung up and Wagner pulled some things from the refrigerator and made himself a sandwich. He stood in the silence of the place, chewing thoughtfully and sipping occasionally from a fresh can of beer. He suddenly missed Veck, wishing for the man's mere presence. To talk with him about this snarl of worms was impossible, of course, and so it would accomplish nothing of practical value to have Veck on hand; but there was this heavy loneliness, this sense of being isolated in a backwater of time and events, and a bit of Veck's zany conversation would have done a lot of good for the old morale. Things were probably not a hell of a lot better for Veck, either, come to think of it. A private investigator's life was a dreariness of cheap motel rooms, all-night diners, solitary vigils in parked cars, calling phones that never answered, tapping on unfriendly doors and hoping that whoever answered wasn't a nut with a gun or a knife or a fireplace poker.

Veck could have cheered him up about now, Wagner judged, but Veck could probably have used a touch of the same medicine out there in Alabama or Louisiana or wherever he said he would be this week. One thing for certain: Veck would have an idea or two on where he might find a Castro agent.

It was a real pain, this having to work so close to the chest, or whatever the idiom was. The only sane move at this point was to set up a parley with the Cuban premier and enlist his help in negating the Squeaky's fuse. Let him have his bomb; let him make his score on the hated Yankees; let him scare the hell out of the whole western hemisphere. But get someone to flip the switch to "off."

Panic-shmanic.

The important thing was to stop the ticking.

He sat on the sofa to do more thinking and fell asleep with the first thought, which was of how tired he was. He was in a large meadow, presumably created by the salami and cheese sandwich, and he was running from a creature that was always behind him and therefore never quite identifiable. His feet were nearly impossible to move because with each step they sank into a taffy-like mud beneath the grass. He was about to give up when the creature stopped its growling and began a soft, rhythmic, insistent clucking sound.

No. A tapping sound.

He came awake.

The room was still dark, and his watch told him he'd been sleeping for no more than twenty minutes.

The tapping was at the door.

"Who is it?"

"I've got to see you," a woman's voice said faintly.

He slid the bolt, leaving the chain fastened, and opened the door a few inches.

"Audrey?"

"Let me in. It's important."

22

"You're alone, aren't you?"

He nodded. "Yes. But. . . ."

"I know Veck's away," she said, unbuttoning her raincoat, "but you might have sneaked a little somebody in for, ah, companionship on these long rainy nights."

"What's going on, Audrey?" he said, taking her coat and continuing to regard her with mild astonishment. "What are you doing out so late? Or early. Or whatever it is."

"Well," she breathed, dropping onto the sofa and leaning back against its cushions in mock weariness, "that's what I want to ask you: What's going on?"

"I don't follow you."

"Do you have anything to drink around here?"

"Beer. Coffee. I think there's a little whiskey somewhere."

"Whiskey's fine. Straight, in a small glass. No ice."

He saw to it, and when she had given the drink a tentative sip and showed an appropriately appreciative expression, she gave him a direct, protracted stare, and he could see that her affability was a pose that was hard for her to maintain.

"All right, Audrey. I've given you your drink. Now you give me an explanation."

"Sure," she said reasonably. "But first I want to make a deal."

"About what?"

"I want firm assurance from you that what I'm about to say to you goes no further."

He shrugged. "I'll have to hear it first. But if you're pregnant and need a loan, I'm afraid you've come to

206

the wrong guy. I'm damned near broke myself."

"No, I'm not pregnant." She laughed with genuine amusement. "I wish it were that simple."

"Where's your hardboiled-waitress-with-a-heart-of-gold, Audrey? You're talking like a schoolmarm."

She tasted the whiskey again. Peering into the glass, she said mildly, "I'm a Cuban agent, Roger. I've been working for Premier Castro for eleven years."

Wagner sat down in the overstuffed chair and tried manfully to look unruffled. It was all he could do to keep from staring at her with an open mouth. "Oh?" he said. "Why do you tell me this?"

"Because my Havana bureau has given me a full make on you. You are recently retired from the Central Intelligence Agency, where you compiled a record of excellent accomplishment, highlighted by your rather spectacular negation of a plot involving Hans Trille, Munich police inspector, and other clandestine Nazis, to kidnap the American President. That was a dilly, really, and I truly admire you for it."

"T'warn't nuthin'."

She raised her hands in a silent and exaggerated parody of applause. "Oh, yes, it was."

"So you think I was a peachy agent. So what do you want from me? An autograph?"

"I've been following you recently. You are a clever fellow. I could use a few men like you."

"Oh, come off it, Audrey. What the hell do you want?"

"A run-down on what you're up to." She said this in an offhand way, as if she had just asked him to pass the salt.

"What do you mean, what I'm up to?"

"It's your turn to come off it, Roger. You've been working on something for the CIA, and I simply must know what it is."

He sniffed and shook his head. "Hoo-boy. Is that the way Fidel's spies work? Just walk in on somebody and say, 'Hey—tell me all your secrets, eh?' If so, you might just have revolutionized the spy biz. Cut out all the cute cloak-and-dagger stuff and get right to the point. Fabulous."

"Be serious," she said irritably. "I. . . ."

He broke in, hot with his own irritability. "Serious? Godamighty, woman! I run my katootie off for a million hours without sleep; I get shot at; I am jazzed by hoods; I live on beer and dry sandwiches; I don't even have the time to watch the cartoons on morning TV. And you say I'm not serious? My aching GI back."

"What are you working on? What was that shoot-'em-up in Daytona all about?"

"None of your frigging business."

"I know where Mrs. Wagner's being held."

He gave her a look, feeling the ice forming behind his belt buckle. "Held?"

"I'll tell you where. If, of course, you tell me what's going on."

"What have you done with my wife?" he managed.

"I haven't done anything with your wife. Somebody else has. All I know is where they're holding her. I had some people tail her when she went to Colorado, on the chance that she might be running an errand for you and your CIA bosses. My people tell me that somebody else seems similarly concerned, since they removed Mrs. Wagner from her Colorado Springs hotel and drove her to a certain address."

Wagner gave himself the customary silent speech he always delivered to himself when facing moments of personal crisis. *Don't panic, Roger. Breathe slowly and evenly, and think of the universal truth: none of this will seem important this time next year. There are always answers, always ways to work things out, either directly or by compromise. Until the answers are forthcoming, breathe slowly and evenly and give not the slightest indication that you've just wet your pants.*

"What's going on, Audrey," he grated, his anger held behind clenched teeth, "is that World War Three is about to begin. Within two days."

She sniffed. "Really, now, Roger. . . ."

"I mean it, Audrey. All the commandos you've brought into Florida, all the bombs you've planted in Miami notwithstanding, your chances of finding the Squeaky here are just about nil. The anti-Castro people in Miami are in the process—right now—of sneaking the damned thing into Havana. And, meanwhile, if that isn't enough, the U.S. of A. is so ticked off about the commandos and your plans to seal off Florida while you look for the Squeaky that every nuke between here and Big Sur is now leveled on Fidel's beard."

Audrey placed her glass on the coffee table, carefully. "Just what in hell are you talking about? Commandos? Bombs in Miami? The Squeaky? What does this mean—?"

"*Where is my wife?*"

"You haven't answered my question."

"I've told you: Cuba is about to be incinerated. Twice. By the Squeaky you dumb bastards stole from us in Germany and which was stolen from you by the Castro opposition in Miami. By the eighty jillion missiles that will come pouring in from the north. How specific can I get, for God's sake?"

"What's a Squeaky?"

"You're joking."

"I'm not joking. My government has told me nothing of all this."

"You're joking."

"Will you stop saying that?" Her face was pink with anger and undisguised confusion. "I'm being very honest with you. I am one of Cuba's ranking intelligence officers, and I have not been told any of this. Why do you think I've been following you around? If I knew what you know, I wouldn't have had to."

Wagner could see her worry now. "It looks to me," he said, putting salt in her wound, "as if you're no longer considered to be such a hotshot by the people in Havana. They've got a major thing going, and you're not clued in. My-oh-my."

"What's a Squeaky?"

"Where's my wife?"

"I'll not tell you until I have your answer."

"And you won't have my answer until I know where my wife is."

Audrey's gray eyes considered him for a long, thoughtful moment. She said finally, "Let's be reasonable about this, Roger. What you're saying has serious implications."

"Serious *implications*? That's like saying the Atlantic Ocean is quite a sink hole. Lordy, Audrey, I'm talking World War *Three*. Don't you understand? This is the *big* one."

210

Audrey stood up, her plain face openly troubled. "I'm going to have to take this up with my superiors."

"You'd better make it fast. Your superiors are due to become wisps of cigar smoke. Remind them that the U.S. of A. is, by law and policy, compelled to use all means to combat international terrorism, including armed force. Assure them that the U.S. of A. is entirely ready to expend Florida and take on the Soviets rather than put up with your invasion. Tell them that a Squeaky is, at this very moment, being smuggled ashore on some sandy beach near Havana, and that it's set to go off in two days. Tell your superiors that their little commando exercise has put them squarely between the rock and the hard place. And then go look for a job where you are trusted enough to be told what's going on."

She crossed the room and stood by the door. "I take it that the Squeaky is a nuclear Doomsday device."

"What else?" he said sourly.

Audrey sighed. "All right, Roger. I'll tell them. But remember your promise. You will tell no one else of this conversation."

"I promised you nothing. You've given me nothing."

"Your wife is being held in a private home on County Road Fourteen east of Colorado Springs near the village of Foley. The number on the rural mail box at the entrance gate is Two-oh-seven. The property is listed at the court house as being owned by a law firm named Winfield and Lindsay."

"All right. I've just promised."

"Good. I'll be back to you."

"As I say, Audrey: make it fast."

* * *

"Groot?"

"What is it, Wagner?"

"That was a rotten trick you pulled."

"Trick? What are you talking about?"

"My wife. Luring her to Colorado. Holding her hostage to make sure I'd do what you wanted me to do."

"I don't follow you."

"Goddamn you, Groot! You're so sneaky you're going to sneak right up your own behind one of these days. Which is where you belong."

"Wagner, what in God's name are you ranting about?"

"My wife. That's what I'm ranting about. You dangle a hundred thousand in front of her just to get her out of town so I can work for you. Well, I tell you one thing, buster: we're going to take that hundred thou."

"I've had nothing whatsoever to do with your wife's leaving town. I'll admit I was pleased by the coincidence, but it was just that. A coincidence."

"Winfield and Lindsay isn't a CIA front?"

"Winfield and Lindsay? Who are they?"

"You mean that, Groot? You don't know?"

"What *is* all this, anyhow—?"

"The CIA did *not* lure my wife to Colorado Springs?"

"Of course not. Why should we?"

"Who did, then?"

"I haven't the slightest notion."

"Jesus God."

"Wagner— *Wagner*?"

212

DAY 8

23

From the phone booth Wagner went back to Veck's house, his weariness almost beyond further management. His mind was entirely on Eva, out there somewhere, alone and frightened and with no understanding of what had happened to her. He looked at himself, trying to find the fury and outrage of a husband whose wife was being abused, but he found none, eventually admitting that he was simply too tired—too weighted down by physical, mental, and spiritual fatigue and the gathering recognition of failure and imminent destruction. He had faced death often in his lugubrious lifetime but never had he perceived the reality of ceasing to be as clearly as he did now. The world was mad, certifably insane, and the stupid goddam noods—whoever they were and whatever their flaky reasons—were about to incinerate half the world. The half Eva was in. The half he was in. Squeaky would squeak, and he and Eva and Groot and all the Dagwoods and Blondies and Ivans and Olgas and Hansels and Gretels and Pedros and Ninas would become cosmic dust. When it happened he must be with her. There was nothing more important. And within the depression and indefinable guilt was the understanding that whatever lay beyond the Squeaky's squeak would have to be better than this madness, and so he would—must—find her, calmed by a do-it-yourself theology that said *When it all comes finally to nothing, it ends up as Something.*

When he opened the door, Veck was there, eating a sandwich and drinking a beer, as usual.

"Well," Veck said through a mouthful, "Little Sheba has come home at last."

"Not for long."

"My God, Wagner. What's the matter with you? You look awful."

"I've got to go out of town."

"To a sanitarium, I hope."

"Did my laundry come back?"

"Yeah. It's on your bed. Where you headed?"

"Colorado Springs. Somebody's kidnapped my wife."

Veck swallowed noisily. "You're kidding."

"No."

"How do you know this? I mean. . . ."

"Where's my suitcase?"

"I put it in your closet there. But what. . . ."

"I'm going to need your help, Robert."

"Name it."

Wagner began throwing things into the overnight bag. "I'm working on a drug caper. A kind of government sting operation. I need to confirm something. It calls for a tail job, but I have to go to Colorado and find Eva, so I can't do it. And time is running out on me. I'm under a hellish deadline."

"So who do you want tailed?"

"Informants tell me that the main druggist sends in his wholesalers from the sea—or from Matanzas bay, actually. They are said to land near the Castillo and go to the Frawley motel for briefing. I want a surveillance of the Frawley. I want a record of who comes and goes. Starting right away."

"O.K. You want pix? Names?"

"Yeah. What happens there from now until, say, day after tomorrow. Anything you can learn, anything you can photo."

"Where'll you be?"

"I'll have to call you."

"So when'll you be back?"

"I'll rent one of those executive jets at the St. Augustine airport. Three hours out, three hours back, whatever it takes between."

Veck polished off his beer and stopped a burp with his fist. "You need any tools? Hardware?"

"I wouldn't know what to take."

"How about a shootin' arn?"

"I never carry a gun."

"But you're going to storm a kidnapper's castle. You can't do it bare-knuckled."

"I'll be all right. Hand me that comb and brush there."

"How about a T-47? A little something you can use to call me if you get in a jam."

Wagner gave him a look. "A T-47? The way I hear it, that's a very new, special, top secret item reserved by the intelligence agencies."

Veck humphed. "Maybe so. But I'm a very efficient fellow with very efficient suppliers."

"Well, I suppose anybody who's got the Mafia in his pocket can get hold of a little old radio."

"The only thing I can't get a hold on, Meester Wagnair, is my own life. I can straighten out everybody's problems but my own."

"I know the feeling."

"When you're finished packing, come into the den. I'll show you how the T-47 works."

"I thought you had all your hardware in your office on the Plaza."

Veck smiled. "All the show-window stuff. The special stuff I keep here. You need something special, just ask.''

"Toss me those slippers, will you?"

"You want me to call the plane rental service for you?"

"Good idea. You do that while I shave."

"Zu Befehl, mein Führer." Veck clicked his heels and bowed stiffly in the old Prussian manner.

"And tell them I'll pay any premium to have the plane and crew ready and waiting in thirty minutes. Tell them I'll want the plane to stand by in Colorado Springs. And tell them to have a rental car waiting for me there."

"Hoo-boy. You talk like a guy with money. Do you know the going rate for jet charters these days?"

"It must run about forty cents an hour, at least."

Veck shrugged, shook his head, and turned for the hall and the phone.

"By the way," Wagner said, "do you have any pals on the Daytona police force?"

"A couple. Why?"

"There was a lot of shooting at a bar down there yesterday. I was caught in the middle of it and got out by the skin of my *tokus.* But there's no mention of it in the papers or on the tube. Maybe one of your pals can tell me why."

"What bar?"

"A grubby little place called the Bon Vivant. On Route One's worst part, with real estate and insurance offices upstairs and a couple of vacant lots around it."

"Who was shooting?"

"Some Cubans."

218

"Hell," Veck grunted, "that's why it's not in the news. Cubans shooting each other is not considered news any more."

"Be serious."

"I am serious. There's been so much killing by and among rival Cuban factions it's no longer of interest to the media. Even morbid interest among the Joe Citizens is a once-upon-a-time thing. A couple weeks ago I saw a Cuban kid with a knife handle sticking out of his chest. He was lying in the parking lot of a Taco Tillie's drive-in. People were stepping over him to get to their cars and driving around him when they left. I checked him out, and he was deader'n a doornail. When I called the cops, they were twenty minutes getting there. Why? He was the fifth Cuban to turn up homicided that morning, and, the prowl car guy told me, he had to wait his turn."

"God."

"It's a cruel world. The weak leave it. The strong stay."

Wagner was immersed in melancholy. "Nobody likes to be helped into leaving," he said abstractly.

"Well, Rawjaw, somebody had better start helping a lot of the weaklings to leave it—soon. Or we won't have a world at all, cruel or otherwise."

"What the hell's that supposed to mean?"

"The world's population. It's growing too big. It's already too big. It's got to be reduced, curbed, controlled. If it isn't we'll starve to death. Soon."

"Oh, come off it, Robert. You sound like Adolf von Hitler."

"He was prejudiced. I'm not talking prejudice, I'm talking survival."

"You're talking horse manure."

"Nope. The world has a beeg problem, my son."

"Balls."

"You'll see."

"Call the airport, will you?"

Veck went off to the Frawley, cameras and gear bouncing on his hips, and Wagner swallowed another cup of coffee before climbing into his rented car and heading for the airport through the misty dawn. The sky over the ocean had turned pink and the street-cleaning trucks were rumbling as he drove west on Carrera and then north on Route 1. There was very little traffic at this early hour and he made all the lights. Perhaps this was an omen, he thought; maybe things would go better than he suspected they might.

The airport, a cross-hatching of blue and green and red and white lights in the fog, was silent. Nothing moved, and the array of private planes, tied down in orderly rows on the concrete apron, glinted dully and looked forlorn and somehow useless. He parked the car by the chain link fence running south from the hangar line, and, after locking the doors, made his way to the dimly-lit building whose sign announced to the sleeping world that this was the operations office and passenger check-in area of Apollo Aircraft Charter—You Doze While We Fly You There.

He pushed through the double glass doors and went to the counter where another sign said Welcome Apollo Passengers: Ring the Bell for Service. He had his hand over the bell—one of those rinky-dink things to be found in rinky-dink hotels or mama-and-papa stores—when he froze.

220

He stood there, hand outstretched, palm down, as if he had been suddenly transformed into a wax figure.

The years were with him again; he felt in his bowels the slow stir of alarm mixed with revelation—an uneasiness he first experienced as a boy when, climbing the wire fence beside a moonlit orchard, he began his ill-fated raid on Mr. Rigley's beautiful apples. The feeling had become a part of him, fine-tuned and ever-present, in the war years and, later, during the long gray span of his time in The Company. With its alarm was a mixture of prescience and expectation of the dreadful, and it had never failed him. *You Have Just Been Told Something,* it announced, unspoken, inaudible, yet clearly and insistently; *You Are On the Verge,* it said.

Here it was a smell.

The strong, unmistakable, sweet-sour trace of pipe tobacco.

He felt the thing in his gut, the turning, and he could virtually see an impression gathering in his mind. No. Not an impression. Clear understanding.

A seeing of what had been eluding him.

"Ha." The sound was soft but it gave substance, authority, confirmation to the nebulousness he was about to call an idea.

It had to be tested.

He turned and eased through the door and into the dawn-light outside, hoping his brief presence in the office hadn't alerted someone. Hurrying now, he went to a phone booth nestled against the corner of a hangar. He checked the yellow pages, dropped a silver dollar in the slot, and dialed, his eyes fixed on the check-in counter inside.

He could hear the phone ringing there.

It rang five times.

On the sixth ring, a girl emerged from a door marked Operations and made her way through the little maze of desks to pick up the phone.

"Apollo Aircraft Charter," she said in the singsong airline way.

"This is Roger Wagner. I've chartered a plane for a run to Colorado Springs this morning."

"Oh, yes, Mr. Wagner. The plane is waiting."

"Well, that's what I'm calling about. I'm being delayed here in St. Augustine and I want you to keep things on hold for a couple of hours."

He could see her turn, rest her elbow against the counter, and begin to scribble a note on a pad there. "Oh, I see. Do you have any idea of when you'll be departing, sir?"

"Not yet. Just tell the crew to stand by and keep the coffee hot."

"Might I remind you, sir, that the charter can't be delayed indefinitely? The company rule is that the. . . ."

Wagner broke in. "Oh, sure. You mean I got to pay. Sure. I know the meter's running. No problem."

She nodded, her tidy hairdo catching the light from overhead. "Very well, Mr. Wagner. We'll hold until we hear from you. Meantime, may I check your charge number?" She read it off a file folder she'd flipped open.

"Yep. That's it. Bye."

He hung up and watched her replace her phone, then turn and call through the door to Operations. After a moment a tall man appeared, crossing the desk maze to stand beside the girl at the counter and regard the note she held. A small Meerschaum dangled from the corner of his mouth, a curl of smoke rising from its well-used bowl.

The face was older, of course. But the unruffled expression, the solemn puffing, the way he reached for the phone and cradled it on his shoulder were the same as they had always been.

Hans Trille, renegade Munich cop.

Returning to his car, Wagner threw whatever will he could muster against the icy rock of sorrow and loss that now occupied his gut.

I love you, Eva. But I can't come to you yet. Hold on, my dear.

24

A rosiness began to show below the band of black, snow-filled clouds that marked the edge of the departing night. It was very cold, and Eva could feel the enormousness around her, the great, frozen expanse of featureless plains. She walked, stiff-legged, picking her way along the highway's gravel berm in a torment of weariness and despondency.

She had abandoned the Ford in a copse after its radiator had begun to steam and a severe clanking had sounded somewhere in its vitals. She had been walking for an hour and ten minutes, eyes straining against the darkness, without once seeing a car. In fact, the only signs of life she'd seen were a rabbit that had huddled, miserable and alone, beside a winter-stiffened clump of weeds, and a bird that circled in the dawn light, crying an unhappy cry, full of solitude and hunger.

She had her own hunger to deal with, remembering sadly the food she had ignored on the tray brought to her by the maid. Her last real meal had been breakfast—when? The day before? The day before what? What day was this? Perhaps she had taken too much of the whiskey; there was a confusion of time in her mind. The bottle, one of those flat little half-pint things, had been in the Ford's glove compartment. Which meant the maid must be an alcoholic, because her Uncle Murph, who often boasted that he'd been with AA since Hannibal crossed the Alps and knew more about drinking than Bacchus himself, claimed that anyone who had to have a bottle under a car seat or in a glove compartment was sure to be in trouble with booze. "Half-pints were invented for alkies," he used to say. "It's hard as hell to carry around a nice, normal quart, or fifth, or even a pint. And who the hell carries hooch around, anyhow, unless he's got the fever."

Well, she thought, *I'm carrying one in my purse, right now. So much for your claim, Uncle Murph. I had one gulp, to make me warmer, and all it did was make me want to throw up. You're a jerk, Uncle Murph. No. No, you're not. You're a dear man, and I'm sorry you know so much about drinking, because it must have cost you a lot of pain to learn.*

She took a deep breath, feeling the icy air in her throat and chest, and it seemed to help, because things became clearer, and the humming she heard proved not to be imaginary but real, a car approaching fast from the west. Its headlights, harshly brilliant, hurt her eyes.

Hands raised, she waved the universal signal to stop.

The car, large and low, passed, slowed, halted, then began to back up, its gears whining. She squinted into the back-up lights and saw the Colorado license plate. The car was a four-door Oldsmobile, dark-hued and sleek.

The door opened and a woman stepped out and seized her roughly.

"There you are, you little bitch," the woman hissed. "I owe you a punch in the nose."

"Just get her in the car, Louise," Lindsay called from the driver's seat, "and stop the horsing around."

"I'll kill her!"

"No you won't. Just get in the car. We've wasted too much time on her as it is."

Eva felt herself shoved into the front seat beside Lindsay, then the slim bulk of the maid hemmed her on the other side. *Like a dishrag, between bookends;* she thought bitterly. *After all my effort, it's come to a pair of bookends.*

Lindsay took up the microphone of the citizens' band radio mounted on the dash. "This is Jolly Roger," he said coolly. "Jolly Roger to Buccaneers: we've got her. Everybody back to the house." Then he eased the big car through a U-turn and sped west toward the graying face of the distant Rockies.

Somewhere in the long ride Eva said, "I've got to go to the bathroom."

But the others seemed not to hear.

The dawn had resolved from suggestion into fact, and the sky, showing faintly blue and cold, seemed to suggest that the dullness of deep winter was a promise soon to be realized. As she rode, Eva became aware of the austere beauty of the land through which she had been fleeing, and her mind, weary and full of defeat, went to a recollection of Havelock Ellis's bitter assurance that the sun and the moon and the stars would have disappeared long ago had they happened to be within reach of predatory human hands. The great mountains ahead, lavender under the brightening sky, would not last for long if the likes of this Lindsay and his woman were to prevail; somehow the evil ones seemed always to find ways to turn beauty to ashes, and the evil ones, she told herself, were all of us. As Pogo once said. Ellis and Pogo. Now *there* was a pair of smart-asses if there ever was one. The human race retches, and Ellis and Pogo diagnose the ailment in a smug word or two and then walk away, leaving us with the awful question of what to do about it. Anybody could see that Lindsay and—what was her name? Louise?—were evil, and that they were evil because they wanted something too badly. But what in hell do you *do* about it? Spouting epigrams isn't enough. . . .

She missed Roger very much, and she knew that she had been trying so desperately to run for the East because that's where he was; she could have fled in any direction if all she'd wanted was escape from the evil ones. But he was there, and he was all she wanted, and if she couldn't have him she wanted nothing.

Well, maybe something.

I could use another swig of the whiskey in my purse.

I'll have to do something to get away, but I'm so tired. I need something to get me moving.

Ha.

There's one for good ole Pogo: "He who fights to save his life shall booze it."

Hee-hee.

They had come into a town, one of those typical Western places with a wide main street and stores with false fronts and hitching rails and pickup trucks and big hats and pointy boots. She thought she recognized it as one she'd driven through in the night, but she couldn't be sure, since all the towns looked so much alike to her.

"I have to go to the bathroom," she said.

Lindsay continued with his driving, remote and preoccupied, and Louise sat in miserable silence.

There was an intersection ahead with a traffic light, and it was red. At the corner by the curb were two white cars emblazoned with large red letters that spelled Police. A pair of officers in Boy Scout hats leaned against the fender of the first car, looking important and cool for the lesser mortals who plodded to work through the morning dimness.

"I have your whiskey in my purse, Louise," Eva said. "Do you mind if I take it out and drink some? I'm cold and tired."

Lindsay gave Louise a sidelong glance. "Have you been at it again?"

"I just had a half-pint in my car. I was taking it to my boy friend."

"You drunken slut. We would have had none of this trouble if you had just kept the cork in the bottle. But no: you had to get a snoot-full and let this dame loose."

"I wasn't even drinking," Louise whined defensively.

"Well, for God's sake," Eva broke in, "can I have a drink or can't I?"

"Oh, go ahead," Lindsay grumped.

Eva moved the purse to her lap, opened it, and took out the half-pint. Unscrewing the top, she glanced at Louise. "You want some, too?"

"No, she doesn't," Lindsay snapped. "She has one more drink—ever—and I'll personally put her under. That's a promise."

Eva raised her left foot and, in a swift, stabbing motion, jammed it down on the toe of Lindsay's highly polished oxford, the one that rested on the accelerator pedal.

The Oldsmobile leaped wildly ahead, and Lindsay, cursing, struggled to control the wheel while trying to free his foot. During the effort, though, the car roared and screeched through the intersection, running the red light and tearing off the fender of a passing blue pickup. There was considerable clatter and the tinkling of shattered glass, and the Olds, slewing sidewise, bounced over the far curb and came to a rest with its nose in the show window of Wild Bill Fiesel's Appliance Shop and Discount Hardware.

"What in hell are you doing, you crazy broad?" Lindsay wailed.

"I'm pouring whiskey on you, you dumb bastard."

"Well, stop it."

A small crowd had gathered, of course, and one of the policemen, an enormous man with beautiful, even teeth under his black mustache, opened the door on Lindsay's side of the car and grated, "O.K., mister, come on out."

Eva said, "Officer, this man has been drinking, and I'm terrified. I refuse to ride another inch with him."

"I have *not* been drinking," Lindsay barked.

"Well," the policeman said, "somebody sure has. Phew."

They all got out of the car and stood in a little circle among the assembled citizens while the policeman and Lindsay and Wild Bill Fiesel and the little lady who had been driving the pickup traded papers and dirty looks.

"I'll have to take you to my car for a balloon-test of your breath," the policeman told Lindsay.

"I haven't been drinking, officer. This woman poured whiskey on my clothes."

"Refusal to take the test is presumed to be evidence of drunken driving, sir."

"Well, for God's sake, then. Take me to your balloon. I'll show you."

"This way, please."

As the cop led Lindsay away, Eva leaned into the Oldsmobile, unplugged the connections, and pulled the CB radio from its mounting.

"Hey," Louise complained, "what's the big idea?"

"Lindsay used this to call his little pals home. I'm not going to leave it here so he can send them back out."

"All I have to do is go to a phone," Louise warned.

"But you won't. You know that the best thing for you is to run like hell. What Lindsay will do to you when he gets you alone wouldn't go down even in a Class-B horror movie."

"Oh, jeez. What'll I do?" Louise whimpered, her swollen eyes and nose showing teary dampness.

Eva reached into her purse and withdrew a fifty-dollar bill. "Here. For the use of your car. Take it, get a ticket on a bus—any bus—and hope Lindsay never sees you again. OK?"

"Oh, jeez!"

Eva slipped away through the crowd, cut through an alley, where she dumped the radio into the lap of a dozing wino, and came upon the Municipal Courthouse, beside which was a cab stand. A Checker sat there, dusty and forlorn.

She leaned through the cabbie's window and said, "How much to the nearest airport? Where I can rent a plane."

The cabbie, a grizzled fellow with bushy eyebrows and a goatee to match, said, "Pinkton Airport. Luke Tooley rents planes there. Ten minute ride."

230

"I'll give you fifty dollars to get me there as fast as you can drive."

"For fifty bucks, lady, I'll go into intergalactic time-warp. Get in."

25

Groot had visited the White House several times in his long career, but never like this—alone, in a rainy dawn, and by way of a vaulted service entrance tucked discreetly under the stairs of the South Portico. He was led into a dimly lit corridor by the two Secret Service men who had picked him up, and in a moment he was admitted to a smallish room with creamy Georgian paneling, Chippendale furniture, and softly glowing lamps. The President was seated at a slant-top desk under a portrait of Benjamin Franklin. He was writing in a small black notebook and looked up only after crossing a T with what to Groot seemed to be a slash of controlled anger. Yet the eyes, the smile, were, as always, serene and benign.

"Ah. Groot. Thank you for coming at this ungodly hour."

"It's good to see you, Mr. President."

"Sit down, sit down. Would you like coffee?"

"No, thank you, sir." He assumed a tentative position on a finely carved chair beside a pie-crust table, praying it would hold his bulk. Despite his intention to remain cool and inscrutable, his gaze wandered about the elegant room as if he were a raggedy-ass tourist from Gump Stump Junction.

"Beautiful, isn't it?"

"Yes, sir."

"It's called the Map Room. It once was a cloak room for the Diplomatic Reception room next door. In 1942, or thereabouts, Franklin Roosevelt converted it into a secret chart room where he could check the progress of World War Two, twice a day. Then it fell into less glamorous duty as a powder room, then a doctor's office, a place for the Secret Service boys to sit with their feet up. That kind of thing. Harry Truman's renovations brought it back to this."

"I'm glad, sir. It's really quite nice."

"I come here when I want to get some real work done. The majesty of the Oval Office can be intrusive, distracting."

"I dare say."

The President sat in the wing-back chair by the small fireplace and gave Groot a brooding glance. "I'm taking our problem to the National Security Council in exactly three hours, Groot. The matter has grown too huge, too unmanageable for just the few of us to continue to deal with it secretly and among ourselves."

"You're right, of course, sir."

"I've called for a briefing on the whole spectrum, from Cuba's current military-economic fever chart to a run-down on the Soviet airlift capabilities after a nuclear exchange. In addition to the regular members of the Council—the emphasis will be on summaries from the Secretaries of State and Defense—I'll be having presentations from the CIA, the DFA, and NSA, and the intelligence chiefs of the armed services. This afternoon will be given to a full cabinet meeting, with State, Defense, Interior, Agriculture, and Commerce reporting on our various disaster preparedness and assistance capabilities. A stand-by alert has already been given the Pentagon and, of course, the West Germans. All embassies have been teletyped to stand by for emergency instructions." The President paused to take a sip of coffee.

"Will you be notifying the West European Alliance,

sir?" Groot wanted to cross his legs, but he feared it might put undue strain on the chair.

"No. Not yet."

"May I ask why, sir?"

"I want first to receive my cabinet and department inputs. Then I'll have to brief congressional leaders, of course. Our own key government structures must be fully informed and primed for action before I take the matter to unfriendly or nonpartisan governments."

Groot nodded. "May I ask how much time you're giving all this, Mr. President?"

"Twenty-four hours."

"That will be calling it close."

"How so?"

"The Cubans are ready to move within thirty-six hours."

The President placed his cup and saucer on a small serving table. His eyes, Groot saw, showed pain. "This is why I've asked you here now, Groot. I want a complete, to-the-minute précis of the situation. I'll also want your recommendations. Not that I'll follow them. But I want them before my meeting."

"Yes, sir."

"Begin, please."

Groot, because he had an orderly mind, rarely used notes. He would not have needed them for this case in any event, since he had lived with it, to the exclusion of all else, for the past week. He merely nodded politely, folded his hands on his belly, and began.

"We have established certain facts. First: Cuban commandos have stolen a Squeaky from our military forces in Germany. All but one of the American soldiers assigned to the transport of the missing bomb were killed outright; the survivor, the colonel who was commanding the convoy, is still in a coma and has barely survived an additional attack on his life by persons unknown but presumed to be allies of the Cubans.

"Secondly: the bomb, while being ferried to Cuba by an amphibian airplane, was intercepted off Florida—I can give you the chart coordinates—by anti-Castro forces operating out of Miami. The anti-Castroites have hidden the bomb, undetected by our most advanced surveillance tools, somewhere in Florida, and are said to plan to smuggle it into Havana and explode it there.

"Third: Castro, having vowed to retrieve the bomb and its special fuse mechanism, has already secretly invaded Florida via St. Augustine and certain inland waterway drop-points. He has placed about a thousand combat troops, disguised as vacationing young people, in a resort area on Lake George south of Palatka. One of our ablest agents, posing as a University of Florida archeologist, has been able to penetrate the camp area with two members of his regular CIA team. He confirms the intruders as Cuban commandos. He sets their number at one thousand twenty-two. He says they are heavily armed. He says that within thirty-six hours they will close Florida—symbolically—by blowing up key overpasses on the main north-south highways—Routes A1A, 1, 95, 17, 301, 27, 25, and 19—on an east-west line of towns: Daytona Beach, Deland, Ocala, Dunnelton, and Crystal River. At that time, Castro will announce that Florida is closed until his troops find the 'stolen Cuban property.' Any U.S. attempt to retaliate will cause instantaneous execution of community leaders who will have been taken hostage and the detonation of a Cuban nuclear device in Miami. And. . . ."

The President interrupted. "What do your field people recommend?"

"My field commander, Morgan, says the situation is critical and calls for immediate military counter-measures. Pre-emptive attack on Cuba before noon today."

"That would cost us Miami, to start. Then all of Florida. Then war. Large-scale war."

"Yes, sir."

The President thought for a time. Then, sighing, he said, "Castro must have lost his mind."

Groot nodded again. "You are not alone in that idea, sir. Wagner, our other man on the case, has used your very words."

"Wagner? The creaky old retired CIA hack who bumbled onto the case?" The President's tensions were beginning to show.

"Wagner's better than that, sir," Groot said abruptly, surprising himself at his inner anger and his quick defense of a man whom the President had aptly characterized. "He's a very loyal, dedicated, and—well—brave man."

The President waved an apologetic hand. "Of course. You're quite right, Groot. It was a gross thing for me to say."

"Wagner is quite vocal on the matter, Mr. President. He says that Castro's too smart, too sophisticated, too cool and wily to swing out in a way that amounts to an open invitation to pre-emptive nuclear war."

"Well, what does Wagner propose we do about

that?" The President's voice still held on edge.

Groot hunched a shoulder. "Nothing dramatic, sir. He simply urges us to go slowly, carefully."

The President sniffed. "Oh, great." He paused, then added, "The point remains: Whoever shoots first, everybody loses. If the anti-Castroites explode the stolen Squeaky in Havana, the Cubans and Soviets will retaliate—a wiping out of Florida at the least and a third of the civilized world at the worst as we retaliate to their retaliation. Who would gain by this, Groot? Who sees nuclear war as a desirable goal? Certainly not the anti-Castroites. Certainly not the Cubans. Both would be atomized in the first ten minutes. Certainly not the Soviets. They—and we—would be gone in the next fifteen minutes. Certainly no one in Europe or the Mideast or India, possibly China and Japan. They go when the rest of us go. Who then? Who is mad enough to see an advantage in murder and suicide?

"A *schmeer*," the President went on. "An incomprehensible *schmeer*. In a world that's a *schmeer* There were times, Groot, when the world was fairly easy to understand—the motives of hate, greed, love, patriotism, idealism, the fear of death, the respect for life provided realistic yardsticks by which to make judgments, whether they were personal or international in scope. But it all started to fall apart when the movies changed."

"I don't follow you on that one, Mr. President. . . ."

"Do you remember the way movies were in the Forties, the Fifties—even the early Sixties? They had what somebody once described as A Beginning, A Muddle, and an Ending. Each movie was a kind of reflection of the national morality and the national yearning for an ultimate order in the seeming chaos about us. You could tell the good guys from the bad guys, not just by the color of the hats they wore but also by the way they walked and talked. But then the anti-hero came along, the hip, the slick, the trendy, the cool; good became bad, bad good; patriotism became gauche, corny, a posture struck by the rednecks who wore white shoes and white belts; evil was groovy, fashionable; motives were no longer clear and cogent, because impulsiveness, mindless ego, blind selfishness were the prevailing national—world-wide, by God!—ethic. People stopped being doers, Groot. They became complainers. Not just here in the States. Everywhere. And, because they have always been an accurate reflection of the nation and its people, the movies became the same—aimless, blurred in motive, indifferent to good or bad, and the most unbearable thing of all: boring. Our movies are aimless and boring and wretched today, Groot, because the world is that way."

The President sipped his coffee again, and Groot found himself fearing for the President's sanity. *Movies?* The world had gone to hell when the *movies* did? Mother of God . . .

"The world, Groot, is in a stupor of weariness and despair. Economic and political stagnation in Europe, Asia, the Soviet Union. A total inertia here Stateside. The Third World awash in plagues, famines, and unfulfilled desires. An elephantiasis of population everywhere—figures compounding exponentially because the only recreation, the only self-expression, the only time of tenderness left to half the people in the

238

world is an act that makes more people. And now, some people have stolen a bomb and stand ready to destroy the world for reasons we can't even fathom, for motives that have no discernible humanity in them—not the slightest relationship to the morality we once saw in our movies. We are going into a nuclear war, Groot, and we're not even sure who's starting it and why."

Groot thought, with a touch of annoyance, *Speaking of motives, I wonder if this is really why I was called here in the middle of the night? To serve as an audience of one for a President who wants to parody Hamlet?...*

"I'd like your recommendations now, Groot."

Groot was ready. "I suggest most respectfully, sir, that we send a message directly to Premier Castro, informing him of the Doomsday mode on the Squeaky and that anti-Castro Cubans are probably at this very moment smuggling the device into Cuba. We should tell him that we are ready to reveal the means by which the bomb can be neutralized so that the Squeaky's custodians can avert the destruction of themselves and much of Cuba. We should suggest that you and he meet—on a boat at sea, perhaps—to discuss means by which we might cooperate in the search for the Squeaky."

"You are serious? You think I should meet with Castro?"

"Yes, sir. You must convince him, on an eyeball basis, that we have had nothing to do with the plot to plant a Squeaky in his country. That we want to do anything possible—anything acceptable to him—to help him negate the bomb before it triggers in Havana."

The President shook his head slowly. "I'm afraid Castro will reject any such overture as merely part of a slick cover-up of a Yankee plot to rationalize the invasion of Cuba. We Americans have never given Castro any real reason to believe us. He won't trust us because we've never given him reason to. It's that simple."

"It's got to start someplace, Mr. President."

"I fear it's too late, Groot. With a Squeaky en route to Havana, a Cuban nuke in Miami, and Cubans amassing at Palatka, we have no recourse but nuclear war. Thank God we have several days in which to prepare."

The phone on the serving table warbled politely and the President picked it up. "Yes?"

He listened for a time, and Groot saw his face grow pale.

The President replaced the phone slowly, his gaze oblique. "Jesus God," he said softly, "we've got stupendous trouble now."

"Sir?"

"That was military intelligence calling from our hospital in Wiesbaden. The colonel who was serving as convoy commander when the Squeaky was stolen on that German road: he's regained consciousness. MI has been able to question him."

"And?"

"He reports that during the shooting he went to the weapons truck. As he was climbing in, he was shot. But he made it to the Squeaky compartment, he says, and, with his waning strength, he sought to deactivate the bomb's fuse, thereby rendering it useless to

240

the hijackers."

"*Sought* to, sir?"

"He says he wanted to set the specifier on Pi-2, which disconnects the bomb's systems and sabotages the fuse so that its secrets can't be studied by un-friendlies. But in his semi-conscious state, he suspects he forgot to put the specifier into override, which clears the systems for a new specification. If so, he says, he could very well have placed the setting on any one of a dozen possible trigger points."

"Which means we might have no time at all."

The President nodded somberly. "Instead of defusing the bomb, the colonel thinks he might very well have reset it to go off sooner. The Squeaky can trigger at any time now."

26

Wagner had driven from the airport directly to Vilano Beach, where he parked the car among a knot of pickup trucks and vans that nuzzled up to the Orange Blossom diner like piglets to a sow. He sat for a time, watching daylight spread across the still-sleeping houses, forcing himself to concentrate on where to go with his gathering awareness. One of his answers came in the form of the James C. Fitzmuller Refuse Collection Company's truck.

He climbed out of the rental Ford and crossed the road to where the big white truck stood, grumbling and shaking and waiting for the pair of trashmen at its rear to throw the bundles and rattle the cans. Swinging up on the cab step, he grinned through the window and said, "Hi, Fitz."

"Well, if it ain't Mr. Wagner. What are you doing out on an early crappy morning like this?" Fitz was openly surprised and pleased—mostly, Wagner suspected, because of the twenty-five-dollar check he'd received from the Wagners as a Christmas remembrance.

"I've got a little problem, Fitz. And it occurred to me that you might be willing to give me a hand with it."

"Sure. You want me to haul away a wilted refrigerator, I betcha."

"Nothing that complicated. I want to borrow your hat and your sweatshirt and a pair of work gloves. Then I want to ride up to my house on the back of your truck."

Fitz's eyes widened. "You lose a bet or suthin?"

"No."

"I get it. You were on the town and you're trying to sneak into the house without your wife sees you."

"Close. Actually, it's my wife who's out of town. But I've got a very nosy neighbor who would be very happy to tell Eva that she saw me coming home at dawn. I've got to pass the old snoop's house to get to my own. I thought this would be a good way to do it."

"Hey, man," Fitz laughed, "right out of a TV sit-com, eh?"

"There's a ten-spot in it for you."

"Hell, Mr. Wagner, you don't have to pay me for something like that. I got a snoopy neighbor or two myself." Fitz took off his cap and passed it through the window. "Here are the gloves, too. The sweat-shirt's pretty dirty, though."

"So's my conscience, Fitz. Especially after last night." He winked.

"Yeah. Ha-ha."

"Before you move on, I want to talk to the boys in the back room."

"Hep yo' sef, as we say in the Deep South."

Wagner went to the rear of the truck and nodded good morning to the two young men who stood there, waiting. One was entirely too large, the other somewhat too small. To the smaller one Wagner said, "Want to make ten bucks?"

"Sure," the kid said, rolling his chewing gum to the other side of his mouth. "What you want me to do? Kill somebody?"

"Later, maybe. But for now all I want you to do is cut through the village to the beach, then walk along the dunes like a tourist. When you get to my house—you know, number ten—just follow the scrub-line to my garage, step under the deck so nobody in the house can see you, and wait until I get there and come in for the trash. You'll put this cap and sweatshirt on and carry the trash back to the truck. OK?"

The kid looked thoughtful. "You're trying to sneak into the house, huh?"

"You got it."

The kid was no dummy. "Hell, if I can go along the beach and up the scrub-line like a tourist, why can't you? Why do you need me?"

"Because my snoopy neighbor knows what I look like. A thousand people pass that way every day, and the old lady's used to it. But not one of those thousand people look like me. Know what I mean?" Wagner winked again.

The kid nodded and chewed a bit. "Sounds like a fifteen-dollar job to me," he said. "These errant-husband cases are always more expensive, tricky. Know what I mean?"

Despite himself, Wagner smiled. "Yeah. I know. What's your name—Jesse James?"

The kid chuckled good-naturedly. "Hell, Mr. Wagner. I was just kidding. You don't have to pay me a cent."

"Fifteen it is. Ten for the job, five for your law school tuition. You *are* going to law school, aren't you?"

"Pre-law, at Flagler."

"You've got a great career ahead of you."

He went up the back stairs from the garage and, with the delicacy of a surgeon, inserted the key and turned it in the lock and let himself into the utility

244

room. Carefully, silently, he opened the kitchen door just enough to permit a view of the counter, the sink, a corner of the refrigerator, and, beyond, a section of hallway and a portion of the living room. There was the smell of coffee and cigarette smoke, and he could hear Eva's radio playing. It was this, more than the bubbling of the coffee maker or the fouling of the place with tobacco or the sound of a faucet gushing in the bathroom, that found and energized whatever gland it is that manufactures anger. The presence of an alien who walked the carpets, rested in the chairs, operated the appliances, ran the water, and breathed the air of his home was cause for calculated action; but the use of the bedside radio was cause for fury. Eva had brought the radio home one day early in their marriage, finally admitting, after all kinds of elaborate explanations and rationalizations, that she liked to hear soft music in the night, especially when making love. It had been a confession of exceptional intimacy, made with a heavy blush, and he could never so much as glance at the dumb little plastic box without a pang of sentimental amusement.

The man came out of the bathroom and Wagner gave him a chop that sent him sprawling. When he rolled him over, Wagner was not surprised to see that it was the Teutonic Charles Atlas ad who had kicked sand in his face and apologized in German. He was not surprised because this had been the elusive wisp that had been nagging him from the first. What was a German-speaking Cuban doing jogging on Vilano Beach, anyhow? The question had eluded him because he'd been snowed by his own familiarity with German; when you speak a language most of your adult life you don't exactly go into crash-dive alert when you hear somebody speaking it, even in off-beat circumstances.

But now he thought he knew what a German-speaking Cuban had been doing on Vilano Beach. For one thing, he'd been getting a good look at old Roger Wagner for future reference, like knowing who among the thousands who resided in old Roger Wagner's homestead was to be knocked off.

Wagner tied the man's wrists behind him with strands of adhesive from the medicine cabinet. Then he lashed the ankles and, straining, attempted to raise the unconscious form to a sitting position on the carpet before the sectional sofa. It was no good, though; the man was too heavy and limp, and so Wagner sat by the seaside window and had a cup of coffee, continuing with his evaluations, speculations, and judgments.

Eva dominated.

For all his emotional need to run immediately to Colorado, his logic, having returned to sluggish life at the moment of his recognition of Hans Trille at the airport, told him sternly that she was better off where she was. The kidnappers would not harm her; clearly, they needed her to exert some kind of control over him. As long as he managed to stay alive, to elude them—whoever they were—Eva would stay alive. And if he didn't stay alive, the entire matter became academic. Moreover, the Squeaky was ticking somewhere and it really made no difference where anyone was if that little rascal performed its ultimate function, and his best service to Eva would be, when all was said, to find the Squeaky and return it to its rightful copyright owners, postage due.

In a silent speech filled with noble phrases and anguished self-pity, Wagner assured himself that if he truly loved Eva he would not career off to Colorado; he would instead concentrate on the need to avert a war—as she most certainly would demand that he do.

The man groaned and opened an eye.

"Good morning," Wagner said in German. "You certainly make rotten coffee."

The other eye opened.

"What's your name?"

The man didn't answer. So Wagner went to the kitchen and returned with one of Eva's large mixing bowls and a sawtooth bread-knife. Placing the bowl under the man's hands, he smiled. "I don't want to get blood on the carpet."

"What are you going to do?"

"I'm going to dismantle your hands. Finger by finger."

"With that bread-knife?"

"Mm-hm."

"That's pretty drastic, isn't it?" the man said, worried.

"Your taking up station in my home, waiting to kill me whenever I might come in, is rather drastic, too, you'll have to admit. One drastic calls for another, I always say. What do you always say?"

"My name is Ludwig Menzing. Where in hell you been? I've been waiting three goddamn days."

"I've been busy. Who told you to stake me out?"

"I can't tell you that."

"You'd better. Or you'll never play the harpsichord again."

"I mean, I don't know. Honest. I get my instructions by way of a typewritten note delivered to my motel."

"Which motel is that?"

"The Pomeroy. On Anastasia Boulevard."

"How come you're here in the States?"

"A man hired me in Munich, paid my air fare. Picks up my expenses."

Wagner switched to English, testing. "How did this guy identify himself?"

"He didn't," Menzing answered readily. "He merely waved money."

"What are you hired to do?" Wagner asked, in German again.

"I don't know yet. I'm waiting to find out."

"Did this man assign you to watch my place?"

"Like I say, I don't know. I just got a note."

"What's the man look like? The one who hired you."

"Stocky. Dark eyes. Mean. I'm not very good at describing people."

"How long have you been in Florida?"

"Ten, eleven days."

"How long did the man say you'd be here? Altogether."

"A month."

"What's he paying you?"

"A thousand dollars a week and expenses."

"Are you the only one he hired?"

"No. There are others. You saw me with some of them. Jogging. I don't know much about them."

"Are they Germans, too?"

"No. South Americans—Cubans. Mexicans. Like that."

248

"Why you? Why a German when everyone else is Latin?"

"I don't ask questions. I just take my pay and wait."

"What did they tell you to do with me?"

"Persuade you to commit suicide. Grieving over your absent wife."

"How?"

"Force a quart of whiskey down you. Whiskey laced with a bottle of sleeping pills."

"You'd do that for a thousand a week?"

"Things are slow these days. A job's a job."

Wagner thought for a moment. "When, where, how do you get together with the other joggers?"

Menzing tried to shift his weight from the shoulder that pressed against the sofa. But he was off balance and it didn't work. "The note gives me directions on where to run each morning and afternoon. I start after breakfast and I always meet some others on my route and we run together—per instructions."

"Are the routes always the same?"

"No. Through town in the morning, along the beaches in the afternoon. Different streets, different times."

"Why so much exercise?"

"I don't know. The man said I must keep in top physical shape. It's part of the deal."

"Have you ever been in military service?"

"The usual stint in the army. The West German army."

"Infantry?"

"Yes. I was a platoon sergeant."

"Are you here on a legal passport?"

"Sure."

"How about the others?"

"I don't know. There's something odd there. I think they come in by boat."

"Which means you're something special, then, eh? Something like a platoon sergeant. A mercenary."

"If I was a mercenary, Herr Wagner, I wouldn't be talking so much."

"Which reminds me: Why *are* you talking so much?"

"A thousand a week isn't enough to pay for a couple of hands. I'm a real harpsichord nut."

"Good thinking. And, as a reward for your cooperative attitude, I won't kill you and sink your body in the marsh. Instead, I'll run you downtown on charges of burglary."

"Burglary? I didn't steal anything."

"You stole about a pound of my coffee and a bunch of food. And my liquor supply seems considerably depleted. You're a naughty boy and I'm going to send you to reform school." Wagner crossed the room, knelt, and slipped the handcuffs on Menzing's wrists—the old CID cuffs Harry Franklin had given him in Augsburg one night. Then he removed the adhesive, not too gently, and Menzing grimaced and hissed.

Wagner checked his watch, saw it was after nine, and went to the kitchen phone extension. He found the number in the directory and dialed it.

"Historic Preservation Board," a woman said.

"I want to talk to someone about the archeology projects around town."

"That would be Dr. Drummond. One moment, please."

Dr. Drummond proved to be a woman, too. She had a nice voice that made "Good morning" sound as if she meant it.

"My name is Oglethorpe," Wagner said. "I'm doing a piece on old St. Augustine for *Chronos Magazine* and I have a few questions about the archeology projects."

"Oh, say, that's just great. *Chronos? Great!*"

"Yeah. Tell me, Dr. Drummond, can anybody just walk into town and start digging for ancient treasure?"

"Oh, my goodness, no. The Board keeps a very close rein on what happens, especially the altering of property, the recovery of artifacts, and so on."

"How about Academe—the universities, and like that?"

"It's mostly grants. The main digs going on right now are being conducted, under a grant from the National Endowment for the Humanities, by Florida State University."

"How about the work being done by Paul Driscoll?"

"Driscoll? Oh. Oh, yes. The man from Washington. He's on a special grant from the Department of the Interior. He's been working here about three months now. I understand he's just left for Washington. Special conference up there, or something."

"And Dr. Samuels and his students?"

There was a pause. Then: "Dr. Samuels?"

"Yeah. From the University of Florida."

"Well, now. I can't rightly say. In fact, I'm not sure I know any Dr. Samuels."

"Little guy. Beard. Easy manner. Has about four or

251

five undergrads working with him on a dig at Trinity Church."

"Oh?" Dr. Drummond seemed flustered. "Well, now. I— Well. That's odd. The digs at Trinity were completed months ago. The last time they were worked, Dr. Langley, of Penn State, was looking for primitive Indian stuff. I. . . ."

"You mean you've never heard of Dr. Samuels?"

"I—I'm looking at the record sheet of projects. It covers the past two years. There's no Dr. Samuels on it anywhere."

"Well," Wagner said, "maybe I got the name wrong."

"But you said he was digging at Trinity. . . ."

"That's right."

"Nobody reported it to us. . . ."

"You'd better look into it, then, eh?"

"You bet, Mr. Oglethorpe. I'm very grateful to you for alerting me. Dr. Samuels is probably a tourist who thinks just anybody's allowed to dig up our town. Well, I'll see that he's straightened out, you can believe that." She paused again, presumably to reassemble her badly shaken pleasantness. "Now: what other questions can I answer for you, Mr. Oglethorpe?"

"I'd like to come by in a day or two. Talk to your people. That kind of thing."

"Wonderful. Come any time. We'll be delighted to see you."

"Right. Bye."

Wagner hung up and returned to the living room to find Menzing gone.

The handcuffs were on the carpet and the key, which he'd left on the lamp table as if in oversight, lay beside

252

them. He had not been overly impressed by Menzing's intelligence, but obviously the fellow had been bright enough to see the key and make the connection and hit the high road for other climes, as the saying had it.

Which was just what the doctor ordered, as the other saying had it.

Mrs. Wagner's little boy, Roger, had a pretty good idea which climes were involved.

Plenty of time to catch up.

Even so, he made a quick work of locking up, and he picked up a few minutes by returning to the Orange Blossom diner and his car by cutting through several back yards.

As he swung onto A1A and headed for town, he felt another attack of depression.

Things were beginning to take form at last.

And they were even worse than he'd feared.

27

It had always been so. A single thread, a tiny wisp of an idea, a feeling, an impression, a hunch. Some fiber of the senses would snag on some condition of the moment and the unraveling would begin.

Pipe smoke.

Not even the smoke itself. Only its spoor.

And in a small interval, his mind had begun to weave the pattern. Quick, sure, undoubting clicks of the intellectual loom.

Strasser's body on the beach: no coincidence. Well-placed boat wreckage with a convenient radio manual: the Miami connection. A young jogger, apologizing reflexively in German: the leadership angle. Eva's timely trip out of town: clearing the decks, setting up a control. A Havana reference and a gun cache on the Lang boat: bringing in Castro. Attempts to kill him—in Miami, in Munich, always after having phoned Groot: signs he had been onto something and had served a purpose. Schattner, the farmer, and his revelation of Spanish being spoken during the raid: the Castro element again. The strange disappearance of prominent Nazis: no coincidence. The unreal ease with which he had obtained information from Dom, the Mafia godfather, and Garcia, the anti-Castro chieftain: the garden path department.

Still to be explained: Where Audrey fitted in; where Dr. Samuels, the phony archeologist, fitted in; where good-natured, accommodating Robert Veck fitted in.

And, of course, where the Squeaky was hidden.

If Ludwig Menzing now performed his function as Teutonic Paul Revere, rushing through the Halls of Frawley alerting his fellow joggers to the oncoming

Roger Wagner, he might even find out more about that.

The post office, being on King Street, was on the way to the Frawley Motel, so Wagner was able to make a fast visit to the General Delivery window. The biographical material he had requested of Klatt was there as promised, and he felt a glow of gratitude for the Munich cop, who, along with Eva and one or two others, represented the last of species *homo straight-shooticus.*

The Frawley was a no-questions establishment that catered to college kids, adult adulterers, and other components of the quickie trade. He parked in the shadows of an abandoned orange-juice-and-curios shop across the road and sat low in his seat, studying the Frawley's art greco tastelessness through eyes that burned, heavy and grainy. There were four cars, each with a St. John's County license tag, and three vans from Duval County. The remaining rooms appeared to be unoccupied, but he couldn't be certain of this because the drapes were drawn—perhaps providing morning dusk for between-classes lovers who had arrived from campus on the bicycles in the rack by the Coke machine.

He looked around for Veck's Buick, but there was no trace of it. Which was not surprising. A pro like Veck would rarely be apparent in any normal stakeout.

He thought about this, putting it high on his list of Things that Would Seem to Confirm.

Since nothing was going on at the Frawley— nothing yet visible, that is—he took some time to consider Klatt's mail facsimiles.

He had read the Siegfried Unger saga during his trip to Munich, and this second reading revealed very little that he hadn't known before. The only notable exception was a somewhat pedantic run-down on Unger's involvement in the World Crusade for the Control of Famine. The WCCF was a murky conglomeration of international gadabouts, professional pietists, and limousine revolutionaries who, according to the organization's own brochure, were essentially United Nations lobbyists intent on persuading Third World nations that overpopulation and under-production of goods were the cause of general starvation. Wagner shook his head in silent disgust. Great thinking, that. It took a lot of sensitivity and perceptiveness to assure dying people that everything would be all right if they (1) stopped visiting each other's beds, and (2) got off their duffs and worked like mad, for a change. With thinking like that, no wonder the world was in trouble.

Klatt had included a sheaf of pictures that showed Unger attending this dinner meeting, that reception, sailing his boat, riding on his 2000-acre Argentine horse ranch.

He stared at these, bothered by something unnameable. But the more he stared the more the something eluded him. So he went on to farmer Ludwig Schattner, whose biography carried only two vaguely interesting notes. He had been an Unteroffizier in the West German Landswehr, a key noncom in a demolitions company. And he had been—still was—a member of the Bund Deutscher Patrioten, a severely right-wing political group generally suspected of being a front for neo-Nazis. *Another great deduction,* Wagner thought dourly. *Who are the geniuses who come up with such audacious thinking?*

He gave considerable time to the files on the young people, Kurt Münser and Loni Riess. Not that there was anything extraordinary there. Two more obscure and unachieving people could probably not be found in Germany, a nation of busybodies. His depression over their murders had long since gone; they were dead, they were without further pertinence, and that was that. But they haunted him for another reason. They had said something, seen something, done something that carried a special significance. He had virtually memorized the tape he had made of his interview with them, but whatever was there eluded him as the truth behind the Unger photos eluded him. Seen, but unseen. Through a glass darkly.

Damn.

The magic struck again.

At that moment. That tiny splinter of time.

It came in the form of a tractor-trailer—hulking, grimy with the road, spouting a plume of sooty exhaust like a coal-choked whale. A dirty grey box on rumbling wheels; a box painted with dirty red letters proclaiming Rumpelmaier's Potato Chips. Snorting, bellowing, shaking the ground in its thunderous passage to some snack-dispensing emporium in some unguessable town somewhere to the north.

There.

That was what he had been missing.

The young people had told him. But he hadn't heard.

A truck. A big truck. Out of sight.

When the raid was done, the commandos had car-

257

ried a box from the shattered weapons trailer. Toward a spot, beyond plain view, from which a helicopter had risen. Then the attackers had assembled—presumably for a roll call—finally to split up and run off through the countryside in every direction.

Then a large truck had started up, somewhere beyond the woods. It had driven off to the south.

What truck?

Who had needed a tractor-trailer? Why?

I know. Wagner's mind stirred with tired elation. *I know now, you sons of bitches. . . .*

The T-47 in his vest pocket vibrated suddenly, as Veck had told him it would. The radio would either warble to announce an incoming call or it would vibrate, depending on the mode specified by the receiver. Warbles were good for wakening a sleeping receiver; vibrations were advisable if the receiver required silence in a tricky situation.

"Wagner, receiving."

"Where in hell are you, buddy-boy?" Veck's tenor sang out. "I just checked my answering service and it tells me the air charter people called, wanting to know when you'd be wanting to leave. *Leave?* I thought you left hours ago."

"I got held up a bit, Robert."

"You OK?"

"Sure. On the way to the airport I realized there was something I'd forgotten. I risked a visit to my house to pick up the something and lo, the place was occupied by a very unfriendly gent. It was all very acrimonious. Not only that, but everybody was madder'n hell, too."

"What happened to the gent?"

"He got away," Wagner said.

"Well, you can't win them all. Where are you now?"

"In Jacksonville. Picking up another something."

"Are you still going to Colorado?"

"Sure. Where are you, by the way, Robert?"

"Where else? You told me to stake out the Frawley, so I'm staking out the Frawley."

"Anything going on there?"

"Nothing that would make headlines. Unless, of course, it was the Hanky-Panky Journal."

"One of my unfriendlies drives a blue van. Do you see one there?"

"There are three vans. One red, one black, another yecch green. There isn't even a blue car."

"All right. Thanks." Veck, Wagner decided, was an absolute perishing magician when it came to stakeouts. There wasn't the slightest trace of Veck anywhere in sight of his own hiding place, yet Veck had precisely described the vehicles parked at the Frawley.

"By the way," Wagner said casually, "I know the Frawley, and there isn't much of any place to set up a stakeout. I mean, there are too many open fields, not many trees, and about the only building that gives a view of the motel's front is an old orange juice stand across the road. Where are you set up?"

There was a blip of silence and then Veck laughed his high-pitched laugh. "You don't think I'm actually so old-fashioned as to sit in a car or hide in a rain barrel on a stakeout, do you? Hell, man, that went out with Sam Spade."

"What are you talking about? A stakeout's a stakeout."

"Not in the sense you old fogies put on it. We of the

259

modern generation use tools, my boy. I am watching the Frawley from my tool shop. Closed-circuit TV, color replay tape, zoom-and-magnify stills capability. Why should I cool my *tokus* in a beat-up Buick when I can be at home, drinking beer and gobbling a hoagie?"

Wagner thought about that, then asked another question. "Well, how about a tail? If somebody at the Frawley goes tootling off in his yecch-colored van, you won't be able to follow him."

"Oh, my, you are antedeluvian, aren't you, my boy? I visited the Frawley in the dark of midnight dreary and planted finks on the interesting vehicles."

"Finks?"

"Electronic signals that enable me to sit at the mighty console and watch where cars go without moving my own butt an inch."

"I wish to hell the CIA was as well equipped as you keyhole-peepers are. Godamighty!"

"Today's CIA has them, dear boy. Your old-time CIA did not."

"Hell, I've only been out of the Company a year and a half."

"But you weren't in the mainstream, obviously. Top people working top priorities are well-equipped. Indians working conventional stuff from provincial wigwams must make do with Sam Spade techniques."

Wagner felt a flare of annoyance, and against his better sense he heard himself saying, "You're full of crap, Robert. You sound like a guy who's making it up as he goes along. I didn't have much in the way of hardware in the CIA because *nobody* had much, damn it."

After another tiny interval, Veck said, somewhat

stiffly, "Have it your way."

Wagner, worried that he might have overplayed his hand, softened his tone. "Do me a favor, will you? Call the airport and tell them I'm still coming. And I know and accept that the meter's running."

"You don't remember anything I tell you, do you. I told you twice: You can jack into the commercial telephone system with the T-47. Just press the theta key with a pencil-point, put the switch on zero, and, again using your pencil-point, dial the area code and number by pressing the appropriate digits on the panel. Do the same for Universal Information."

"Oh, yeah."

"But I'll call for you, if you're busy."

"I'm busy. The Jacksonville traffic is a demolition derby today."

"O.K. Let me know when you get back from Colorado."

"Sure. Bye."

Wagner returned the radio to his breast pocket, feeling one of the deepest-hurting depressions he had experienced in his long history of depressions.

Veck was lying.

He was lying about all the fancy cameras and instruments.

If he truly had been scanning the Frawley and its environs, there was no way he could have missed seeing Roger Wagner and his merry Hertzmobile tucked in beside the orange juice stand. If Veck could see the Frawley's line-up of vans and cars, he could also see the orange juice stand from virtually any camera angle.

He was lying, too, therefore about watching the

Frawley from his mighty console. And if he was not watching his closed-circuit TV, as claimed, and yet was able to describe the cars and vans parked at the motel, he would have to be nearby.

Which nearby?

There was only one which could guarantee his invisibility.

The Frawley Motel itself.

From which he could *not* see Wagner's car, parked as it was behind and to one side of the orange juice stand.

So what else was Veck lying about?

28

When he arrived at Veck's house on St. George Street, Wagner was still taut with the excitement of having at last seen through all the dazzle and flim-flam. These were the moments—fleeting, ethereal, tantalizing—that would make life in the Company worthwhile. In the thirty-some years, he'd had these times; not many, to be sure, but a number sufficient to hold him fast during the rest of it—the decades of doorbell-ringing, paper-shuffling, behind-kissing, and monotony. The crystal moments of perception, recognition, revelation, and triumph. They would come in a flutter of the clock; they would be enjoyed, cherished, for all of a day, or a night, or, at best, a week. And then the plodding would resume, and the magic would have gone, lost again in the compressed-lip coping that marked the days and years.

He had hoped that, by allowing Menzing to escape, the German would flee to the Frawley and trigger some action by reporting what he'd heard Wagner say on the phone. But nothing had come of it, and street savvy told Wagner now that Menzing, fearing his bosses' punishment for failing to kill Wagner, was somewhere near Toronto and still headed north. Any mob devours its bumblers, a fact no doubt well known to Ludwig Menzing.

Which, all in all, facilitated Wagner's present errand, which was to find a Disty-List, a portable device designed to pick up conversations behind walls and in vehicles up to five hundred yards away. There was no doubt Veck would have one—the tool was superb for recording the sounds of clandestine passion and therefore a standard item in the private-eye's inventory.

And now, with Veck virtually guaranteed to be at the Frawley, this was an excellent time to break into Veck's private stores and rummage a bit.

Veck proved to have not only a Disty-List but also just about anything else dear to the heart of an eavesdropper and spy. There were electronics, from Jensen beepers to cough-drop microphones; he had infra-red scanners, black-light cameras, pillow mikes, bedspring graphs, phone-dial recorders, binoculars, telescopes, phone taps, heart-beat counters, radar sets, TV scans, movie cameras, and a complete darkroom and Movieola editing machine.

Wagner examined all this with a kind of grouchy envy. Veck must really have a business, he thought sourly; nobody could afford such an array, unless he had a corner on all the divorce work between Key West and Vancouver and his name was really Veckefeller. A search of the files disclosed nothing interesting or illuminating: a folder of photos catching a bald-headed banker type arriving for, performing during, and leaving from an afternoon of fun and games on a waterbed with an extraordinarily limber brunette; a great clump of pages from hotel registers; a card catalog of equipment suppliers; stationery; film packs; and phone books for New York, Washington, Chicago, Atlanta, L.A., Denver, and Orlando.

Colorado Springs, too.

Beside the phone itself was a memo pad and a stack of unpaid bills, none for a large amount. Beneath these was a brochure for Disneyland and, paperclipped to it, a penciled list of twenty names, most of them of Latin derivation. At the top of the list was Schattner. Ludwig Schattner, and after his name, a check mark.

There were four other German names, each separated from the others by four Latin names. One was Menzing, who, like the other Germans, had the check mark. At the bottom were today's date and *ETA: 1500 hrs.*

Operations schedule?

Why not?

Wagner understood then that it was time to make his move. The time for guessing, speculating, anguishing had passed. The world had need of straight-line action.

He found the number on the inside cover of the St. Augustine phone book, and he dialed it, thinking as he did that now was when he would have been praying if he'd known how to.

"State Police," a woman said.

"I want to report a crime. I mean, a crime that's about to take place. Or is taking place. I don't know which."

"I'll connect you with the duty officer."

There was a click, a buzz. Then: "Samson speaking."

"I can't give you the exact time," Wagner said, "but in an hour or so—sometime before noon, I'd guess—a convoy of three vans will be headed south on Route 1 out of St. Augustine. There will be twenty men aboard, along with a large amount of explosives and automatic weapons. The men are illegal aliens and the guns are contraband."

"May I ask your name, please?"

"Roger Wagner, Vilano Beach. I'm a special operative, CIA. For confirmation, check this number." He read off Groot's.

"The vans—can you describe them?"

"One's red, one's black, one's yecch green. They all have Duval County tags. Numbers as follows." He read his list. "They'll probably be traveling in tandem and wearing Cuban uniforms."

"What is their mission?"

"Terrorism. To embarrass Cuba. I'd suggest a road-block near the I-95 connection on Route 1, where there's nothing but palmettos and scrub oak. If these guys fight you, you won't want a lot of citizens around."

"These men are dangerous?"

"Since when were twenty hired killers, armed with tommy-guns and carrying grenades and plastique, dangerous? They're the kind of guys you'd like to introduce to Mom."

"I mean. . . ."

Wagner hung up.

Because he had an aversion to leaving even electronic collect-call traces on somebody else's phone records, Wagner took the T-47 from his pocket and punched into the commercial phone system, as Veck had instructed. It took about three minutes by the wall clock before Groot came on the line.

"Hi, Groot. This is Roger Wagner, president of the American Association of Retired Spies."

"Wagner, where in hell's name have you been? My God, I've been turning Colorado inside out, looking for you!"

"I'm not there. I'm here."

"Where's here? My God. . . ."

"I have very little time, Groot. I want to tell you something."

"Time? Little *time*? Oh, dear Lord—Do you have

any idea how little time we *all* have? I. . . ."

"What's the situation up there?"

Groot, his voice thick with anger and what Wagner heard as frustration, rasped, "In exactly one hour the President of the United States is going into a meeting of the National Security Council. He will inform the Council of the occupation of a part of Florida south of Palatka by a large concentration of Cuban commandos who, at noon, will begin to attack our highway system and key communities. At this very moment a courier is standing by to carry notification to the House and Senate leadership that, under the Emergency and Anti-Terrorism Act of 1985, the President has put the Armed Forces on Red Alert, and that Miami can expect a nuclear explosion within an hour of the assault's beginning. Missile attacks from Cuba and the Soviet Union will probably be launched simultaneously. The President will, therefore, ask Red Alert authorization under Public Law Two Thousand Four to send a pre-emptive strike against all Cuban military bases and air and sea forces. He will also ask authority for retaliation on an as-needs basis against the Soviet Union and its allies. Elements of the 82nd Airborne Division are already emplaned and standing by at Fort Benning for a counter-attack to be launched against the enemy's Palatka concentration at 11:27 a.m. All U.S. Forces abroad are now in combat mode, and alert messages to friendly foreign governments have been composed and T-47'd to our embassies for courier delivery on signal. And. . . ."

Wagner broke in. "Who knows about all this, as of this time?"

"The President. Six people in The Company, including you and me. The C.O. and his ordnance section at Wolfratshausen. The Security Council meeting will be the first disclosure to anyone outside those twelve, fifteen people."

"Well, Groot, tell the President to keep his pants on. Tell him to call off the meeting. Somebody's been feeding him a line."

"Are you insane?"

"Yep. But I've also figured this thing out."

"What are you talking about?"

Wagner sighed. "Listen to this, Groot. And act on it at once. Every minute counts."

"Oh, dear Lord! Do you imagine for a moment that. . . ."

"Call the commanding general at the U.S. Army station in Wolfratshausen. Have him initiate an immediate and intensive search of all trucks, all trailers, all cargo-carrying vehicles in his various motor pools. All of them. Every one."

"Why?"

"The Squeaky is hidden in one of them."

"*What?*"

"Probably in a trailer. A trailer parked in storage. That would be most likely. A trailer in mothballs, unused, held in reserve, parked among a hundred others. That's my guess."

"What. . . ."

"The Squeaky never was stolen. It was taken back to Wolfratshausen in a GI vehicle immediately after the raid. The commandos only made it *look* as if they'd stolen it, flown it out of Germany."

"How do you know this, Wagner? And how was it done?"

"I haven't got time to tell you. And you haven't got the time to dawdle. You have to get to the President. You have to tell him to postpone the Security Council meeting and to suspend the 82nd Airborne counterattack on Palatka and the Red Alert and all that crap."

"The commandos in Palatka. . . ."

"There *are* no commandos in Palatka. That's just part of the flim-flam. There are no more than twenty terrorists, mercenaries from South America officered by Germans, riding south on Route 1 in three vans. From what I can put together, I'd guess they were on their way to shoot up and terrorize—get this— Disneyland."

"Have you been drinking?"

"Say, now there's a great idea."

Groot coughed. "All right. You claim the Squeaky never left Germany. . . ."

". . . and is stored snugly at Wolfratshausen. The commandos didn't need a Squeaky—only the *illusion* that they had one."

"Which means, the commandos had help from inside. From some American military types at Wolfrathausen."

"I suggest you start with the nuclear ordnance officer and work your way down. My guess is that it was a transportation officer, or a motor pool chief. Somebody like that, who needed lots of coin to pay lots of bills."

"What about the vans—the Route 1, ah, Disneyland thing. . . ."

"The State Police are setting up a roadblock for what should prove to be a rather colorful pinch."

Groot was silent for an interval, and Wagner gave him the time, knowing that everything hinged on Groot's making the call to Germany and his dissuading the President. If he did neither, there would be nuclear war before nightfall.

"Are you absolutely positive of all this, Wagner?"

"Yep," Wagner said, dying a little.

"No doubts at all?"

"Nope," he lied.

"If we stand down, as you recommend, and there is a nuclear attack, we'll not be ready. Doomsday retaliation, yes. But not ready. Which means not only Miamians but millions of Americans will die without a chance to take cover. Civil defense. . . ."

"Groot, would you please stop talking and get going? Tell the President. Guard the highway overpasses if it makes all you Washington cats feel better, but call off the Airborne, call off any meetings, any alerts. Not to do so will cause publicity, and publicity causes cries of outrage—panic. It is even at times known to cause heartburn and constipation."

"You're impossible, Wagner."

"Yep."

"You've got names to go with all these purported machinations, I suppose."

"Tell your recorder to sit up and pay attention, because here they are: One of the leaders seems to be Hans Trille, the renegade Munich cop, one-time Luftwaffe pilot, and, until his forced resignation, one-time head of Das Greuelverbündnis—the ill-reputed Terror Alliance. Trille seems to do the flying chores for this current caper, and he hangs out at St. Augustine airport.

270

"Then we have Robert Veck, a St. Augustine shamus, whose drawers I'm going through right now. He has a number of underworld contacts and appears to be the arranger for the terrorists—the guy who sets things up, provides supplies, that kind of thing.

"Next is Dominick Clemente, a Mafia boss who's located in Eustis. He may be a legitimate Cosa Nosta figure, or he may be a fakeroo, planted to give me a bum steer. Either way, he's in on this Disneyland gavotte.

"And Carlos Garcia, who has an office over the Bon Vivant on Route One in Daytona. He's pretending to be an anti-Castro Cuban, but after looking at a lot of pictures, I'm willing to bet he's the much-discussed Siegfried Unger, all duded up in a paste-on mustache and a dyed marcel.

"Put down all the personnel at the Lang and Ace Boat Rentals in Miami. They run guns and dope, and are auxiliaries to this thing. And be sure to add your friend and mine, Ludwig Schattner, the Bavarian so-called damn-old farmer. He was a terrorist plant, and he's here in town now to perform his real skill, learned in the West German army: demolitions. He's being backed up by another Ludwig named Menzing, registered at the Pomeroy Motel in St. Augustine, who is a mercenary hired as troop leader. And here are the names of the other paid soldier boys." He read the list by Veck's telephone.

"Anything else?" Groot asked after he'd finished.

"One more thing. There's a so-called archeologist puttering around town. Name: Dr. Samuels. Said to be a University of Florida prof presiding over a field tour by several undergrads. I've established that Samuels is a phony, and so, probably, are his undergrads. They've shown no direct connection, but I suspect they're involved with the terrorists."

"Very well," Groot said. "We'll look into it. What are your plans now?"

"I'll be here, in the very private workshop of my one-time friend and landlord, Robert Veck. I suspect I'll find a lot of goodies here."

"Where are you going from there?"

"I'm taking one of Veck's Distys to the Frawley Motel. That's the barracks of this naughty little army. I want to hear and record some of their conversation, then I may follow them on their jaunt to Disneyland."

"All right," Groot said. "Call me back in fifteen minutes. I should have the President's reaction by then, and he may have some questions for you."

"I'll call from here. Before I leave for the Frawley."

He hung up and began to read one of a stack of pamphlets Veck had placed on a corner of his work table. It was all about the world overpopulation problem and how everybody was going to be dead of starvation by 7 p.m., October 23rd, 2017.

God.

What a sick bastard.

What a sick world.

29

While he waited for O'Malley to raise Morgan on the Communications Room's T-47, Groot sat at his desk, moving his file of papers from one side of the blotter to the other. Then he sank back in his chair, swiveled toward the window, and let his gaze roam across the winter-sullen shopping plaza. A misty rain was falling, turning the pavements to oily mirrors and causing automobile tires to hiss, and those few shoppers in evidence moved slowly, huddled in their coats and stepping with care, like misshapen pigeons. It was always the same, he was thinking. It always came down to an absolute, often spit-in-the-wind choice, where you looked at the people in the equation and you weighed them, one against the other, and then decided where to place your bet. There were no short-cuts; it took the long run to reveal who stood on the side of truth and loyalty and achievement. Here—now—the evidence seemed in balance between Morgan and Wagner. He thought of Morgan, picturing him as he walked the halls of Langley, neat in his gray suit, beard carefully barbered, mincing his steps as if his highly polished oxfords hurt him slightly. A creased and business-like type, with a professorial air and a reverence for the practical; cool of mien and, Groot suspected, singleminded and ruthless in his pursuit of the things important to Rufus Morgan. Then he considered Wagner, lounging in whatever chair of the moment, rumpled and tweedy, with a shirt that always seemed a size too small and a nondescript tie that was always askew and a prevailing air of intelligent, somewhat charming contempt for The Establishment and The System. The touseled idealist, Wagner was, wearing his good-guy heart on a sleeve tattered by thirty years of disillusionment and bureaucratic abuse. An intuitive mechanic, who could listen to the engine of intrigue and sniff its exhaust and then tell you what was out of tune.

Morgan was rarely wrong. Wagner was usually right.

Still, Armageddon could be upon us, Groot thought, and it's no longer a matter of flipping a coin or going with your hunches. There was no room for wrongness in this choice; he would have to know that what he told the President was correct and most likely to avert a nuclear shootout.

The buzzer buzzed. "Mr. Morgan on Two, sir."

"Hello, Morgan."

"I'm glad you called, sir. I was about to call you. All hell is about to break loose."

"Oh? Where are you?"

"At the Palatka site. In an observation screen my people have established on the perimeter." Morgan's voice was heavy with excitement.

"So what's going on?"

"The Cubans have assembled, at least a thousand of them, and are being loaded into trucks and buses—some of them school buses. They are in Cuban uniform and are carrying their weapons openly. It seems that they will be moving out in a very short time now. A matter of minutes."

"What do you recommend?"

"An immediate airstrike, sir. Followed by paratroops and light armor. I implore you to signal the President the need for a pre-emptive strike worldwide. War is upon us."

274

"You're sure?"

"Absolutely. To delay another moment is risking the lives of millions. We must strike now. Here, first, then Cuba, then at the Soviets. At once." Morgan added, a brittleness in his tone, the touch of impatience and anger. "The Cubans will detonate the Miami nuclear device at precisely noon."

"Where did you get that?"

"From Carlos Garcia, an anti-Castroite who has penetrated the Palatka group. He reported this to me only ten minutes ago."

"I see. Do I have time to jet down there for a personal reconnaissance prior to making presentations to the President?"

There was a moment of shocked silence. Then: "My God, no, sir, you don't! We are working against *minutes* You must tell the President now. Exactly what I've told you."

"The reason I'm hesitating, Morgan, is that I've just received a T-47 from Wagner in St. Augustine. He tells me that he is just now searching the files of a private investigator named Veck. He says he has already run across some sensational revelations and he plans to T-47 me"—Groot glanced at the desk clock, doing some rapid calculations—"in exactly ten minutes. I do not want to go to the President with your recommendations, Morgan, until I hear what Wagner has to say about the Disneyland angle."

There was another taut moment. *"Disneyland?"*

"Wagner said there was something about to happen there, too. It may bear on what you're observing."

"Ten minutes, sir?"

"Nine minutes, thirty seconds, as of now."

"I'll call you back, sir."

"No. I'll call you. I'll listen to Wagner, then call you to see if what he says jibes with what you're watching there."

"Ah—Very well, sir. I'll be waiting for your call."

"By the way: What does your informant Garcia say about the Squeaky?"

"He confirms my earlier report, sir. It's in Havana."

"Oh, God!"

"When it goes off, the Cubans and Soviets will definitely nuke us. It's not a question of *whether* we should nuke Cuba. It's *when.* And I recommend that we do it now. At the latest, with the very first shot fired by the Palatka group. Which, as I say, will probably be in minutes. Less than an hour, certainly."

"All right, Morgan. All we can do is our best. Stick with it, and I'll call you very shortly now."

"Yes, sir."

Groot hung up and sat quietly, watching the mist turn to wet snow.

What a rotten day for the end of the world.

His tendency was to believe Wagner. The conditions, the timing, the threats described by Morgan were simply too far-out.

But one must go carefully.

Within ten minutes he would know which of the two, Morgan or Wagner, was telling the truth.

If he heard from Wagner at all, it would be Morgan. If he did not hear from Wagner, it would be Wagner.

But then, it would be entirely too late for it to make any difference to Wagner.

Poor fellow.

Thirty years a loser.

30

Veck had a lot of sophisticated gear, certainly, but there was none of the fancy TV surveillance gadgets he'd made so much of in his T-47 talk with Wagner. The closed-circuit cameras and receivers were quite basic, and there was no way Veck could sit in his shop and watch the Frawley—or even the street outside, for that matter. Wagner used the waiting time for a fast but comprehensive examination of the workshop and the house itself, assuring himself that there were no surprises to deal with, and although Veck's inventory was extensive and expensive, it did not include a Squeaky or any of its components. For all his confidence in his own theory as to the Squeaky's whereabouts he was still Roger Wagner, and Roger Wagner had an enormous capacity for second-thought, diffidence, and doubt. His mind went to the day of his graduation from OCS, the Benning School for Boys, circa 1943, when he had first donned the pinks-and-greens of a second lieutenant and stood in line in the sun and waited through the dreadful, organ-toned reading of the list. He had stood there, with top ratings in leadership, a wizard's academic record, and expert classification in all infantry weapons, and felt absolutely sure in his belly that between this spot, here, and the platform where General Somebody-or-Other was presenting certificates and exchanging salutes, he would somehow fail. Even when his mother had pinned the gold bars to his shoulders he felt secretly that the General would suddenly materialize and say, "Sorry, Mrs. Wagner, but there's been a mistake and I'll have to have those bars." In later years he had learned to sublimate—overcoming his unsureness with deliberate physical action, audacious and iconoclastic thought, and careful planning. Still, the old character defect would rise up once in awhile, and this was one of the times.

Was the Squeaky really hidden on the back of a truck in Germany?

Of course. Where else could it be?

Still—

The prescribed ten minutes had passed, and it was time to call Groot.

He did not call, however.

He chose to let the time elapse and move on. And he waited, knowing that everything was now in the hands of God and Groot, and not necessarily in that order.

Easily, unhurriedly, he left the workshop and moved through the house for the doorway that opened on the balcony and the stairway to St. George Street. He glanced about the rooms, giving them a final, thoughtful inspection, and, turning, opened the door.

Menzing was there, a pistol in one hand, with the other reaching for the knob. He was partially bent, as if in an attitude of listening.

Menzing was surprised. Wagner was not.

Wagner kicked the German in the stomach, and the man erupted—a terrible, wind-filled burst of breath and pain—and the pistol clattered to the board flooring, bouncing wildly.

Wagner kicked him again, and Menzing staggered backward, eyes bulging, mouth agape and working, like a fish's, and he went against the railing, which collapsed into a splintery confetti that followed him, crashing and slamming, into the street below. Some women squealed, a man shouted, and there was a running and a clamor of voices as the tourists formed the inevitable yammering circle.

Wagner picked up the pistol and went through the garden to Spanish Street, where he doubled back and, skirting the crowd, sauntered to the parking lot across from the Oldest Schoolhouse. He climbed into the Ford and in moments was on his way to the airport.

St. Augustine's airport was not a commercial facility, in the sense that scheduled national airlines included it on their routes. It was designed to accommodate private pilots and the operators of small charter services, as well as factory and maintenance facilities for several aircraft manufacturers. Neither was it a prepossessing place, composed as it was of a scattering of tin buildings, a clutch of standard hangars, and an operations center that evoked the ricky-ticky air mail service of the early 30's. The most impressive aspect was the array of aircraft of all sizes and descriptions, from antique biplanes to the latest and sleekest of the so-called executive jet transports. The planes stood in orderly rows, their wing tips and tails tied to concrete-mounted anchor loops, and as he drove through the gate and moved along the flight line, Wagner's eyes sought out the ships bearing the ensign of Apollo Aircraft Charter. There were two, both twin-engine jets of the Cessna family, low-slung, sleek, and seeming to be all angles and points in design. One was tied down and obviously undergoing maintenance, since several side panels in its right engine nacelle were open and dangling a spaghetti of cables. The other, gleaming white in the morning sunlight, poised virtually at the door of the operations center, its passenger hatch open, its boarding steps lowered. Wagner assumed that this was the ship that had been on hold for him and was now standing ready for a much more pressing duty.

He steered the Ford into the blue shadows of a factory building so that it would escape the attention of whoever might be on hand in the Apollo operations room. Driving slowly, he circled the building and pulled into a small parking area marked Grumman Business Only. He left the car and went to the rear door of Apollo Operations and found it open.

He went along an inner corridor, slowly, keeping close to the wall. Somewhere a teletype clacked, and there was the murmur of voices. Quietly he eased along the wall until he came to a corner. Peering around this, he could see the blonde girl leaning on the service counter, talking earnestly with Hans Trille and, beside him, Bob Veck. In the passenger waiting room beyond, pacing at the large window and slapping his leg with a newspaper, was the man who called himself Garcia.

Across the corridor, on the opposite wall, was a door marked Janitor. Wagner judged that, if he could be in that closet with the door only slightly ajar, he could see most of the two rooms and anybody in them without being seen himself. The trick would be to cross the narrow space and enter the closet without the motion catching someone's eye. He stood there, thinking about this, tense but somehow calm, unspeakably weary yet curiously bright and alert.

The problem was solved by the arrival of a car—a

decelerating whine, the crunching of tires on gravel, the slamming of a door. The girl and the three men turned and went to the entrance, and during the interval Wagner quick-stepped to the janitor's closet. He swung inside and peered out to see Dr. Samuels enter the waiting room, nervous and agitated and pale above his beard.

"It is time to go, gentlemen," he heard Samuels say. "The situation is beyond management now, and, for better or worse, it's time for us to fly to Herr Unger's island."

Trille rumbled, "The plane is ready, sir. The engines are warm. We've been waiting for you."

"How about the man Wagner?" Garcia/Unger asked.

"By now he's dead," Samuels said. "I sent Menzing to finish him off."

"Let's hope the idiot did it this time," Veck said.

Wagner stepped into the corridor, leveled the automatic he had retrieved after Menzing's fall, and said coolly, "No, Robert, he missed again. As has Herr Trille and his crew, who've been waiting in vain all these hours to take me up, probably over the ocean, and dump me from the airplane you hired to fly me to Colorado."

The five pairs of eyes came about in a lugubrious unity of motion, each pair reflecting its owner's astonishment. Veck's hand made a reflexive move for his pocket, and Wagner snapped, "Don't do it."

Veck froze, then slowly raised both hands.

"All of you move to the other side of the room," Wagner ordered, marveling at the calmness of his own voice. "That's the way. Now sit. You, Trille; you, Veck;

you, Garcia or Unger or whatever name you're using today: all of you on the sofa. You, young lady, in that chair next to them. And you, Dr. Samuels, in that chair by the drinking fountain. That's the way. Good."

Wagner stepped behind the service desk and picked up the phone, keeping his gaze riveted on the sullen group facing him from across the room. Then, in a quick glance, he established the position of the 0-button, and punched it.

"Operator."

"I want the police."

"You can dial that number directly, sir."

"I cannot dial the number directly, lady. I am holding a gun on five people who have been trying to kill me."

"May I have your name and the number you're calling from, sir?"

"My God, this is an emergency! I can't tell you the numbers because I can't take my eyes off my prisoners."

"Well, sir, if I'm to help you, you must cooperate."

"Oh, hell. My name is Roger Wagner. I am a Federal agent. I am in the operations and reception room of Apollo Aircraft Charter, St. Augustine airport. I am holding four men and a woman for Federal prosecution. They are killers, and I need help. And if you don't find some way to get some kind of police here as fast as possible, I'll tear, fold, and spindle my next bill from you people."

He slammed down the phone and told the blonde, "You: go to the sofa and take the gun out of Veck's shoulder holster."

The girl arose from her chair, her lip trembling, her

eyes teary, and, fumbling, withdrew the revolver, holding it between her fingertips, as if it were a dead mouse.

"All right, now slide it across the floor to me."

She did it just the way he wanted, and he kicked the weapon under the counter. There was an interval of silence, and Wagner perceived that they were all listening for the sound of police sirens—an absurdity, since he'd only hung up a moment before, but also a revelation of the tension that had entered the room.

Samuels broke the spell. "So then," he said in his pedantic way, "I see that Groot has told you I am—or was—a CIA agent."

Wagner, because he'd had thirty years of practice, did not permit his surprise to show. "Of course," he lied.

"It's a mistake for you to hold us like this," Samuels said evenly. "If you understood the seriousness of things, you'd be with us—not against us."

"I'm nuts, Samuels, but I'm not a nut."

"Morgan. My name is Morgan."

Veck stirred, annoyed. "Oh, come off it, Morgan. You're wasting your time talking to this guy. He's the original Clark Kent."

Wagner moved around the counter and stood facing the group, arms crossed, pistol at the ready. "You're all wasting your time. The plot's fizzled out. The war's been called off on account of nobody showing up."

"That's what you think," Veck snapped.

Wagner humphed. "You people are really too much. You are all upset over the population explosion, so you decide to get the U.S. to nuke Cuba, the Soviets to nuke the U.S., the U.S. to nuke the Soviets, and the rest of the countries in the northern hemisphere to nuke each other. Then you crawl out from under your rocks in the Southern hemisphere and take over what's left, including the poor fish who are bumbling aimlessly about in the Third World. Godamighty."

Garcia-Unger bridled, "The world's population is on a runaway basis. There will be nearly fifteen billion people by early in the next century. We are already stifling, starving, choking with less than half that number. The only way for the earth to survive at all is to decimate its population."

"By nuclear war?"

"By any means possible. With today's clean bombs, it should be no big thing."

"Oh, Jesus."

Veck said, "Don't be so upset, Rawjaw. Come with us. Now. If you stay, the war will wipe you out."

"Don't you understand? There will *be* no war. We know the Squeaky you people are supposed to have stolen is still at Wolfratshausen. We know that everything that's happened—from Strasser's body on the beach to the phony reports of commandos at Palatka—has been orchestrated by you people, with emphasis on realism that would convince the authorities that your shell game was legitimate. And we know that your real action—the twenty mercenaries terrorizing Disneyland in Cuban uniforms—won't come off because they've all just been arrested at a State Police road block on Route One. I repeat, lady and gentlemen, the war's been called off. There is no need for you to go flying off to whatever island the rich Herr Unger has provided for your sitting-out of the, ah, holocaust. There *is* a need for you, Dr.

Samuels-Morgan, to be hung for treason. There *is* a need for the rest of you to pay the piper for everything from conspiracy to attempted mass murder."

An oppressive silence took over the room, and Wagner could see that they all were struggling to deal with the reality of their disaster. They glared at him, presumably in hate, but with eyes he felt were not truly seeing him.

It was in this muted moment of realization that Wagner heard a voice behind him, piping, "All right, all of you: Stick 'em up."

He turned, startled.

She stood there at the entrance to the corridor. Her legs were spread and slightly bent, her hands held together in front of her in the attitude struck by policemen on TV when they command a crook to freeze. Only in this instance, she held no gun—only a purse with one hand tucked inside.

"Eva?"

"Damn you, Roger. I'd been waiting at the highway gate for an hour and a half for a taxi to come from town. And you drive right past me without so much as a glance my way."

"I—"

"Do you have any *idea* how hard it is to get a cab to come out to this godforsaken place? And why, for God's sake, haven't you answered the *phone?* You're lucky I'm here to save you from these creeps."

"Eva, if you really have a gun in that purse, put it down. I'm not their prisoner. They're mine!"

He should have known better. He could see it coming, but in some peculiar independence his body and mind refused to react, and so it happened anyway.

Veck had another gun, and in a flash of movement and a squeaking of the plastic-and-aluminum sofa and a hissing of breath, he was in a crouch, and the gun had boomed—a terrible sound so huge and complete it seemed to fill the room with something as tangible as Jello. There was a burning of the air beside Wagner's face, and he went down in the kind of instinctive ducking compelled by a flash of lightning. And a second shot sounded, almost as a continuation of the first, and he was aware of Eva spinning around, her skirt flaring, and then going down in a sprawling of legs and arms.

"Eva!"

He fired at Veck, and the bald man yelped.

"To the plane!" Trille roared.

"I've been hit," Veck groaned.

"Help him to the plane," Garcia yelled. "Quickly. Quickly. Before the police get here!"

Wagner fired again, but his aim had not been steady and the others were gone, clattering madly across the concrete apron beyond the door, making a rush for the waiting airplane.

Wagner ran to Eva, and he was vaguely conscious of a sobbing, and as he knelt beside her he realized it was his own.

"Eva."

Her face was a dreadful white, her eyes were half closed and indirect, and a curl of drool was at the corner of her slack mouth.

Rage and grief took over and he began to move and do despite the absolute need to collapse.

As if watching someone else, he saw himself dashing to the door, careening as the handle caught his jacket pocket, stumbling on the concrete, falling and stinging. Running again, shouting soundless curses at the airplane as it squealed and whined and turned slowly to point its nose toward the south and the wind that came from there. There was a glimpse of Trille, staring from the cockpit window, impassive, his jaws clenching the ever-present pipe. He thought he saw Trille's stony expression break, a small smile showing.

He wavered, consumed by fury and loss and the knowledge that the plane was leaving and he was powerless to stop it.

Wait.

On the ground there.

A wedge of wood. Red, with a length of rope attached.

A control-locking wedge. A simple chunk of wood, which, when inserted between a parked airplane's elevators and horizontal stabilizer, kept the controls from banging in the wind.

He snatched it up and ran and leaped, catching the plane's tail and falling onto the broad white expanse of the stabilizer. As the machine began to roll faster, he fought for balance, struggling to hold on with one hand while he used the other to jam the wooden wedge into the elevator hinge area.

And then he fell away, rolling on the sandy concrete, fighting for breath and consciousness.

Lying there, sobbing again, he watched the beautiful white airplane begin its rush down the long band of pavement, rumbling and shaking the ground. It rolled, raised a bit, kissed the runway again with a tiny chirp of its tires, then rose, carried aloft by the thundering.

It went up, and then it seemed to hang, and after a split of time it wheeled sideways in a kind of horrid majesty, returning to earth in a slamming, a bouncing, a disintegration in which the whiteness shattered like frosted glass.

There was a flash, and then a gigantic ball of flame, and only then did the sound of police sirens reach him.

When he returned to the waiting room, Eva was sitting in one of the plastic chairs, her face still white.

"My God," he said, stupefied.

"Are you all right, Roger?"

"I thought you'd been shot. . . ."

"I was. But he hit my purse and blew it out of my hands, and I fainted, I guess. Did you know that fainting runs in my family?"

"No."

"It's ridiculously Victorian."

"Eva. . . ."

"My hands tingle. They still tingle from the shot."

"How did you get here?"

"I rented a plane, dummy."

"Eva. . . ."

"Take me home, will you?"

DAY 9

31

Eva lay listening to the wind's restless fretting at the windows, half-awake in the dawn light and content with her closeness to Roger and the soft sound of his breathing. She could sense the spread of the sea beyond the curtains' stirring, and the room held the smell of salt and fish and kelp—distant and not unpleasant. There was a pattering of rain against the house, and she snuggled deeper under the covers, luxuriating in the prospect of a lazy, damp day in her own home with her own man.

The terror and loneliness of the past days were unreal, like recollections of a horror film that had been endured, then dismissed as an inexplicable aberration. It was as if it all had happened to someone else, and yet the experience had endowed her personally with enlarged perceptions of her life and how it should now be spent. She knew now that Roger loved her. She knew now that she loved him. These twin facts had been established beyond any further vulnerability to doubt and misconception. For them both there would be no other life but that which their love would compel. The simplicity of this was liberating, exhilarating.

He stirred, and she felt his kiss.

"Guten Morgen, gnädige Frau," he said softly. "Iss you dere?"

"Yes-indeedy-von-doody, Herr Hero."

The quiet resumed, and she could sense his awakeness, the energy of his mind, sorting and considering and categorizing. It was his way, no more to be denied or altered than that calling of the gulls circling in the leaden sky above the surf.

"Did they abuse you?" he asked.

"No. They only wasted time I could have spent with you."

"Who is Lindsay?"

"A lawyer, as he claims. A lawyer who has lots of money and a big house and expensive cars and who worries a lot about the population explosion."

"How did you know I was in a confrontation with those people at the airport?"

"The tall man with the pipe and the bald man were in Lindsay's office one day. And at his home. I saw them both places. When I saw them lined up, glowering at you in that airport room, I knew you had to be in danger. I did what I could. What I thought was right."

There was another interval. Then: "How did you manage to get there?"

"I was able to escape from Lindsay's house and make my way to an airport. I hired a funny fat fellow in a cowboy hat to fly me to St. Augustine. It cost me a fortune, and we'll be eating beans for months."

"Maybe we can still get your inheritance out of Lindsay."

"Don't count on it, buddy. He's probably in Patagonia by now."

He became silent again, and she remembered the night, in which, during the deep and dreamless sleep of exhaustion, they had awakened, as if in some secret, long-established agreement, to lose themselves in the busy-ness of lovers. She wondered if he had any true appreciation of how much they had meant to her, the tenderness and languid exchanges in the darkness.

"Know something?" he said, breaking into

her thought.

"What?"

"You're one hell of a woman."

"Yep."

They dozed again.

The phone rang, and Wagner reached across Eva's form to lift it. "Yes?"

"Good morning. The Republic has been saved."

"Groot, don't you *ever* go to bed?" He yawned.

"Beds are for weaklings and lovers."

"Well, I'm both."

"I want to clear up a few details."

"Like what?"

He could hear Groot's asthmatic breathing, a sign that the lumpy, gray man was assembling his thoughts.

"Well," Groot said, "I'd appreciate your running through the high-spots for me. The President and I think we have it generally in hand, but there are a few things that we can clarify as you go along."

"It's not so complicated," Wagner said through another yawn. "Morgan, Unger, Trille, Veck, and Lindsay were nuts on the overpopulation thing, and— thanks to Unger's fascistic orientation, Morgan's overweaning ambitions, Lindsay's money, Veck's opportunism, and Trille's Nazism—they conspired to trigger a war between the U.S. and the Soviets over Cuba. They figured that would accomplish two major ends for them: a decimation of the world's population and a chance for Unger's European and American fascists to assume leadership of the world's demoralized survivors. A new world. Literally.

"Their problem was to create the spark for general war in a credible way. They had to do something that would cause the secrecy and suspiciousness and distrust between the U.S. and the Soviets to work against—to overwhelm—logic and patience. The mere theft of a Squeaky by terrorists wouldn't do it. It had to look as if the theft was masterminded by Castro, with the resultant panic and rashness of action. And they couldn't simply announce that 'Castro did it.' They had to lead the U.S. down a carefully contrived garden path, in which ace intelligence officers—that's me—and stupid, patriotic zealots—that's you—discovered, step by step, that 'Castro did it.' They counted on the expectation that, once a Squeaky was thought to have been stolen, the U.S. would work in desperate secrecy to find it and get it back. Exploiting this mania for secrecy, they—the bad guys—found it easy to create the illusion that the Squeaky had been planted in Havana; they could use twenty guys, jogging around town at different times and in different clothes, to suggest an influx of mysterious foreigners who were forming an army at Palatka; they could convince us that a Cuban nuke had been installed in Miami. It was all a flim-flam aimed at the deliberate instigation of nuclear war—the ultimate act of terrorism." He paused.

Eva murmured, "God. You sound like Walter Cronkite."

"Who's he?"

"My hairdresser."

"You mean," Groot said, "that everything that happened to you had been set up, orchestrated by the group?"

"I'd thought you'd have got that idea by now." Wagner kissed the tip of Eva's nose.

Groot said, "If Morgan, et al, were working a scheme to delude the President through me, why did they bring in you?"

"The way I see it," Wagner said, "I was to Morgan what the waving wand is to the magician. While all my running around distracted you and the President, Morgan's sleight-of-hand had a better chance of fooling all of us. Also, it's much more believable when a retired agent—savvy enough to recognize something significant—'stumbles' onto the body of a key foreign intelligence agent and is led, step by step, along a fast-track scam. If Morgan had simply set up his Palatka fiction unabetted by all my gyrations, you and the President would have focused on Palatka and therefore more readily seen through Morgan's tricks. Morgan worked pretty much alone, keeping his CIA team in the dark and involved in seemingly relevant but really unimportant duties. Meanwhile, I was—often entirely under Morgan's and Veck's control—reporting 'independently' on stuff that gave substance to what you were receiving from Morgan himself. And Morgan kept me alive as long as I suited this purpose, staging a couple of attempts on my life simply to convince us that I was on to something and should be given maximum attention. As insurance against the unlikely event that I might break through to the truth, or become otherwise unmanageable, Morgan lured Eva to Colorado and held her as a kind of unwitting hostage. As it was, both Eva and I proved to be too unmanageable too soon, and so Morgan's razzmatazz began to unravel. He had to hurry things along, and he got sloppy, and I saw through the holes."

Groot murmured, as if to himself, "They did everything they could to present us with a believable, yet completely unfathomable and unreasonable mishmash. Nothing made sense because it wasn't supposed to make sense."

"Oh, God, Groot: You're so veddy clever."

"The one thing they *didn't* count on was your surviving long enough to see through the scam."

"I'm fussy about things like that. By the way: Why didn't you tell me Samuels, or Morgan, or whatever, was a CIA man? It could have saved me a lot of wasted energy."

"Standard operating procedures, my friend. You know that as well as I do. It usually pays to have parallel investigations, each unaware of the other. It can give the Front Office additional dimensions of thought and action."

Wagner rubbed his eyes with his free hand, suddenly tired of this dull old man and his silly questions. "Well, the Front Office can't be doing a hell of a lot of thinking if it can have a fanatical, wheeling-and-dealing revolutionary like Morgan on its employee rolls for twenty-five years."

"Men change. Men get self-righteous, fearful, pious; they change their points of view, their convictions. Time and living and need do those things to men."

"Time hasn't done a perishing thing for you, has it?"

"I'm afraid not."

Wagner detected a great loneliness in Groot's words, and his only slightly good-natured jeering seemed suddenly to be working a cruelty on the old fellow. "Well," he said, his tone softer, "we all live life as we see it."

"I risked your life. You know that, don't you, Wagner?"

"When?"

"I set you up. Morgan was telling me one thing, you were telling me another. I figured that, if Morgan tried to take you out, you were the one I should believe."

"Oh. You mean *that* when. Hell, Groot, you've set me up so many times I'd have been very worried about you if you hadn't sicced Morgan on me. You would have been entirely out of character."

"Well, I had to tell you that."

"Careful. You'll be turning into an old softie. And I like you better as a mean, calculating, Machiavellian, ruthless, arbitrary, lying son of a bitch. That's the Groot I know and love."

"Watch your language, buster," Eva said. "There are women present."

"Show me one," he challenged. "Just one."

She flipped back the covers, then pulled them to her again.

"Oo. You're right," Wagner said. "That's a woman if I ever saw one. A lady flasher, yet."

"What are you saying, Wagner?" Groot asked.

"I'm saying goodbye. If you have to ask any more questions to understand this caper, you're in the wrong business. And that goes for your silver-haired, golden-tongued, bubble-headed president, too."

"The President speaks very highly of you, Wagner."

"Tell him not to waste his breath. I'm a Coolidge man."

"The President has authorized me to allow you to keep the two hundred and fifty thousand dollar advance you received. He says it was you, and you alone, who discovered where the Squeaky was hidden and you deserve a reward."

"Tell the President I've just become his most rabid fan."

"It might interest you to know, also, that the State Police arrested the Disneyland raiders without the slightest fuss. And the Colorado people, Lindsay et al, are right now under interrogation in Denver. So is the motor officer at Wolfratshausen."

"All right, Groot. Office hours are over. Tell the President to send a money order. I don't accept personal checks." He hung up and, peering with lowered brows at Eva, he yanked away the blankets and said, "If I'm going to believe that, I've got to see it closer."

She was reaching for him when the phone rang again.

"Damn!" Wagner groped and brought the instrument to him. "I said the office was closed," he barked.

"Roger?"

"Oh. Audrey. Is that you?"

"It's me. I've just returned from a personal interview with you-know-who."

"The Big Cigar?"

"The Big Cigar says that what you've told me is nothing but a cheap, gringo trick to cast aspersions on him and to rationalize an invasion of Cuba."

"I figured he might take it that way."

"Moreover, he says, the idea that he might have to steal a Squeaky is absurd. And, Roger, he absolutely astonished me with his next words. He gave me a di-

298

rect order to tell my North American contact—meaning you, I suppose—that Cuba has no need to steal a Squeaky, since Cuba has possessed a weapon of that type for a year now, thanks to his glorious, steadfast, and adored brothers in the Soviet Union."

"Boy, he must have been really ticked off to let a goody like that slip out, eh?"

"I've never seen him so furious. He fired me on the spot for blowing my cover over such a silly trick."

"He fired you, then let you come back to tell me all this?"

"Well. . . ."

Wagner humphed. "Audrey-baby: You're in the wrong business. You don't think I believe all this do you?"

She sighed, then laughed softly. "I didn't expect you would. Any more than we believe your administration would be so upset about the mere theft of a Squeaky when we naturally assume you now have something ever so much more advanced."

"I don't believe you. You don't believe me. I don't believe you don't believe me. You don't believe I don't believe you don't believe that I don't believe you don't believe. Let's just forget the whole thing and start over. You go back to slinging dishes, I'll go back to reading rotten best-sellers and walking the beach."

"No hard feelings?"

"Goodbye, Audrey."

He rested back against his pillow, sighing a sigh of his own.

"Who's Audrey, Mr. Wagner?"

"Lady downtown. She says that if Mrs. Wagner ever neglects me, I should stop around."

"That'll be the day."

THE MOBIUS MAN

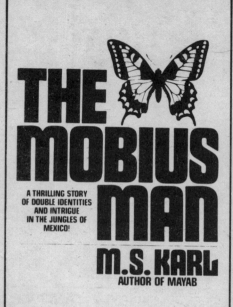

THE
MOBIUS
MAN

A THRILLING STORY
OF DOUBLE IDENTITIES
AND INTRIGUE
IN THE JUNGLES OF
MEXICO!

M.S. KARL
AUTHOR OF MAYAB

When CIA operative David
Dennison was sent to Mexico to
investigate the murder of another
agent, he was soon convinced that
Harold Bassett, the jailed suspect,
was innocent. Then Bassett
suddenly escaped. Dennison chased
him through the Mexican jungle with
the aid of Bassett's Indian mistress.

By
M.S.
Karl

PRICE: $2.50
0-8439-1038-0
CATEGORY:
Mystery

THE SPY WHO NEVER WAS

By
Sheila Martin

PRICE: $2.25   0-8439-1036-4   **CATEGORY:** Espionage

Brad Stevenson and Chris Borchardt
had one thing in common — Chris's wife,
Lia, with whom Brad was having an affair.
When Lia disappeared, her husband and
lover buried their differences as they joined
forces to search for her. As Brad and
Chris pursued their investigations, they
stumbled on a CIA plot of such intricacy
and magnitude that they could hardly
believe its implications.

THE RIGHT TO KILL

Manhattan detective Michael O'Daley deemed it a routine murder case. But he had yet to discover the hit-and-run death . . . the professor with an assassin's past . . . the KGB and Israeli SS agents who tailed him everywhere . . . or that trained killers from four countries had arrived in New York.

Scott Jansen

PRICE: $2.25
0-8439-1112-3

CATEGORY:
Espionage

SEND TO: **LEISURE BOOKS**
P.O. Box 511, Murray Hill Station
New York, N.Y. 10156-0511

Please send the titles:

Quantity	Book Number	Price
_____	_____	_____
_____	_____	_____
_____	_____	_____
_____	_____	_____
_____	_____	_____

In the event we are out of stock on any of your
selections, please list alternate titles below.

_____	_____	_____
_____	_____	_____
_____	_____	_____
_____	_____	_____

Postage/Handling_____

I enclose_____

**FOR U.S. ORDERS, add 75¢ for the first book and 25¢ for
each additional book to cover cost of postage and handling.
Buy five or more copies and we will pay for shipping. Sorry,
no. C.O.D.'s.**

**FOR ORDERS SENT OUTSIDE THE U.S.A., add $1.00
for the first book and 50¢ for each additional book. PAY BY
foreign draft or money order drawn on a U.S. bank, payable
in U.S. ($) dollars.**

☐ **Please send me a free catalog.**

NAME _____
(Please print)

ADDRESS _____

CITY _____STATE _____ZIP_____
Allow Four Weeks for Delivery